JORROCKS'S JAUNTS AND JOLLITIES

JORROCKS'S
JAUNTS AND JOLLITIES

THE HUNTING, SHOOTING, RACING, DRIVING, SAILING,
EATING, ECCENTRIC AND EXTRAVAGANT EXPLOITS OF
THAT RENOWNED SPORTING CITIZEN, MR. JOHN
JORROCKS OF ST. BOTOLPH LANE AND
GREAT CORAM STREET

BY

R. S. SURTEES

WITH FIFTEEN COLOURED ILLUSTRATIONS BY
HENRY ALKEN

METHUEN & CO. LTD. LONDON
36 Essex Street, Strand, W.C.2

NOTE

THIS Issue is founded on the Edition
published by R. Ackermann in the
year 1843.

First Published by Methuen & Co.   July 1903
Reprinted November 1906 and December   1910
First Issued in this form . . . . April 1911
Reprinted July 1913, July 1916, September 1918,
*   June 1919, September 1923 March 1928.*
*   July 1933, January 1942, December 1944 and*
*   1948*
Fourteenth Edition 1951

CATALOGUE No. 3487/U

PRINTED IN GREAT BRITAIN

CONTENTS

	PAGE
SWELL AND THE SURREY	I
THE YORKSHIREMAN AND THE SURREY	15
SURREY SHOOTING—MR. JORROCKS IN TROUBLE	36
MR. JORROCKS AND THE SURREY STAG-HOUNDS	54
THE TURF : MR. JORROCKS AT NEWMARKET	68
AQUATICS : MR. JORROCKS AT MARGATE	91
THE ROAD : ENGLISH AND FRENCH	116
MR. JORROCKS IN PARIS	146
SPORTING IN FRANCE	168
MR. JORROCKS'S DINNER PARTY	186

v

COLOURED ILLUSTRATIONS

Illustrated Title-page

FACING PAGE

Mr. Jorrocks telegraphs the Fox 26

The Appearance of Swell astonishes the Surrey Hunt 27

Mr. Jorrocks introduces the Yorkshireman to the
    Surrey 58

Squire Cheatum's Keeper attacks the Murderer of
    Old Tom 59

Mr. Jorrocks declares his inability to subscribe to the
    Surrey Stag-Hounds 90

The Baron ' Vills his Wet ' 91

Mr. Jorrocks makes his Entrée into the Newmarket
    Betting Ring 122

' O Gentlemen ! Gentlemen ! here's a lamentable
    occurrence ' 123

' Water I do declare—with worms in it ' . . . 154

Mr. Jorrocks renounces the acquaintance of the
    Yorkshireman 155

Mr. Jorrocks makes a Faux Pas 186

Mr. Jorrocks beats the Baron for Speed . . . 187

Mr. Jorrocks takes a ride at St. Cloud . . . 206

' Lift Me Up ! Tie Me in my Chair ! Fill my Glass ' 207

SWELL AND THE SURREY

WHAT true-bred city sportsman has not in his day put off the most urgent business—perhaps his marriage, or even the interment of his rib—that he might ' brave the morn ' with that renowned pack, the Surrey subscription fox-hounds ? Lives there, we would ask, a thorough-bred, prime, bang-up, slap-dash, break-neck, out-and-out *artist*, within three miles of the Monument, who has not occasionally ' gone a good un ' with this celebrated pack ? And shall we, the bard of Eastcheap, born all deeds of daring to record, shall we, who so oft have witnessed—nay, shared—the hardy exploits of our fellow cits, shall we sit still, and never cease the eternal twirl of our dexter around our sinister thumb, while other scribes hand down to future ages the paltry feats of beardless Meltonians, and try to shame old Father Thames himself with muddy Whissen-dine's foul stream ? Away ! thou vampire, Indolence, that suckest the marrow of imagination, and fattenest on the cream of idea ere yet it float on the milk of reflection. Hence ! slug-begotten hag, thy power is gone,—the murky veil thou'st drawn o'er memory's sweetest page is rent !

' Harp of Eastcheap, awake ! '

Our thoughts hark back to the coverside, and our heart o'erflows with recollections of the past, when life rode the pace through our veins, and the bark of the veriest mongrel, or the bray of the sorriest coster-monger's sorriest ' Jerusalem,' were far more musical sounds than Paganini's pizzicatos or Catalini's clamorous caterwaulings.

And thou, Goddess of the Silver Bow—chaste Diana —deign to become the leading star of our lucubrations ; come perch upon our grey goose-quill : shout in our ear the maddening Tally-ho ! and ever and anon give a salutary ' refresher ' to our memory with thy heaven-

wrought spurs—those spurs old Vulcan forged when in
his maddest mood—whilst we relate such feats of town-
born youths and city squires as shall ' harrow up the
souls ' of milk-sop Melton's choicest sons, and ' fright
their grass-galloping garrons from their propriety.' But
gently, Pegasus ! *Here again*, boys, and ' let's to business,'
as they say on 'Change.

'Twere almost needless to inform our readers that
such portion of a county as is hunted by any one pack of
hounds is technically denominated their *country* ; and of
all *countries* under the sun, that of the Surrey subscription
fox-hounds undoubtedly bears the bell. This superiority
arises from the peculiar nature of the soil—wretched
starvation stuff most profusely studded with hugh sharp
flints,—the abundance of large woods, particularly on
the Kent side, and the range of mountainous hills that
run directly through the centre, which afford accommodation to the timid, and are unknown in most counties and
unequalled in any.

One of the most striking features in the aspect of this
chosen region of fox-hunting, is the quiet, easy manner
in which the sportsmen take the thing. On they go—
now trotting gently over the flints—now softly ambling
along the grassy ridge of some stupendous hill—now
quietly following each other in long-drawn files, like
geese, through some close and deep ravine or intermin-
able wood, which re-echoes to their never-ceasing holloas
—every man shouting in proportion to the amount of
his subscription, until day is made horrible with their
yelling. There is no pushing, jostling, rushing, cramming,
or riding over one another ; no jealousy, discord, or
daring ; no ridiculous foolhardy feats ; but each man
cranes and rides, and rides and cranes, in a style that
would gladden the eyes of a director of an insurance
office.

The members of the Surrey are the people that
combine business with pleasure, and even in the severest
run can find time for sweet discourse, and talk about the
price of stocks or stockings. ' Yooi, wind him there,
good dog, yooi, wind him.'—' Cottons is fell.'—' Hark
to Cottager ! Hark ! '—' Take your bill at three months,

or give you three-and-a-half discount for cash.'—' Eu in there, eu in, Cheapside, good dog.'—' Don't be in a hurry, sir, *pray* ! He may be in the empty casks behind the cooper's. Yooi, try for him, good bitch. Yooi, push him out.'—' You're not going down that bank, sure*ly*, sir ? Why, it's almost perpendicular ! For God's sake, sir, take care—remember you are not insured. Ah ! you had better get off—here, let me hold your nag, and when you're down you can catch mine ;—*that's your sort*, but mind he doesn't break the bridle. He won't run away, for he knows I've got some sliced carrots in my pocket to reward him if he does well.—Thank you, sir, and now for a leg up—there we are—*that's your sort* —I'll wait till you are up also, and we'll be off together.'

It is this union of the elegant courtesies and business of life with the energetic sports of the field, that constitutes the charm of Surrey hunting ; and who can wonder that smoked-dried cits, pent up all the week, should gladly fly from their shops to enjoy a day's sport on a Saturday ? We must not, however, omit to express a hope that young men, who have their way to make in the world, may not be led astray by its allurements. It is all very well for old-established shopkeepers ' to do a bit of pleasure ' occasionally, but the apprentice or journeyman, who understands his duties and the tricks of his trade, will never be found capering in the hunting field. He will feel that his proper place is behind the counter ; and while his master is away enjoying the pleasures of the chase, he can prig as much ' pewter ' from the till as will take both himself and his ' woman ' to Sadler's Wells Theatre, or any other place she may choose to appoint.

But to return to the Surrey. The town of Croydon, nine miles from the standard in Cornhill, is the general rendezvous of the gallant sportsmen. It is the principal market town in the eastern division of the county of Surrey ; and the chaw-bacons who carry the produce of their acres to it, instead of to the neighbouring *village* of London, retain much of their pristine barbarity. The town furnishes an interesting scene on a hunting morning, particularly on a Saturday. At an early hour

groups of grinning cits may be seen pouring in from the
London side, some on the top of Cloud's coaches, some
in taxed carts, but the greater number mounted on
good serviceable-looking nags, of the invaluable species
calculated for sport or business, ' warranted free from
vice, and quiet both to ride and in harness ' ; some few
there are, who, with that kindness and considerate
attention which peculiarly mark this class of sportsmen,
having tacked a buggy to their hunter and given a seat
to a friend, who, leaning over the back of the gig, his
jocund phiz turned towards his *fidus Achates*, leads his
own horse behind, listening to the discourse of ' his
ancient,' or regaling him ' with sweet converse ' ; and
thus they onward jog, until the sign of the Greyhound,
stretching quite across the main street, greets their
expectant optics, and seems to forbid their passing the
open portal below.   In they wend then, and having
seen their horses ' sorted,' and the collar marks (as much
as may be) carefully effaced by the shrewd application
of a due quantity of grease and lamp black, speed into
' mine host,' and order a sound repast of the good things
of this world ; the which to discuss, they presently
apply themselves with a vigour that indicates as much
a determination to recruit fatigue endured, as to lay in
a stock against the effects of future exertion.   Meanwhile the bustle increases ; sportsmen arrive by the
score, fresh tables are laid out, covered with ' no end ' of
vivers ; and towards the hour of nine may be heard to
perfection that pleasing assemblage of sounds issuing
from the masticatory organs of a number of men stead-
fastly and studiously employed in the delightful occupation of preparing their mouthfuls for deglutition.   ' O
noctes cœnæque Deûm,' saith friend Flaccus.   Oh,
hunting breakfasts ! say we.   Where are now the jocund
laugh, the repartee, the oft-repeated tale, the last debate ?
As our sporting contemporary, the *Quarterly*, said, when
describing the noiseless pursuit of old Reynard by the
Quorn :—' Reader, there is no crash *now*, and not much
music.'   It is the tinker that makes a great noise over a
little work, but, at the pace these men are eating, there
is no time for babbling.   So, gentle lector, there is now

no leisure for bandying compliments, 'tis your small eater alone who chatters o'er his meals ; your true-born sportsman is ever a silent and, consequently, an assiduous grubber. True it is that occasionally space is found between mouthfuls to vociferate ' WAITER ! ' in a tone that requires not repetition ; and most sonorously do the throats of the assembled eaters re-echo the sound ; but this is all—no useless exuberance of speech ;—no, the knife or fork is directed towards what is wanted, nor needs there any more expressive intimation of the applicant's wants.

At length the hour of ten approaches ; bills are paid, pocket-pistols filled, sandwiches stowed away, horses accoutred, and our bevy straddle forth into the town, to the infinite gratification of troops of dirty-nosed urchins, who, for the last hour, have been peeping in at the windows, impatiently watching for the *exeunt* of our worthies.—They mount, and away—trot, trot,—bump, bump,—trot,—bump, bump,—over Addington Heath, through the village and up the hill to Hayes Common, which having gained, spurs are applied, and any slight degree of pursiness that the good steeds may have acquired by standing at livery in Cripplegate or else-where, is speedily pumped out of them by a smart brush over the turf to the Fox, at Keston, where a numerous assemblage of true sportsmen patiently await the usual hour for throwing off. At length time being called, say twenty minutes to eleven, and Mr. Jorrocks, Nodding Homer, and the principal subscribers having cast up, the hounds approach the cover. ' *Yooi in there !* ' shouts Tom Hill, who has long hunted this crack pack ; and crack ! crack ! crack ! go the whips of some scores of sportsmen. ' Yelp, yelp, yelp,' howl the hounds ; and in about a quarter of an hour Tom has not above four or five couple at his heels. This number being a trifle, Tom runs his prad at a gap in the fence by the woodside ; the old nag goes well at it, but stops short at the critical moment, and, instead of taking the ditch, bolts and wheels round. Tom, however, who is ' large in the boiling-pieces,' as they say at Whitechapel, is prevented by his weight from being shaken out of his

saddle ; and, being resolved to take no denial, he lays
the crop of his hunting-whip about the head of his beast,
and runs him at the same spot a second time, with an
obligato accompaniment of his spur-rowels, backed by a
' *curm along, then !* ' issued in such a tone as plainly
informs his quadruped he is in no joking humour. These
incentives succeed in landing Tom and his nag in the
wished-for spot, when immediately the wood begins to
resound with shouts of ' Yoicks True-bo-y, yoicks
True-bo-y, yoicks push him up, yoicks wind him ! ' and
the whole pack begin to work like good uns. Occasionally may be heard the howl of some unfortunate hound
that has been caught in a fox-trap, or taken in a hare-
snare ; and not unfrequently the discordant growls of
some three or four more, vociferously quarrelling over
the venerable remains of some defunct rabbit. ' Oh,
you rogues,' cries Mr. Jorrocks, a cit rapturously fond of
the sport. After the lapse of half an hour the noise in
the wood for a time increases audibly. 'Tis Tom
chastising the *gourmands*. Another quarter of an hour,
and a hound that has finished his coney bone slips out
of the wood, and takes a roll upon the greensward,
opining, no doubt, that such a pastime is preferable to
scratching his hide among brambles in the covers.
' Hounds have no right to *opine*,' *opines* the head
whipper-in ; so clapping spurs into his prad, he begins
to pursue the delinquent round the common, with
' Markis, Markis ! what are you at, Markis ? Get into
cover, Markis ! ' But ' it's no go ' ; Marquis creeps
through a hedge, and ' grins horribly a ghastly smile '
at his ruthless tormentor, who wends back, well pleased
at having had an excuse for taking ' a bit gallop ' !
Half an hour more slips away, and some of the least
hasty of our cits begin to wax impatient in spite of the
oft-repeated admonition, ' *don't be in a hurry !* ' At
length a yokel pops out of the cover, and as soon as he
has recovered breath, informs the field that he has been
' a hollorin' to 'em for half an hour,' and that the fox
had ' gone away for Tatsfield, 'most as soon as ever the
'oounds went into 'ood.'

All is now hurry-scurry,—girths are tightened,—

reins gathered up,—half-munched sandwiches thrust into the mouth,—pocket-pistols applied to,—coats comfortably buttoned up to the throat ; and, these preparations made, away goes the whole field, ' coolly and fairly,' along the road to Leaves Green and Crown Ash Hill,—from which latter spot the operations of the pack in the bottom may be comfortably and securely viewed,—leaving the whips to flog as many hounds out of cover as they can, and Tom to entice as many more as are willing to follow the ' twang, twang, twang ' of his horn.

And now, a sufficient number of hounds having been seduced from the wood, forth sallies ' Tummas,' and making straight for the spot where our yokel's ' mate ' stands leaning on his plough-stilts, obtains from him the exact latitude and longitude of the spot where Reynard broke through the hedge. To this identical place is the pack forthwith led ; and, no sooner have they reached it, than the wagging of their sterns clearly shows how genuine is their breed. Old Strumpet, at length, first looking up in Tom's face for applause, ventures to send forth a long-drawn howl, which, coupled with Tom's screech, setting the rest agog, away they all go, like beans ; and the wind, fortunately setting towards Westerham, bears the melodious sound to the delighted ears of our ' roadsters,' who, forthwith catching the infection, respond with deafening shouts and joyous yells set to every key, and disdaining the laws of harmony. Thus, what with Tom's horn, the halloaing of the whips, and the shouts of the riders, a very pretty notion may be formed of what Virgil calls—

' Clamorque virûm clangorque tubarum '—

A terrible noise is the result !

At the end of nine minutes or so, the hounds come to fault in the bottom, below the blacksmith's at Crown Ash Hill, and the fox has a capital chance ; in fact, they have changed for the blacksmith's tom cat, which rushed out before them, and, finding their mistake, return at their leisure. This gives the most daring of the field, on the eminence, an opportunity of descending to view the sport more closely ; and being assembled in the bottom, each congratulates his neighbour on the excellent condition and staunchness of the hounds, and the admirable view that has been afforded them of their peculiar style of hunting. At this interesting period, a ' regular swell ' from Melton Mowbray, unknown to everyone except his tailor, to whom he owes a long tick, makes his appearance and affords abundance of merriment for our sportsmen. He is just turned out of the hands of his valet, and presents the very *beau idéal* of his caste—' quite the lady,' in fact. His hat is stuck on one side, displaying a profusion of well-waxed ringlets ; a corresponding infinity of whisker, terminating at the chin, there joins an enormous pair of moustaches, which give him the appearance of having caught the fox himself and stuck its brush below his nose. His neck is very stiff ; and the exact Jackson-like fit of his coat, which almost nips him in two at the waist, and his superlatively well-cleaned leather Andersons,[1] together with the perfume and the general puppyism of his appearance, proclaim that he is a ' swell ' of the very first water, and one that a Surrey sportsman would like to buy at his own price and sell at the other's. In addition to this, his boots, which his ' fellow ' has just denuded from a pair of wash-leather covers, are of the finest, brightest, blackest patent leather imaginable ; the left one being the identical boot by which Warren's monkey shaved himself, while the right is the one at which the game-cock pecked, mistaking its own shadow for an opponent, the mark of its bill being still visible above the instep ; and the tops—whose pampered appetites have been fed on champagne—are of the most delicate cream-colour, the whole devoid of mud or speck. The animal he bestrides is no less calculated than himself to excite the risible faculties of the field, being a sort of mouse colour, with dun mane and tail, got by Nicolo out of a Flibberty-gibbet mare, and he stands seventeen hands and an inch. His head is small and blood-like, his girth a mere

---

[1] Anderson, of South Audley Street, is considered to be the only man capable of cutting ' unmentionables ' worthy the wear of a gentleman.

trifle, and his legs, very long and spidery, of course, without any hair at the pasterns to protect them from the flints ; his whole appearance bespeaking him fitter to run for half-mile hunters' stakes at Croxton Park or Leicester, than contend for foxes' brushes in such a splendid country as the Surrey. There he stands, with his tail stuck tight between his legs, shivering and shaking for all the world as if troubled with a fit of ague. And well he may, poor beast, for—oh, men of Surrey, London, Kent, and Middlesex, hearken to my word—on closer inspection he proves to have been shaved ! ! ! [1]

After a considerable time spent in casting to the right, the left, and the rear, ' True-*bouy* ' chances to take a fling in advance, and, hitting upon the scent, proclaims it with his wonted energy, which drawing all his brethren to the spot, they pick it slowly over some brick-fields and flint-beds, to an old lady's flower-garden, through which they carry it with a surprising head into the fields beyond, when they begin to fall into line, and the sportsmen doing the same—' one at a time, and it will last the longer '—' Tummas ' tootles his horn, the hunt is up, and away they all rattle at ' Parliament pace,' as the hackney-coachmen say.

Our swell, who flatters himself he can ' ride a few,' according to the fashion of his country, takes up a line of his own, abreast of the leading hounds, notwithstanding the oft-vociferated cry of ' Hold hard, sir ! ' ' *Pray*, hold hard, sir ! ' ' For God's sake, *hold hard*, sir ! ' ' G—d d—n you, *hold hard*, sir ! ' ' Where the *h—ll* are you going to, sir ? ' and other familiar inquiries and benedictions, with which a stranger is sometimes greeted who ventures to take a look at a strange pack of hounds.

In the meantime the fox, who had often had a game at romps with his pursuers, being resolved this time to give them a tickler, bears straight away for Westerham, to the infinite satisfaction of the ' hill folks,' who thus have an excellent opportunity of seeing the run without putting their horses to the trouble of ' rejoicing in their

[1] Shaving was in great vogue at Melton some seasons back. It was succeeded by clipping, and clipping by singeing.

strength, or pawing in the valley.' But who is so fortunate as to be near the scene of action in this second scurry, almost as fast as the first ? Our fancy supplies us, and there not being many, we will just initialize them all, and let him whom the cap fits put it on.

If we look to the left, nearly abreast of the three couple of hounds that are leading by some half-mile or so, we shall see ' Swell '—like a monkey on a giraffe— striding away in the true Leicestershire style ; the animal contracting its stride after every exertion in pulling its long legs out of the deep and clayey soil, until the Bromley barber, who has been quilting his mule along at a fearful rate, and in high dudgeon at any one presuming to exercise his profession upon a dumb brute, overtakes him, and in the endeavour to pass, lays it into his mule in a style that would insure him rotatory occupation at Brixton for his spindles, should any member of the Society for the Prevention of Cruelty to Animals witness his proceedings ; while his friend and neighbour old B., the tinker, plies his little mare with the Brummagems, to be ready to ride over ' Swell ' the instant the barber gets him down. On the right of the leading hounds are three crack members of the Surrey, Messrs. B—e, S—bs, and B—l, all lads who *can* go ; while a long way in the rear of the body of the pack are some dozen, who, while they sat on the hills, thought *they could also*, but who now find out their mistake. Down Windy Lane, a glimpse of a few red coats may be caught passing the gaps and weak parts of the fence, among whom we distinctly recognize the worthy master of the pack, followed by Jorrocks, with his long coat laps floating in the breeze, who thinking that ' catching-time ' must be near at hand, and being dearly fond of blood, has descended from his high station to witness the close of the scene. ' Vot a pace ! and vot a country ! ' cries the grocer, standing high in his stirrups, and bending over the neck of his chestnut as though he were meditating a plunge over his head ; ' how they stick to him ! vot a pack ! by Jove, they are at fault again. Yooi, Pilgrim ! Yooi, Warbler, ma *load !* (lad). Tom, try down the hedge-row.' ' Hold your jaw, Mr. J.,' cries Tom, ' you are always throwing that red rag of yours. I wish you would keep your potato-trap shut. See ! you've made every hound throw up, and it's ten to one that ne'er a one among 'em will stoop again.' 'Yonder he goes,' cries a cock of the old school, who used to hunt with Colonel Jolliffe's hounds, and still sports the long blue surtout lined with orange, yellow-ochre unmentionables, and mahogany-coloured knee-caps, with mother-of-pearl buttons. ' Yonder he goes among the *ship* (sheep), for a thousand ! see how the skulking waggabone makes them scamper.' At this particular moment a shrill scream is heard at the far end of a long shaw, and every man pushes on to the best of his endeavour. ' Holloo *o-o-u, h'loo o-o-u, h'loo, o-o-u,* gone away ! gone away ! for*rard* ! for*rard* ! hark back ! hark for*rard* ! hark for*rard* ! hark back ! ' resounds from every mouth. ' He's making for the 'oods beyond Addington, and we shall have a rare teaser up these hills,' cries Jorrocks, throwing his arms around his horse's neck as he reaches the foot of them. ' D—n your hills,' cries ' Swell,' as he suddenly finds himself sitting on the hind quarters of his horse, his saddle having slipped back for want of the hunting martingal [1] ; ' I wish the hills had been piled on your back, and the flints thrust down your confounded throat, before I came into such a cursed provincial.' ' Haw, haw, haw ! ' roars a Croydon butcher,—' what, don't 'e like it, sir, eh ? too sharp to be pleasant, eh ?—Your nag should have put on his boots before he showed among *us.*'

' He's making straight for Fuller's Farm,' exclaims a thirsty veteran on reaching the top, ' and I'll pull up and have a nip of ale, please God.' ' Hang your ale,' cries a certain sporting cheesemonger, ' you had better come out with a barrel of it tacked to your horse's tail.' —' Or 'unt on a steam engine,' adds his friend the omnibus proprietor, ' and then you can brew as you go.' ' We shall have the Croydon Canal,' cries Mr. H—n, of Tottenham, who knows every flint in the country, ' and how will you like that, my hearties ? ' ' Curse the

[1] Hunting martingale.

Croydon Canal,' bawls the little Bromley barber, ' my
mule can swim like a soap-bladder, and my toggery
can't spoil, thank God ! '

The prophecy turns up.   Having skirted Fuller's
Farm, the villain finds no place to hide ; and in two
minutes or less, the canal appears in view.   It is full of
craft, and the locks are open, but there is a bridge about
half a mile to the right.   ' If my horse can do nothing
else he can jump [1] this,' cries Swell, as he gathers him
together and prepares for the effort.   He hardens his
heart and goes at it full tilt, and the leggy animal lands
him three yards on the other side.   ' Curse this fellow,'
cries Jorrocks, grinning with rage as he sees ' Swell '
skimming through the air like a swallow on a summer's
eve, ' he'll have a laugh at the Surrey for ever and ever,
Amen.   Oh dear ! oh dear ! I wish I *durst* leap it.   What
shall I do ?   Here, Bar*gee*,' cries he to a bargeman, ' lend
us a help over, and I'll give you ninepence.'   The bargeman takes him at his word, and getting the vessel close
to the water's edge, Jorrocks has nothing to do but ride
in, and the opposite bank being accommodating, he
lands without difficulty.   Ramming his spurs into his
nag, he now starts after ' Swell,' who is sailing away with
a few couple of hounds that took the canal ; the body
of the pack, and all the rest of the field—except the
Bromley barber, who is now floundering in the water—
having gone round to the bridge.

The country is open, the line being across commons
and along roads, so that Jorrocks, who is not afraid of
' the pace ' so long as there is no leaping, has a pretty
good chance with ' Swell.'   The scene now shifts.   On
turning out of a lane, along which they have just rattled,
a fence of this description appears : the bottom part is
made of flints, and the upper part of mud, with gorse
stuck along the top, and there is a gutter on each side.
Jorrocks, seeing that a leap is likely, hangs astern, and
' Swell,' thinking to shake off his only opponent, and to
have a rare laugh at the Surrey when he gets back to
Melton, puts his nag at it most manfully, who, though

---

[1] ' Jumping ' is Leicestershire for leaping—leaping provincial
for jumping.

somewhat blown, manages to get his long carcass over, but, unfortunately alighting on a bed of flints on the far side, cuts a back sinew, and 'Swell' measures his length on the head-land. Jorrocks then pulls up.

The tragedy of *George Barnwell* ends with a death, and we are happy in being able to gratify our readers with a similar entertainment. Already have the best-mounted men in the field attained the summit of one of the *Mont Blancs* of the country, when, on looking down the other side of the 'mountain's brow,' they, to their infinite astonishment, espy at some distance our 'Swell' dismounted and playing at 'pull-devil, pull baker,' with the hounds, whose discordant bickerings rend the skies. '*Whoo-hoop !*' cries one ; '*whoo-hoop !*' responds another ; '*whoo-hoop !*' screams a third ; and the contagion spreading and each man dismounting, they descend the hill with due caution, whoo-hooping, hallooing, and congratulating each other on the splendour of the run, interspersed with divers surmises as to what mighty magic had aided the hounds in getting on such good terms with the *warmint* ; and exclamations at the good fortune of the stranger, in being able (by nicking,[1] and the fox changing his line) to get in at the finish.

And now some dozens of sportsmen, quietly ambling up to the scene of action, view with delight (alone equalled by their wonder at so unusual and unexpected an event) the quarrels of the hounds, as they dispute with each other the possession of their victim's remains, when suddenly a gentleman, clad in a bright green silk-velvet shooting coat, with white leathers, and Hessian boots with large tassels, carrying his Joe Manton on his shoulder, issues from an adjoining coppice, and commences a loud complaint of the ' unhandsome conduct of the gentlemen's 'ounds in devouring the 'are (hare) which he had taken so much pains to shoot.' Scarcely are these words out of his mouth than the whole hunt, from Jorrocks downwards, let drive such a rich torrent of abuse at our unfortunate *chasseur*, that he

[1] A stranger *never* rides straight if he beats the members of the hunt.

is fain to betake himself to his heels, leaving them
undisputed masters of the field.

The visages of our sportsmen become dismally
lengthened on finding that their fox has been 'gathered
unto his fathers' by means of hot lead and that villain-
ous saltpetre 'digged out of the bowels of the harmless
earth'; some few, indeed, there are, who are bold
enough to declare that the pack has actually made a
meal of a hare, and that their fox is snugly earthed in
the neighbouring cover. However, as there are no
'*relliquias Danaum*' to prove or disprove this assertion,
Tom Hill, having an eye to the cap-money, ventures to
give it as his opinion, that pug has fairly yielded to his
invincible pursuers, without having 'dropped to shot.'
This appearing to give very general satisfaction, the
first whip makes no scruple of swearing that he saw the
hounds *pull him down* fairly; and Peckham, drawing
his mouth up on one side with his usual intellectual
grin, takes a similar affidavit. The Bromley barber too,
anxious to have it to say that he has for once been in at
the death of a fox, vows by his beard that he saw the
'varmint' *lathered* in style; and these protestations
being received with clamorous applause, and every one
being pleased to have so unusual an event to record to
his admiring spouse, agrees that a fox has not only been
killed, but killed in a most sportsmanlike, workman-like,
business-like manner; and long and loud are the
congratulations, great is the increased importance of
each man's physiognomy, and thereupon they all lug
out their half-crowns for Tom Hill.

In the meantime our 'Swell' lays hold of his nag—
who is sorely damaged with the flints, and whose wind
has been pretty well pumped out of him by the hills—
and proceeds to lead him back to Croydon, inwardly
promising himself for the future most studiously to
avoid the renowned county of Surrey, its woods, its
barbers, its mountains, and its flints, and to leave more
daring spirits to overcome the difficulties it presents;
most religiously resolving, at the same time, to return as
speedily as possible to his dear Leicestershire, there to
amble o'er the turf, and fancy himself an 'angel on

horseback.' The story of the country mouse, who must needs see the town, occurs forcibly to his recollection, and he exclaims aloud—

> ' me sylva, cavusque
> Tutus ab insidiis tenui solabitur ervo,'

on overhearing which, Mr. Jorrocks hurries back to his brother subscribers, and informs them, very gravely, that the stranger is no less a personage than ' Prince Matuchevitz, the Russian ambassador and minister plenipotentiary extraordinary,' whereupon the whole field join in wishing him safe back in Russia—*or anywhere else*—and wonder at his incredible assurance in supposing that he could cope with

The Surrey Hunt.

THE YORKSHIREMAN AND THE SURREY

IT is an axiom among fox-hunters that the hounds *they* individually hunt with are *the best*—compared with them all others are ' *slow.*'

Of this species of pardonable egotism, Mr. Jorrocks —who in addition to the conspicuous place he holds in the Surrey Hunt, as shown in the preceding chapter, we should introduce to our readers as a substantial grocer in St. Botolph's Lane, with an elegant residence in Great Coram Street, Russell Square—has his full, if not rather more than his fair share. Vanity, however, is never satisfied without display, and Mr. Jorrocks longed for a customer before whom he could exhibit the prowess of *his* [1] pack.

Chance threw in his way a young Yorkshireman who, frequently appearing in subsequent pages, we may introduce as a looseish sort of hand, up to anything in the

---

[1] Subscribers, speaking to strangers, always talk of the hounds as *their own.*

way of a lark, but rather deficient in cash—a character so common in London as to render further description needless.

Now it is well known that a Yorkshireman, like a dragoon, is nothing without his horse, and if he does understand anything better than racing—it is hunting. Our readers will therefore readily conceive that a Yorkshireman is more likely to be astonished at the possibility of fox-hunting from London, than captivated by the country, or style of turn-out; and in truth, looking at it calmly and dispassionately, in our easy-chair drawn to a window which overlooks the cream of the grazing grounds in the Vale of Whitehorse, it does strike us with astonishment that such a thing as a fox should be found within a day's ride of the suburbs. The very idea seems preposterous, for one cannot but associate the charms of a ' find ' with the horrors of ' going to ground ' in an omnibus, or the fox being headed by a great Dr. Eady placard, or some such monstrosity. Mr. Mayne,[1] to be sure, has brought racing home to every man's door, but fox-hunting is not quite so tractable a sport. But to our story.

It was on a nasty, cold, foggy, dark drizzling morning in the month of February that the Yorkshireman, having been offered a ' mount ' by Mr. Jorrocks, found himself shivering under the Piazza in Covent Garden about seven o'clock, surrounded by cabs, cabbages, carrots, ducks, dollys, and drabs of all sorts, waiting for his horse and the appearance of the friend who had seduced him into the extraordinary predicament of attiring himself in top-boots and breeches in London. After pacing up and down some minutes, the sound of a horse's hoofs were heard turning down from Long Acre, and reaching the lamp-post at the corner of James Street, his astonished eyes were struck with the sight of a man in a capacious, long, full-tailed, red frock coat reaching nearly to his spurs, with mother-of-pearl

[1] [The promoter of] the Hippodrome, a new establishment in the fields, near Bayswater, which may be described as a course for the promotion of illegitimate racing [a speculation that soon came to grief].

buttons with sporting devices,—which afterwards proved to be foxes, done in black,—brown shag breeches, that would have been spurned by the late worthy master of the Hurworth,[1] and boots that looked for all the world as if they were made to tear up the very land and soil, tied round the knees with pieces of white tape, the flowing ends of which dangled over the mahogany-coloured tops. Mr. Jorrocks—whose dark collar, green, to his coat, and *tout-ensemble*, might have caused him to be mistaken for a mounted general postman—was on a most becoming steed,—a great raking, raw-boned chestnut, with a twisted snaffle in his mouth, decorated with a faded yellow silk front, a nose-band, and an ivory ring under his jaws, for the double purpose of keeping the reins together and Jorrocks's teeth in his head,— the nag having flattened the noses and otherwise damaged the countenances of his two previous owners, who had not the knack of preventing him tossing his head in their faces. The saddle—large and capacious —made on the principle of the impossibility of putting a round of beef upon a pudding-plate—was 'spick and span new,' as was an enormous hunting-whip, whose iron-headed hammer he clenched in a way that would make the blood curdle in one's veins, to see such an instrument in the hands of a misguided man.

'Punctuality is the politeness of princes,' said Mr. Jorrocks, raising a broad-brimmed, lowish-crowned hat, as high as a green hunting-cord which tackled it to his yellow waistcoat by a fox's tooth would allow, as he came upon the Yorkshireman at the corner, 'My soul's on fire and eager for the chase ! By heavens, I declare I've dreamt of nothing else all night, and the worst of it is, that in a par-ox-ism of delight, when I thought I saw the darlings running into the warmint, I brought Mrs. J. such a dig in the side as knocked her out of bed, and she *swears* she'll go to Jenner and the court for the protection of injured *ribs* ! But come—jump up—where's your nag ? Binjimin, you blackguard, where are you ? The

---

[1] The late Mr. Wilkinson, commonly called 'Matty Wilkinson,' master of the Hurworth fox-hounds, was a rigid adherent of the 'd—n-all-dandy' school of sportsmen.

fog is blinding me, I declare ! Binjimin, I say ! Binjimin !
you willain, where are you ? '

'Here, sir ! coming ! ' responded a voice from the
bottom of one of the long mugs at a street breakfast
stall, which the fog almost concealed from their view,
and presently an urchin in a drab coat and blue
collar came towing a wretched, ewe-necked, hungry-
looking roan rosinante along from where he had
been regaling himself with a mug of undeniable bohea,
sweetened with a composition of brown sugar and
sand.

'Now be after getting up,' said Jorrocks, 'for time
and the Surrey 'ounds wait for no man. That's not a
werry elegant tit, but still it'll carry you to Croydon well
enough, where I'll put you on a most undeniable bit of
'orse flesh—a reg'lar clipper. That's a hack,—what they
calls three-and-sixpence a side, but I only pays half
a crown. Now, Binjimin, cut away home, and tell
Batsay to have dinner ready at half-past five to a
minute, and to be most particular in doing the lamb
to a turn.'

The Yorkshireman having adjusted himself in the old
flat-flapped hack saddle, and got his stirrups let out
from 'Binjimin's' length to his own, gathered up the
stiff weather-beaten reins, gave the animal a touch with
his spurs, and fell into the rear of Mr. Jorrocks. The
morning appeared to be getting worse. Instead of the
grey day-dawn of the country, when the thin transparent
mist gradually rises from the hills, revealing an un-
clouded landscape, a dense, thick, yellow fog came
rolling in masses along the streets, obscuring the gas
lights, and rendering every step one of peril. It could
be both eat and felt, and the damp struck through their
clothes in the most summary manner. 'This is *bad*,'
said Mr. Jorrocks, coughing as he turned the corner by
Drury Lane, making for Catherine Street, and upsetting
an early breakfast and periwinkle stall, by catching one
corner of the fragile fabric with his toe, having ridden too
near to the pavement. 'Where are you for now ? and
bad luck to ye, ye boiled lobster ! ' roared a stout Irish
wench, emerging from a neighbouring gin-palace, on

seeing the dainty viands rolling in the street. '*Cut away!*' cried Jorrocks to his friend, running his horse between one of George Stapleton's dust-carts and a hackney-coach, ' or the Philistines will be upon us.' The fog and crowd concealed them, but ' Hulloa ! mind where you're going, you great haw-buck,' from a buy-a-hearthstone boy, whose stock-in-trade Jorrocks nearly demolished as he crossed the corner of Catherine Street before him, again roused his vigilance. ' The deuce be in the fog,' said he, ' I declare I can't see across the Strand. It's as dark as a wolf's mouth.—Now, where are you going to with that measly-looking cab of yours ? —you've nearly run your shafts into my 'oss's ribs ! ' cried he to a cabman who nearly upset him. The Strand was kept alive by a few slip-shod housemaids, on their marrow-bones, washing the doorsteps or ogling the neighbouring pot-boy on his morning errand for the pewters. Now and then a crazy jarvey passed slowly by, while a hurrying mail, with a drowsy driver and sleeping guard, rattled by, to deliver their cargo at the post office. Here and there appeared one of those beings, who, like the owl, hide themselves by day and are visible only in the dusk. Many of them appeared to belong to the other world. Poor, puny, ragged, sickly-looking creatures, that seemed as though they had been suckled and reared with gin. ' How different,' thought the Yorkshireman to himself, ' to the fine, stout, active labourer one meets at an early hour on a hunting morning in the country ! ' His reverie was interrupted on arriving opposite *The Morning Chronicle* Office, by the most discordant yells that ever issued from human beings, and on examining the quarter from whence they proceeded, a group of fifty or a hundred boys, or rather little old men, were seen with newspapers in their hands and under their arms, in all the activity of speculation and exchange. ' A clean *Post* for Tuesday's *Times* ! ' bellowed one. ' I want the *Hurl* (*Herald*) for the *Satirist* ! ' shouted another. ' *Bell's Life* for the *Bull* ! The *Spectator* for the *Sunday Times* ! '

The approach of our sportsmen was the signal for a change of chorus, and immediately Jorrocks was assailed

with ' A hunter ! a hunter ! crikey, a hunter ! My eyes !
there's a gamecock for you ! Vot a beauty ! Vere do
you turn out to-day ? Vere's the stag ? Don't tumble
off, old boy ! 'Ave you got ever a rope in your pocket ?
Take *Bell's Life in London*, vot contains all the sporting
news of the country ! Vot a vip the gemman's got ! vot
a precious *basternadering* he could give us—my eyes, vot
a swell !—vot a shocking bad hat ! ¹—vot shocking bad
breeches ! '

The fog, which became denser at every step, by the
time they reached St. Clement's Danes rendered their
further progress almost impossible.—' Oh dear ! oh dear !
how unlucky,' exclaimed Jorrocks. ' I would have given
twenty pounds of best Twankay for a fine day—and see
what a thing we've got ! Hold my 'oss,' said he to the
Yorkshireman, ' while I run into the Angel and borrow
an argand burner, or we shall be endorsed ² to a dead
certainty.' Off he got and ran to the inn. Presently he
emerged from the yard—followed by horse-keepers,
coach-washers, porters, cads, waiter, and others, amid
loud cries of ' *flare up, flare up*, old cock ! tallyho fox-
hunter ! '—with a bright mail-coach foot-board lamp
strapt to his middle, which, lighting up the whole of his
broad back, now cased in scarlet, gave him the appearance of a gigantic red-and-gold insurance office badge, or
an elderly cherub without wings.

The hackney-coach and cab-men, along whose lines
they passed, could not make him out at all. Some
thought he was a mail-coach guard riding post with the
bags ; but, as the light was pretty strong, he trotted on
regardless of observation. The fog, however, abated
none of its denseness even on the ' Surrey side,' and
before they reached the Elephant and Castle, Jorrocks
had run against two trucks, three water-cress women,
one pies-all-*ot* ! all-*ot* ! man, dispersed a whole covey of
Welsh milk-maids, and rode slap over one end of a
buy *'at* (hat) box ! bonnet box ! man's pole, damaging
a dozen paste-boards, and finally upsetting Balham

¹ ' Vot a shocking bad hat ! '—the slang cockney phrase of
1831.
² City—for having a pole run into one's rear.

Hill Joe's ' Barcelona come, crack 'em and try 'em '
stall at the door of the inn, for all whose benedictions,
the Yorkshireman, as this great fox-hunting knight-
errant's ' Esquire,' came in.

Here the Yorkshireman would fain have persuaded
Mr. Jorrocks to desist from his Quixotic undertaking,
but he turned a deaf ear to his entreaties. ' We are
getting fast into the country, and I hold it to be utterly
impossible for this fog to extend beyond Kennington
Common—'twill ewaporate, you'll see, as we approach
the open. Indeed, if I mistake not, I begin to sniff the
morning air already, and hark ! there's a lark carolling
before us ! ' ' Now, spooney ! where are you for ? '
bellowed a carter, breaking off in the middle of his
whistle, as Jorrocks rode slap against his leader, the
concussion at once dispelling the pleasing pastoral
delusion, and nearly knocking Jorrocks off his horse.

As they approached Brixton Hill, a large red ball
of lurid light appeared in the firmament, and just at
the moment up rode another member of the Surrey hunt,
in uniform, whom Jorrocks hailed as Mr. Crane. ' By
Jave, 'ow beautiful the moon is,' said the latter, after
the usual salutations. ' Moon ! ' said Mr. Jorrocks,
' that's not never no moon—I reckon it's Mrs. Graham's
balloon.' ' Come, that's a good un,' said Crane ;
' perhaps you'll lay me an 'at about it.' ' Done ! '
said Mr. Jorrocks, ' a guinea one—and we'll ax my
friend here.—Now, what's that ? ' ' Why, judging
from its position and the hour, I should say it is the
sun ! ' was the reply.

We have omitted to mention that this memorable
day was a Saturday, one on which civic sportsmen
exhibit. We may also premise that the particular hunt
we are about to describe took place when there were
very many packs of hounds within reach of the Metropolis,
all of which boasted their respective admiring subscribers.
As our party proceeded, they overtook a gentleman
perusing a long bill of the meets for the next week, of at
least half a dozen packs, the top of the list being decorated
with a cut of a stag-hunt, and the bottom containing a
notification that hunters were ' carefully attended to by

Charles Morton,[1] at the Derby Arms, Croydon,' a snug, rural *auberge*, near the barrack. On the hunting bill of fare were Mr. Jolliffe's fox-hounds, Mr. Meager's harriers, the Derby stag-hounds, the Sanderstead harriers, the Union fox-hounds, the Surrey fox-hounds, rabbit beagles on Epsom Downs, and dwarf fox-hounds on Woolwich Common. What a list to bewilder a stranger! The Yorkshireman left it all to Mr. Jorrocks.

'You're for Jolliffe, I suppose,' said the gentleman with the bill, to another with a blue coat and buff lining; 'he's at Chipstead church—only six miles from Croydon, a sure find and good country.' 'What are you for, Mr. Jorrocks?' inquired another in green, with black velvet breeches, Hessian boots, and a red waistcoat, who just rode up. '*My own*, to be sure,' said Jorrocks, taking hold of the green collar of his coat, as much as to say, 'How can you ask such a question?' 'Oh no,' said the gentleman in green, 'come to the stag—much better sport—sure of a gallop—open country—get it over soon—back in town before the post goes out.' Before Mr. Jorrocks had time to make a reply to this last interrogatory, they were overtaken by another horseman, who came hopping along at a sort of butcher's shuffle, on a worn-out, three-legged, four-cornered hack, with one eye, a rat-tail, and a head as large as a fiddle-case—'Who's for the blue mottles?' said he, casting a glance at their respective coats, and at length fixing it on the Yorkshireman. 'Why, Dickens, you're not going thistle-whipping with that nice 'orse of yours,' said the gentleman in the velvets; 'come and see the stag turned out—sure of a gallop—no hedges—soft country —plenty of publics—far better sport, man, than potter-ing about looking for your foxes and hares, and wasting your time; take my advice, and come with me.' 'But,' says Dickens, 'my 'orse won't stand it; I had him in the shay till eleven last night, and he came forty-three

[1] Where the carrion is, there will be the crow, and on the demise of the 'Surrey *stag*gers,' Charley brushed off to the west, to valet the gentlemen's hunters that attend the Royal Stag-Hunt.—*Vide* Sir F. Grant's picture of the Meet of the Royal Stag-Hounds.

mile with our traveller the day before, else he's a " good un to go," as you know. Do you remember the *ow*-dacious leap he took over the tinker's tent, at the Epping 'unt, last Easter ? How he astonished the natives within ! ' ' Yes ; but then, you know, you fell head-foremost through the canvas, and no wonder that your ugly mug frightened them,' replied he of the velvets. ' Ay ; but that was in consequence of my riding by balance, instead of gripping with my legs,' replied Dickens ; ' you see, I had taken seven lessons in riding at the school in Bidborough Street, Burton Crescent, and they always told me to balance myself equally on the saddle, and harden my heart, and ride at whatever came in the way ; and the tinker's tent coming first, why, naturally enough, I went at it. But I have had some practice since then, and, of course, can stick on better. I have 'unted regularly ever since, and can " do the trick " now.' ' What, summer and winter ? ' said Jorrocks. ' No,' replied he, ' but I have 'unted regularly every fifth Saturday since the 'unting began.'

After numerous discourses similar to the foregoing, they arrived at the end of the first stage on the road to the hunt, namely, the small town of Croydon, the rendezvous of London sportsmen. The whole place was alive with red coats, green coats, blue coats, black coats, brown coats—in short, coats of all the colours of the rainbow. Horsemen were mounting, horsemen were dismounting, one-horse ' shays ' and two-horse chaises were discharging their burthens, grooms were buckling on their masters' spurs, and others were pulling off their overalls. Eschewing the Greyhound, they turn short to the right, and make for the Derby Arms' hunting stables.

Charley Morton, a fine old boy of his age, was buckling on his armour for the fight ; his soul, too, was ' on fire, and eager for the chase.' He was for the ' venison ' ; and having mounted his ' deer-stalker,' was speedily joined by divers perfect ' swells,' in beautiful leathers, beautiful coats, beautiful tops, beautiful everything, except horses, and off they rode to cut in for the first course,—a stag-hunt on a Saturday being usually divided into three.

The ride down had somewhat sharpened Jorrocks's appetite ; and feeling, as he said, quite ready for his dinner, he repaired to Mr. Morton's house,—a kind of sporting snuggery, everything in apple-pie order, and very good,—where he baited himself on sausages and salt herrings, a basin of new milk, with some ' sticking-powder,' as he called it, *alias* rum, infused into it ; and having deposited a half-quartern loaf in one pocket, as a sort of balance against a huge bunch of keys which rattled in the other, he pulled out his watch, and, finding they had a quarter of an hour to spare, proposed to *chaperone* the Yorkshireman on a tour of the hunting stables. Jorrocks summoned the ostler, and with great dignity led the way. ' Humph,' said he, evidently disappointed at seeing half the stalls empty, ' no great show this morning—pity—gentleman come from a distance—should like to have shown him some good nags.—What sort of a devil's this ? ' ' Oh, sir, he's a good un, and nothing but a good un !—Leap ! Lord love you, he'll leap anything. A railway cut, a windmill with the sails going, a navigable river with ships— anything in short. This is the 'orse wot took the line of houses down at Beddington the day they had the *tre*mendous run from Reigate Hill.' ' And wot's the grey in the far stall ? ' ' Oh, that's Mr. Pepper's old nag— Pepper-*Castor*, as we call him, since he threw the old gemman, the morning they met at the Leg-of-Mutton at Ashstead. But he's good for nothing. Bless ye ! his tail shakes for all the world like a pepper-box afore he's gone half a mile. Those be yours in the far stalls, and since they were turned round I've won a bob of a gemman who I bet I'd show him two 'osses with their heads vere their tails should be.[1] I always says,' added he, with a leer, ' that you rides the best 'osses of any gemman vot comes to our governor's.' This flattered Jorrocks, and sidling up, he slipped a shilling into his hand, saying, ' Well, bring them out, and let's see how they look this morning.' The stall reins are slipped, and out they step with their hoods on their quarters.

[1] A favourite joke among grooms when a horse is turned round in his stall.

One was a large, fat, full-sized chestnut, with a wide ratch down the full extent of his face, a long square tail, bushy mane, with untrimmed heels. The other was a brown, about fifteen-two, coarse-headed, with a rat tail, and collar-marked. The tackle was the same as they came down with. ' You'll do the trick on that, I reckon,' said Jorrocks, throwing his leg over the chestnut, and looking askew at the Yorkshireman as he mounted. ' Tatt., and old Tatt., and Tatt. sen. before him, all agree that they never knew a bad 'oss with a rat tail. But, let me tell you, you must be *werry* lively, if you mean to live with our 'ounds. They go *like the wind*. But come ! touch him with the spur, and let's do a trot.' The Yorkshireman obeyed, and getting into the main street, onwards they jogged, right through Croydon, and struck into a line of villas of all sorts, shapes, and sizes, which extend for several miles along the road, exhibiting all sorts of architecture—Gothic, Corinthian, Doric, Ionic, Dutch, and Chinese. These gradually diminished in number, and at length they found themselves on an open heath, within a few miles of the meet of the ' *Surrey* fox-hounds.' ' Now,' says Mr. Jorrocks, clawing up his smalls, ' you will see the werry finest pack of hounds in all England ; I don't care where the next best are ; and you will see as good a turn-out as ever you saw in your life, and as nice a country to ride over as ever you were in.'

They reach the meet,—a wayside public-house on a common, before which the hounds with their attendants and some fifty or sixty horsemen, many of them in scarlet, were assembled. Jorrocks was received with the greatest cordiality, and whoops and halloas, and cries of, ' Now Twankay ! now Sugar !—now Figs ! ' Waving his hand in token of recognition, he passed on and made straight for Tom Hill, with a face full of importance, and nearly rode over a hound in his hurry. ' Now, Tom,' said he, with the greatest energy, ' *do*, my good fellow, strain every nerve to show sport to-day. A gentleman has come all the way from the north-east side of the town of Boroughbridge, in the county of York, to see our excellent 'ounds, and I would fain have

him galvanized. *Do* show us a run, and let it end with
blood, so that he may have something to tell the natives
when he gets back to his own parts. That's him, see,
sitting under the yew-tree, in a bottle-green coat with
basket buttons, just striking a light on the pommel of
his saddle to indulge in a fumigation.—Keep your eye
on him all day, and if you can lead him over an awkward
place, and get him a purl, so much the better.—If he'll
risk *his* neck, I'll risk *my* oss's.'

The Yorkshireman, having lighted his cigar and
tightened his girths, rode leisurely among the horsemen,
many of whom were in eager council, and a gentle
breeze wafted divers scraps of conversation to his ear.

What is that hound got by ? No. How is that horse
bred ? No. What sport had you on Wednesday ? No.
Is it a likely find to-day ? No, no, no ; it was not
where the hounds, but what *the consols*, left off at ; what
the four per cents., and not the four horses, were *up to* ;
what the condition of the money, not the horse, market.
' Anything doing in Danish bonds, sir ? ' said one.
' You must do it by lease and release, and levy a fine,'
replied another. Scott *v.* Brown, *crim. con.*, to be heard
by the Chief Justice on or before Wednesday next.—
Barley thirty-two to forty-two.—Fine upland meadow
and rye-grass hay, seventy to eighty.—The last pocket
of hops I sold brought seven pounds fifteen shillings.
Sussex bags six pounds ten shillings. There were only
twenty-eight and a quarter ships at market, ' and coals
are coals.' ' Glad to hear it, sir, for half the last you
sent me were slates.'—' Best qualities of beef four
shillings and eightpence a stone—mutton three shillings
and eightpence to four shillings and sixpence.—He was
exceedingly ill when I paid my last visit ; I gave him
nearly a stone of Epsom salts, and bled him twice.—
This horse would suit you to a T, sir, but my skip-jack
is coming out on one at two o'clock that can carry a
house.—See what a *bosom* this one's got.—Well, Gunter,
old boy, have you *iced* your horse to-day ?—Have you
heard that Brown and Co. are in the *Gazette* ? No,
which Brown—not John Brown ? No, William Brown.
What, Brown of Goodman's Fields ? No, Brown of

MR JORROCKS "TELEGRAPHS" THE FOX

THE APPEARANCE OF SWELL ASTONISHES THE SURREY HUNT

—— of Street—Browne with an *e* ; you know the man
I mean.—Oh ! Lord, ay, the man wot used to be called
nosey Browne.' A general move ensued, and they left
' the meet.'

' Vere be you going to turn out, pray, sir, may I
inquire ? ' said a gentleman in green to the huntsman,
as he turned into a field. ' Turn out,' said he, ' why, ye
don't suppose we be coming calf-hunting, do ye ? We
throws off some two stones' throw from here, if so be you
mean what cover we are going to draw.' ' No,' said the
green-coat, ' I mean, where do you turn out the stag ? '
—' D—n the stag, we know nothing about such matters,'
replied the huntsman. ' Ware wheat ! ware wheat !
ware wheat ! ' was now the general cry, as a gentleman
in nankeen pantaloons and Hessian boots, with long
brass spurs, commenced a navigation across a sprouting
crop. ' Ware wheat, ware wheat ! ' replied he, considering part of the ceremony of hunting, and continuing his
forward course. ' Come to my side,' said Mr. —— to
the whipper-in, ' and meet that gentleman as he arrives
at yonder gate ; and keep by him while I scold you.'—
' Now, sir, most particularly d—n you, for riding slap-
dash over the young wheat, you most confounded
insensible ignorant tinker, isn't the headland wide
enough both for you and your horse, even if your spurs
were as long again as they are ? ' Shouts of ' Yooi over,
over, over hounds—try for him—yoicks—wind him !
good dogs—yoicks !—stir him up—*have at him* there ! '
—here interrupted the jawbation, and the whip rode
off shaking his sides with laughter. ' Your horse has got
a stone in each fore-foot, and a thorn in his near hock,'
observed a dentist to a wholesale haberdasher from
Ludgate Hill, ' allow me to extract them for you—no
pain, I assure—over before you know it.' ' Come away,
hounds ! come away ! ' was heard, and presently the
huntsman, with some of the pack at his horse's heels,
issued from the wood playing ' Rule Britannia ' on a
key bugle, while the cracks of heavy-thonged whips
warned the stragglers and loiterers to follow. ' Music
hath charms to soothe the savage *beast*,' observed
Jorrocks, as he tucked the laps of his frock over his

thighs, ' and I hope we shall find before long, else that
quarter of house-lamb will be utterly ruined. Oh dear,
they are going below him, I do believe ! why, we shall
never get home to-day, and I told Mrs. Jorrocks half-
past five to a minute, and I invited old Fleecy, who is a
most punctual man.'

Jorrocks was right in his surmise. They arrived on
the summit of a range of steep hills commanding an
extensive view over the neighbouring country—almost,
he said, as far as the seacoast. The huntsman and
hounds went down, but many of the field held a council
of war on the top. ' Well ! who's going down ? ' said
one. ' I shall wait for the next turn,' said Jorrocks,
' for my horse does not like collar work.' ' I shall go
this time,' said another, ' and the rest next.' ' And so
will I,' said a third, ' for mayhap there will be no second
turn.' ' Ay,' added a fourth, ' and he may go the other
way, and then where shall we all be ? ' ' Poh ! ' said
Jorrocks, ' did you ever know a Surrey fox not to take
to the hills ?—If he does not, I'll eat him without mint
sauce,' again harping on the quarter of lamb. ' *Facilis
descensus Averni* ';—two-thirds of the field went down,
leaving Jorrocks, two horse-dealers in scarlet, three
chicken-butchers, half a dozen swells in leathers, a whip,
and the Yorkshireman on the summit. ' Why don't you
go with the hounds ? ' inquired the latter of the whip.
' Oh, I wait here, sir,' said he, ' to meet Tom Hills as he
comes up, and to give him a fresh horse.' ' And who is
Tom Hills ? ' inquired the Yorkshireman. ' Oh, he's
our huntsman,' replied he ; ' you know Tom, don't
you ? ' ' Why, I can't say I do, exactly ' ; ' but tell
me, is he called Hills because he rides up and down these
hills, or is that his real name ? ' ' Hought ! you know
as well as I do,' said he, quite indignantly, ' that Tom
Hills is his name.'

The hounds, with the majority of the field, having
effected the descent of the hills, were now trotting on
in the valley below, sufficiently near, however, to allow
our hill party full view of their proceedings. After
drawing a couple of osier-beds blank, they assumed a line
parallel to the hills, and moved on to a wood of about

ten acres, the west end of which terminated in a natural
gorse. 'They'll find there to a certainty,' said Mr.
Jorrocks, pulling a telescope out of his breeches' pocket,
and adjusting the sight. 'Never saw it blank but once,
and that was the werry day the commercial panic of
twenty-five commenced—I remember making an entry
in my ledger when I got home to that effect. Humph!'
continued he, looking through the glass, 'they are
through the wood, though, without a challenge.—Now,
my *booys*, push him out of the gorse! Let's see vot
you're made of.—There goes the first 'ound in.—It's
Galloper, I believe.—I can almost see the bag of shot
round his neck.—Now they all follow.—One—two—three
—four—five—all together, my beauties. Oh, vot a
sight! Peckham's cap's in the air, and *it's a find, by
heavens!*' Mr. Jorrocks is right.—The southerly wind
wafts up the fading notes of the Huntsman's Chorus in
Der Freischütz, and confirms the fact.—Jorrocks is in
ecstasies.—' Now,' said he, clawing up his breeches
(for he dispenses with the article of braces when out
hunting), 'that's what I calls fine. Oh, beautiful!
beautiful!—Now, follow me if you please, and if yon
gentleman in drab does not shoot the fox, he will be on
the hills before long.' Away they scampered along the
top of the ridge, with a complete view of the operations
below. At length Jorrocks stopped, and, pulling the
telescope out, began making an observation. ' There he
is, at last,' cried he, ' just crossed the corner of yon
green field—now he creeps through the hedge by the
fir-tree, and is in the fallow one. Yet stay—that's no
fox—it's a hare : and yet Tom Hills makes straight for
the spot—and did you hear that loud tallyho ? Oh !
gentlemen, gentlemen, we shall be laughed to scorn—
what can they be doing ?—see, they take up the scent,
and the whole pack have joined in chorus. Great
heavens, it's no more a fox than I am !—No more brush
than a badger ! Oh dear ! oh dear ! that I should live
to see my old friends, the Surrey fox-'ounds, 'unt hare,
and that too in the presence of a stranger.' The animal
made direct for the hills ;—whatever it was, the hounds
were on good terms with it, and got away in good form.

The sight was splendid—all the field got well off, nor between the cover and the hills was there sufficient space for tailing. A little elderly gentleman, in a pepper-and-salt coat, led the way gallantly—then came the scarlets, then the darks—and then the fustian-clad countrymen. Jorrocks was in a shocking state, and rolled along the hill-tops, almost frantic. The field reached the bottom, and the foremost commenced the steep ascent.

'O Tom Hills!—Tom Hills!—what *are* you at? what *are* you *arter*?' demanded Jorrocks, as he landed on the top; 'here's a gentleman come all the way from the north-east side of the town of Boroughbridge, in the county of York, to see our excellent 'ounds, and here you are running a hare. O Tom Hills! Tom Hills! ride forward, ride forward, and whip them off, ere we eternally disgrace ourselves.' 'Oh,' says Tom, laughing, 'he's a fox! but he's so tarnation frightened of *our* hounds, that his brush dropped off through very fear, as soon as ever he heard us go into the wood; if you go back, you'll find it somewhere, Mr. Jorrocks; haw, haw, haw! No fox, indeed!' said he, 'forrard, hounds, forrard!' and away he went—caught the old whipper-in, dismounted him in a twinkling, and was on a fresh horse with his hounds in full cry. The line of flight was still along the hill-tops, and all eagerly pressed on, making a goodly rattle over the beds of flint. A check ensued. 'The guard on yonder nasty Brighton coach has frightened him with his horn,' said Tom; 'now we must make a cast up to yonder garden, and see if he's taken shelter among the geraniums in the green-house. As little damage as possible, gentlemen, *if you please*, in riding through the nursery grounds. Now, hold hard, sir—pray do—there's no occasion for you to break the kale pots; he can't be under them. Ah, yonder he goes, the tail-less beggar; did you see him as he stole past the corner out of the early-cabbage bed? Now bring on the hounds, and let us press him towards London.'

'See the conquering hero comes,' sounded through the avenue of elms as Tom dashed forward with the merry, merry pack. 'I shall stay on the hills,' said one,

' and be ready for him as he comes back ! I took a good deal of the shine out of my horse in coming up this time.' ' I think I will do the same,' said two or three more. ' Let's be doing,' said Jorrocks, ramming his spurs into his nag to seduce him into a gallop, who, after sending his heels in the air a few times in token of his disapprobation of such treatment, at last put himself into a round-rolling sort of canter, which Jorrocks kept up by dint of spurring and dropping his great *bastinaderer* of a whip every now and then across his shoulders. Away they go pounding together !

The line lies over flint fallows occasionally diversified with a turnip-field or market-garden, and every now and then a ' willa ' appears, from which emerge footmen in jackets, and in yellow, red, and green plush breeches, with no end of admiring housemaids, governesses, and nurses with children in their arms.

Great was the emulation when any of these were approached, and the rasping sportsmen rushed eagerly to the ' fore.' At last they approach ' Miss Birchwell's finishing and polishing seminary for young ladies,' whose great flaring blue and gold sign, reflecting the noon-day rays of the sun, had frightened the fox, and caused him to alter his line and take away to the west. A momentary check ensued, but all the amateur hunts-men being blown, Tom, who is well up with his hounds, makes a quick cast round the house, and hits off the scent like a workman.[1] A private road and a line of gates through fields now greet the eyes of our M'Adamizers. A young gentleman on a hired hunter, very nattily attired, here singles himself out and takes place next to Tom, throwing the pebbles and dirt back in the eyes of the field. Tom crams away, throwing the gates open as he goes, and our young gentleman very coolly passes through without a touch, letting them bang-to behind him. The Yorkshireman, who has been gradually creeping up until he has got the third place, having opened two or three, and seeing another likely to close for want of a push, cries out to our friend as he

[1] Joking apart, Tom is an excellent huntsman and worthy of a better country.

approaches, ' *Put out your hand, sir !* ' The gentleman immediately extends his limb like the arm of a telegraph, and rides over half the next field with his hand in the air ! The gate, of course, falls to.

A stopper appears—a gate locked and spiked, with a downward hinge to prevent its being lifted. To the right is a rail, and a ha-ha beyond it—to the left a quick fence. Tom glances at both, but turns short, and, backing his horse, rides at the rail. The Yorkshireman follows, but Jorrocks, who espies a weak place in the fence a few yards from the gate, turns short, and, jumping off, prepares to lead over. It is an old gap, and the farmer has placed a sheep-hurdle on the far side. Just as Jorrocks has pulled that out, his horse, who is a bit of a rusher, and has now got his ' monkey ' completely up, pushes forward while his master is yet stooping—and hitting him in the rear, knocks him clean through the fence, head-foremost into a squire-trap beyond ! [1]— ' Non *redolet* sed *olet* ! ' exclaims the Yorkshireman, who dismounts in a twinkling, lending his friend a hand out of the unsavoury cesspool. ' That's what comes of hunting in a new [2] saddle, you see,' added he, holding his nose. Jorrocks scrambles upon *terra firma*, and exhibits such a spectacle as provokes the shout of the field. He has lost his wig, his hat hangs to his back, and one side of his person and face is completely japanned with black, odoriferous mixture. ' My vig ! ' exclaims he, spitting and spluttering, ' but that's the nastiest hole I ever was in ; Fleet ditch is lavender-water compared to it ! Hooi yonder ! ' hailing a lad ; ' catch my 'oss, *boouy* ! ' Tom Hills has him ; and Jorrocks, pocketing his wig, remounts, rams his spurs into the nag, and again tackles with the pack, which had come to a momentary check on the Eden Bridge road. The fox had been headed by a party of gipsies, and, changing his point, bends southward and again reaches the hills, along which

[1] ' Cockney-Trap ' would be a more correct appellation, but we adhere to the Leicestershire diction. In this instance the trap was placed as well to secure the fence, as the rich runnings of a neighbouring parish ' midden,' or dung-heap.

[2] There is a superstition among sportsmen that they are sure to get a fall the first day they appear in anything new.

some score of horsemen have planted themselves in the likeliest places to head him. Reynard, however, is too deep for them, and has stolen down unperceived. Poor Jorrocks, what with the violent exertion of riding, his fall, and the *souvenir* of the cesspool that he still bears about him, pulls up fairly exhausted. ' Oh dear,' says he, scraping the thick of the filth off his coat with his whip, ' I'm *reglarly* blown ; I carn't go down with the 'ounds this turn ; but, my good fellow,' turning to the Yorkshireman, who was helping to purify him, ' don't let me stop *you* ; go down by all means, but *mind*, bear in mind the quarter of house-lamb—at half-past five to a *minute*.'

Many of the cits now gladly avail themselves of the excuse of assisting Mr. Jorrocks to clean himself for pulling up, but as soon as ever those that are going below the hill are out of sight, and they have given him two or three wipes, they advise him to let it ' dry on,' and immediately commence a different sort of amusement—each man dives into his pocket and produces the eatables.

Part of Jorrocks's half-quartern loaf was bartered with the captain of an East Indiaman for a slice of buffalo-beef. The dentist exchanged some veal sand-wiches with a Jew for ham ones ; a lawyer from the Borough offered two slices of toast for a hard-boiled egg ; in fact, there was a pretty market ' *ouvert* ' held. ' Now, Tomkins, where's the bottle ? ' demanded Jenkins. ' Vy, I thought *you* would bring it out to-day,' said he, ' I brought it last time, you know.' ' Take a little of mine, sir,' said a gentleman, presenting a leather-covered flask—' real Thomson and Fearon, I assure you.' ' I wish some one would fetch an ocean of porter from the nearest public,' said another. ' Take a cigar, sir ? ' ' No ; I feel werry much obliged, but they always make me womit.' ' Is there any gentleman here going to Halifax, who would like to make a third in a new yellow barouche, with lavender-coloured wheels, and pink lining ? ' inquired Mr. ——, the coachmaker. ' Look at the hounds, gentlemen sportsmen, my noble sportsmen ! ' bellowed out an Epsom Dorling's correct-listseller—and, turning their eyes in the direction in

which he was looking, our sportsmen saw them again
making for the hills. Pepper-and-salt first, and oh,
what a goodly tail was there !—three quarters of a mile
in length, at the least. Now up they come—the ' *corps
de reserve* ' again join, and again a party halt upon the
hills. Again Tom Hills exchanges horses ; and again
the hounds go on in full cry. ' I must be off,' said a
gentleman in balloon-like leathers to another tiger ; ' we
have just time to get back to town, and ride round by the
park before it is dark—much better than seeing the end
of this brute. Let us go ' ;—and away they went to
canter through Hyde Park [1] in their red coats. ' I must
go and all,' said another gentleman ; ' my dinner will
be ready at five, and it is now three.' Jorrocks was
game ; and, forgetting the quarter of house-lamb, again
tackled with the pack. A smaller sweep sufficed this
time, and the hills were once more descended, Jorrocks
the first to lead the way. He well knew the fox was
sinking, and was determined to be in at the death.
Short running ensued—a check—the fox had lain down,
and they had overrun the scent. Now they were on him,
and Tom Hills's whoop confirmed the whole.

' Ah ! Tom Hills, Tom Hills ! ' exclaimed Jorrocks,
as the former took up the fox, ' 'ow splendid, 'ow truly
brilliant—by Jove, you deserve to be Lord Hill—oh,
had he but a brush that we might present it to this
gentleman from the north-east side of the town of
Boroughbridge, in the county of York, to show the
gallant doings of the men of Surrey.' ' Ay,' said Tom,
' but Squire ——'s keeper has been before us for it.' [2]

' Now,' said a gentleman in a cap, to another in a hat,
' if you will ride up the hill and collect the money there,
I will do so below—half a crown, if you please, sir ;—

---

[1] It is a melancholy fact that three-fourths of the red-coated
gentry who attend hounds go out on a similar principle.

[2] A ' pump ' who used to scribble under the signature of ' The
Spectator,' in the *Old Sporting Magazine*, once essayed to write
a graphic description of a day with these hounds which was to
put Leicestershire men out of conceit with their country ; and
so by way of preserving the wild characteristic of the chase, he
introduced a fox that had been deprived of his brush by a keeper
when a cub, and ' hand fed ' for aught we know to the contrary.

half a crown, if you please, sir.—Have I got your half a
crown, sir ? '—' Here's three shillings if you will give me
sixpence.' ' Certainly, sir—certainly.' ' We have no
time to spare,' said Jorrocks, looking at his watch,
' good afternoon, gentlemen, good afternoon,'—muttering as he went, ' a quarter of house-lamb at half-past
five—Mrs. Jorrocks werry punctual—old Fleecy werry
particular.' They cut across country to Croydon, and
as they approached the town innumerable sportsmen
came flocking in from all quarters. ' What sport have
you had ? ' inquired Jorrocks of a gentleman in scarlet,
' have you been with Jolliffe ? ' ' No, with the stag-
hounds ! three beautiful runs ; took him once in a mill-
pond, once in a barn, and once in a brickfield—altogether
the finest day's sport I ever saw in my life.' ' What
have you done, Mr. J. ? ' ' Oh, we have had a most
gallant thing ! a brilliant run *indeed*—three hours and
twenty minutes without a check—over the finest country
imaginable.' ' And who got the brush ? ' inquired the
stag-man. ' Oh, it was a gallant run,' said Jorrocks, ' by
far the finest I ever remember.' ' But did you kill ? '
demanded his friend. ' Kill ! to be sure we did. When
don't the Surrey kill, I should like to know ? ' ' And
who got his brush, did you say ? ' ' I can't tell,' said
he ; ' didn't hear the gentleman's name.' ' What
sport has Mr. Meager had to-day ? ' inquired he of a
gentleman in trousers who issued from a side lane into
the high road. ' I have been with the Sanderstead, sir,
a very *capital* day's sport ;—run five hares and killed
three. We should have killed four—only—we didn't.'
' I don't think Mr. Meager has done anything to-day.'
' Yes, he has,' said a gentleman who just joined, with a
hare buckled on in front of his saddle, and his white
cords all stained with blood. ' We killed this chap after
an hour and forty-five minutes' gallop ; and accounted
for another by losing her after upwards of three-quarters
of an hour.' ' Well, then, we have all had sport,' said
Jorrocks, as he spurred his horse into a trot, and made
for Morton's stables—' and if the quarter of house-
lamb is but right, then indeed am I a happy man.'

2*

SURREY SHOOTING—MR. JORROCKS IN TROUBLE

OUR readers are now becoming pretty familiar with our principal hero, Mr. Jorrocks, and we hope he improves on acquaintance. Our fox-hunting friends, we are sure, will allow him to be an enthusiastic member of the brotherhood, and though we do not profess to put him in competition with Musters, Osbaldiston, or any of those sort of men, we yet mean to say that had his lot been cast in the country instead of behind a counter, his keenness would have rendered him as conspicuous— if not as scientific—as the best of them.

For a cockney sportsman, however, he is a very excellent fellow—frank, hearty, open, generous, and hospitable, and with the exception of riding up Fleet Street one Saturday afternoon with a cock-pheasant's tail sticking out of his red coat pocket, no one ever saw him do a cock-tail action in his life.

The circumstances attending that exhibition are rather curious.—He had gone out as usual on a Saturday, to have a day with the Surrey, but on mounting his hunter at Croydon, he felt the nag rather queer under him, and thinking he might have been pricked in the shoeing, he pulled up at the smith's at Addington to have his feet examined. This lost him five minutes, and unfortunately when he got to the meet he found that a ' travelling [1] fox ' had been tallied at the precise moment of throwing off, with which the hounds had gone away in their usual brilliant style, to the tune of ' Blue bonnets are over the border.' As may be supposed, he was in a deuce of a rage ; and his first impulse prompted him to withdraw his subscription and be done with the hunt altogether, and he trotted forward ' on the line,' in the hopes of catching them up to tell them so. In this he was foiled, for after riding some distance, he overtook

---

[1] He might well be called a ' travelling fox,' for it was said he had just travelled down from Herrings, in the New Road, by the Bromley stage.

a string of Smithfield horses journeying 'foreign for Evans,' whose imprints he had been taking for the hoof-marks of the hunters. About noon he found himself dull, melancholy, and disconsolate, before the sign of the Pig and Whistle, on the Westerham Road, where, after wetting his own whistle with a pint of half-and-half, he again journeyed onward, ruminating on the un-certainty and mutability of all earthly affairs, the comparative merits of stag, fox, and hare hunting, and the necessity of getting rid of the day somehow or other in the country.

Suddenly his reverie was interrupted by the discharge of a gun in the field adjoining the hedge along which he was passing, and the boisterous *whirring* of a great cock-pheasant over his head, which caused his horse to start and stop short, and to nearly pitch Jorrocks over his head. The bird was missed, but the sportsman's dog dashed after it, with all the eagerness of expectation, regardless of the cracks of the whip—the ' comes to heel ' and ' downs to charge ' of the master. Jorrocks pulled out his hunting telescope, and having marked the bird down with the precision of a billiard-table keeper, rode to the gate to acquaint the shooter of the fact, when to his infinite amazement he discovered his friend, Nosey Browne (late of ' The Surrey '), who, since his affairs had taken the unfortunate turn mentioned in the last paper, had given up hunting and determined to confine himself to shooting only. Nosey, however, was no great performer, as may be inferred when we state that he had been in pursuit of the above-mentioned cock-pheasant ever since daybreak, and, after firing thirteen shots at him, had not yet touched a feather.

His dog was of the right sort—for Nosey at least— and hope deferred had not made his heart sick ; on the contrary, he dashed after his bird for the thirteenth time with all the eagerness he displayed on the first. ' Let *me* have a crack at him,' said Jorrocks to Nosey, after their mutual salutations were over. ' I know where he is, and I think I can floor him.' Browne handed the gun to Jorrocks, who, giving up his hunter in exchange, strode off, and, having marked his bird accurately, he kicked him up out of a bit of furze, and knocked him down as ' dead as a door-nail.' By that pheasant's *tail* hangs the present one.

Now, Nosey Browne and Jorrocks were old friends, and Nosey's affairs having gone crooked, why, of course, like most men in a similar situation, he was all the better for it ; and while his creditors were taking twopence-halfpenny in the pound, he was taking his diversion on his wife's property, which a sagacious old father-in-law had secured to the family in the event of such a con-tingency as a failure happening ; so, knowing Jorrocks's propensity for sports, and being desirous of chatting over all his gallant doings with ' The Surrey,' shortly after the above-mentioned day he despatched a ' two-penny,' offering him a day's shooting on his property in Surrey, adding that he hoped he would dine with him after. Jorrocks being invited himself, with a freedom peculiar to fox-hunters, invited his friend the Yorkshire-man, and, visiting his armoury, selected him a regular shot-scatterer of a gun, capable of carrying ten yards on every side.

At the appointed hour on the appointed morning the Yorkshireman appeared in Great Coram Street, where he found Mr. Jorrocks in the parlour, in the act of settling himself into a new spruce green cut-away gambroon butler's pantry-jacket, with pockets equal to holding a powder-flask each, his lower man being attired in tight drab stocking-net pantaloons, and Hessian boots with large tassels—a striking contrast to the fustian pocket-and-all-pocket jackets marked with game-bag strap and shot-belt, and the weather-beaten, many-coloured breeches and gaiters, and hob-nail shoes, that compose the equipment of a shooter in Yorkshire. Mr. Jorrocks not keeping any ' sporting dogs,' as the tax-papers call them, had borrowed a fat house-dog—a cross between a setter and a Dalmatian—of his friend Mr. Evergreen, the greengrocer, which he had seen make a most undeniable point one morning in the Copenhagen Fields at a flock of pigeons in a beet-root garden. This valuable animal was now attached by a trash-cord through a ring in his brass collar to a leg of the sideboard, while a clean-licked dish at his side showed that Jorrocks had been trying to attach him to himself, by feeding him before starting.

' We'll take a coach to the Castle,' said Jorrocks, ' and then get a " go-cart " or a cast somehow or other to Streatham, for we shall have walking enough when we get there. Browne is an excellent fellow, and will make us range every acre of his estate over half a dozen times before we give in.' A coach was speedily summoned, into which Jorrocks, the dog Pompey, the Yorkshireman, and the guns were speedily placed, and away they drove to the Elephant and Castle.

There were short stages about for every possible place except Streatham, Greenwich, Deptford, Blackheath, Eltham, Bromley, Footscray, Beckenham and Lewisham, —all places but the right. However, there were abundance of ' go-carts,' a species of vehicle that ply in the outskirts of the Metropolis, and which, like the watering-place ' fly,' take their name from the contrary—in fact, a sort of *lucus a non lucendo*. They are carts on springs, drawn by one horse (with curtains to protect the company from the weather), the drivers of which, partly by cheating, and partly by picking pockets, eke out a comfortable existence, and are the most lawless set of rascals under the sun. Their arrival at the Elephant and Castle was a signal for a general muster of the fraternity, who, seeing the guns, were convinced that their journey was only what they call ' a few miles down the road,' and they were speedily surrounded by twenty or thirty of them, all with excellent ' 'osses, vot vould take their honours fourteen miles an hour.' All men of business are aware of the advantages of competition, and no one more so than Jorrocks, who stood listening to their offers with the utmost *sang-froid*, until he closed with one to take them to Streatham church for two shillings, and deliver them within the half-hour, which was a signal for all the rest to set-to and abuse them, their coachman, and his horse, which they swore had been carrying ' stiff-uns ' [1] all night, and ' could not go not none at all.' Nor were they far wrong ; for the horse, after scrambling

---

[1] Doing a bit of resurrection work.

a hundred yards or two, gradually relaxed into something between a walk and a trot, while the driver kept
soliciting every passer-by to ' ride,' much to our sportsmen's chagrin, who conceived they were to have the
' go ' all to themselves. Remonstrance was vain, and
he crammed in a master chimney-sweep, Major Ballenger,
the licensed dealer in tea, coffee, tobacco, and snuff, of
Streatham (a customer of Jorrocks), and a wet nurse ;
and took up an Italian organ-grinder to ride beside himself on the front, before they had accomplished Brixton
Hill. Jorrocks swore most lustily that he would fine
him, and at every fresh assurance the driver offered a
passer-by a seat ; but having enlisted Major Ballenger
into their cause, they at length made a stand, which,
unfortunately for them, was more than the horse could
do, for just as he was showing off, as he thought, with
a bit of a trot, down they all soused in the mud. Great
was the scramble ; guns, barrel-organ, Pompey, Jorrocks,
driver, master chimney-sweep, Major Ballenger, were all
down together, while the wet nurse, who sat at the end
nearest the door, was chucked clean over the hedge
into a dry ditch. This was a signal to quit the vessel,
and, having extricated themselves the best way they
could, they all set off on foot, and left the driver to right
himself at his leisure.

Ballenger looked rather queer when he heard they
were going to Nosey Browne's, for it so happened that
Nosey had managed to walk into his books for groceries
and kitchen-stuff to the tune of fourteen pounds, a large
sum to a man in a small way of business ; and to be
entertaining friends so soon after his composition,
seemed curious to Ballenger's uninitiated suburban
mind.

Crossing Streatham Common, a short turn to the left
by some yew trees leads, by a near cut across the fields,
to Browne's house ; a fiery-red brick castellated cottage,
standing on the slope of a gentle eminence, and combining almost every absurdity a cockney imagination can
be capable of. Nosey, who was his own ' Nash,' set out
with the intention of making it a castle and nothing
but a castle, and accordingly the windows were made in

the loophole fashion, and the door occupied a third of the whole frontage. The inconvenience of the arrangements were soon felt, for while the light was almost excluded from the rooms, ' rude Boreas ' had the complete run of the castle whenever the door was opened. To remedy this, Nosey increased the one and curtailed the other, and the Gothic oak-painted windows and door flew from their positions to make way for modern plate-glass in rich pea-green casements, and a door of similar hue. The battlements, however, remained, and two wooden guns guarded a brace of chimney-pots and commanded the wings of the castle, one whereof was formed into a *green-*, the other into a *gig-*house.

The peals of a bright brass-handled bell at a garden-gate, surmounted by a holly-bush with the top cut into the shape of a fox, announced their arrival to the inhabitants of ' Rosalinda Castle,' and on entering, they discovered young Nosey in the act of bobbing for gold-fish, in a pond about the size of a soup-basin ; while Nosey senior, a fat, stupid-looking fellow with a large corporation and a bottle nose, attired in a single-breasted green cloth coat, buff waistcoat, with drab shorts and continuations, was reposing, ' *sub tegmine fagi*,' in a sort of tea-garden arbour overlooking a dung-heap, waiting their arrival to commence an attack upon the sparrows which were regaling thereon. At one end of the garden was a sort of temple, composed of oyster-shells, contain-ing a couple of carrier-pigeons, with which Nosey had intended making his fortune by the early information to be acquired by them ; but ' there is many a slip,' etc., as Jorrocks would say.

Greetings being over, and Jorrocks having paid a visit to the larder, and made up a stock of provisions equal to a journey through the Wilderness, they ad-journed to the yard to get the *other* dog, and the man to carry the game—or rather, the prog, for the former was but problematical. He was a character, a sort of chap of all work, one, in short, ' who has no objection to make himself generally useful ' ; but if his genius had any decided *bent*, it was, perhaps, an *inclination* towards sporting.

Having to act the part of groom and gamekeeper during the morning, and butler and footman in the afternoon, he was attired in a sort of composition dress, savouring of the different characters performed. He had on an old white hat, a groom's fustian stable-coat cut down into a shooting-jacket with a whistle at the button-hole, red plush smalls, and top-boots.

There is nothing a cockney delights in more than aping a country gentleman, and Browne fancied himself no bad hand at it ; indeed, since his London occupation was gone, he looked upon himself as a country gentleman, in fact. ' Vell, Joe,' said he, striddling and sticking his thumbs into the arm-holes of his waistcoat, to this invaluable man of all work, ' we must show the gemmen some sport to-day : vich do you think the best line to start upon—shall we go to the ten h'acre field, or the plantation, or Thompson's stubble, or Timms' turnips, or my meadow, or vere ? ' ' Vy, I doesn't know,' said Joe ; ' there's that old hen-pheasant as we calls Drab Bess, vot has haunted the plantin' these two seasons, and none of us ever could 'it (hit), and I hears that Jack, and Tom, and Bob, are still left out of Thompson's covey : but my eyes ! they're 'special vild ! ' ' Vot ! only three left ? where is old Tom, and the old ramping hen ? ' inquired Browne. ' Oh, Mr. Smith, and a party of them 'ere Bankside chaps, com'd down last Saturday's gone a week, and rattled nine-and-twenty shots at the covey, and got the two old uns ; at least it's supposed they were both killed, though the seven on 'em only bagged one bird ; but I heard they got a goose or two as they vent home. They had a shot at Old Tom, the hare, too, but he is still alive ; at least I pricked him yesterday morn across the path into the turnip field. Suppose we goes at him first ? '

The estate, like the game, was rather deficient in quantity, but Browne was a wise man and made the most of what he had, and when he used to talk about his ' manor ' on 'Change, people thought he had at least a thousand acres—the extent a cockney generally advertises for, when he wants to take a shooting place. The following is a sketch of what he had :—The east, as

far as the eye could reach, was bounded by Norwood,
a name dear to cockneys, and the scene of many a furtive
kiss ; the hereditaments and premises belonging to
Isaac Cheatum, Esq., ran parallel with it on the west,
containing sixty-three acres, ' be the same more or less,'
separated from which, by a small brook or runner of
water, came the estate of Mr. Timms, consisting of
sixty acres, three roods, and twenty-four perches,
commonly called or known by the name of Fordham ;
next to it were two allotments in right of common, for
all manner of cattle except cows, upon Streatham
Common, from whence up to Rosalinda Castle, on the
west, lay the estate of Mr. Browne, consisting of fifty
acres and two perches. Now, it so happened that Browne
had formerly the permission to sport all the way up to
Norwood, a distance of a mile and a half, and consequently he might have been said to have the right of
shooting in Norwood itself, for the keepers only direct
their attention to the preservation of the timber and
the morals of the visitors ; but since his composition
with his creditors, Mr. Cheatum, who had ' gone to the
wall ' himself in former years, was so scandalized at
Browne doing the same, that no sooner did his name
appear in the *Gazette*, than Cheatum withdrew his
permission, thereby cutting him off from Norwood, and
stopping him in pursuit of his game.

Joe's proposition being duly seconded, Mr. Jorrocks,
in the most orthodox manner, flushed off his old flint
and steel fire engine, and proceeded to give it an uncommon good loading. The Yorkshireman, with a look
of disgust mingled with despair, and a glance at Joe's
plush breeches and top-boots, did the same, while Nosey,
in the most considerate, sportsmanlike manner, merely
shouldered a stick, in order that there might be no
delicacy with his visitors as to who should shoot first—
a piece of *etiquette* that aids the escape of many a bird in
the neighbourhood of London.

Old Tom—a most unfortunate old hare, that what
with the harriers, the shooters, the snarers, and one
thing and another, never knew a moment's peace, and
who must have started in the world with as many lives

as a cat—being doomed to receive the first crack on this occasion, our sportsmen stole gently down the fallow, at the bottom of which were the turnips wherein he was said to repose ; but scarcely had they reached the hurdles which divided the field, before he was seen legging it away clean out of shot. Jorrocks, who had brought his gun to bear upon him, could scarcely refrain from letting drive, but thinking to come upon him again by stealth as he made his circuit for Norwood, he strode away across the allotments and Fordham estate, and took up a position behind a shed which stood on the confines of Mr. Timms' and Mr. Cheatum's properties. Here, having procured a rest for his gun, he waited until Old Tom, who had tarried to nip a few blades of green grass that came in his way, made his appearance. Presently he came cantering along the outside of the wood at a careless, easy sort of pace, betokening either perfect indifference for the world's mischief, or utter contempt of cockney sportsmen altogether.

He was a melancholy, woe-begone looking animal, long and lean, with a slight inclination to grey on his dingy old coat, one that looked as though he had survived his kindred and had already lived beyond his day. Jorrocks, however, saw him differently, and his eyes glistened as he came within range of his gun. A well-timed shot ends poor Tom's miseries ! He springs into the air, and with a melancholy scream rolls neck over heel. Knowing that Pompey would infallibly spoil him if he got up first, Jorrocks, without waiting to load, was in the act of starting off to pick him up, when, at the first step, he found himself in the grasp of a Herculean monster, something between a coalheaver and a game-keeper, who had been secreted behind the shed. Nosey Browne, who had been watching his movements, holloaed out to Jorrocks to ' hold hard,' who stood motionless on the spot from whence he fired, and Browne was speedily alongside of him. ' You are on Squire Cheatum's estate,' said the man ; ' and I have authority to take up all poachers and persons found unlawfully trespassing ; what's your name ? ' ' He's not on Cheatum's estate,' said Browne. ' He is,' said the man.

'You're a liar,' said Browne. 'You're another,' said the man. And so they went on ; for when such gentlemen meet, compliments pass current. At length the keeper pulled out a foot-rule, and keeping Jorrocks in the same position he caught him, he set-to to measure the distance of his foot from the boundary, taking off in a line from the shed ; when it certainly did appear that the length of a big toe was across the mark, and putting up his measure again, he insisted upon taking Jorrocks before a magistrate for the trespass. Of course, no objection could be made, and they all adjourned to Mr. Boreem's, when the whole case was laid before him. To cut a long matter short,—after hearing the pros and cons, and referring to the act of parliament, his worship decided that a trespass had been committed ; and though, he said, it went against the grain to do so, he fined Jorrocks in the mitigated penalty of one pound one.

This was a sad damper to our heroes, who returned to the castle with their prog untouched, and no great appetite for dinner. Being only a family party, when Mrs. B. retired the subject naturally turned upon the morning's mishap, and at every glass of port Jorrocks waxed more valiant, until he swore he would appeal against the 'conwiction' ; and remaining in the same mind when he awoke the next morning, he took the Temple in his way to St. Botolph Lane and had six-and-eightpence worth with Mr. Capias the attorney, who very judiciously argued each side of the question without venturing an opinion, and proposed stating a case for counsel to advise upon.

As usual, he gave one that would cut either way, though if it had any tendency whatever, it was to induce Jorrocks to go on ; and he not wanting much persuasion, it will not surprise our readers to hear that Jorrocks, Capias, and the Yorkshireman were seen a few days after crossing Waterloo Bridge in a yellow post-chaise, on their way to Croydon sessions.

After a 'guinea' consultation at the Greyhound, they adjourned to the Court, which was excessively crowded, Jorrocks being as popular with the farmers and people

as Cheatum was the reverse. Party feeling too running
high at the time, there had been a strong ' whip '
among the magistrates to get a full attendance to
reverse Boreem's conviction, who had made himself
rather obnoxious on the blue interest at the election.
Of course they all came in new hats,[1] and sat on the
bench, looking as wise as gentlemen judges generally do.

One hundred and twenty-two affiliation cases (for
this was in the old poor law time) having been disposed
of, about one o'clock in the afternoon, the chairman,
Mr. Tomkins of Tomkins, moved the order of the day.
He was a perfect prototype of a county magistrate—
with a bald, powdered head covered by a low-crowned,
broad-brimmed hat, hair terminating behind in a *queue*,
resting on the ample collar of a snuff-brown coat, with
a large bay-window of a corporation, with difficulty
retained by the joint efforts of a buff waistcoat and the
waisband of a pair of yellow leather breeches. His
countenance, which was solemn and grave in the extreme,
might either be indicative of sense, or what often serves
in the place of wisdom—when parties can only hold their
tongues—great natural stupidity. From the judge's
seat, which he occupied in the centre of the Bench, he
observed, with immense dignity, ' There is an appeal of
Jorrocks against Cheatum, which we, the Bench of
Magistrates of our Lord the King, will take if the parties
are ready,' and immediately the court rang with
' Jorrocks and Cheatum ! Jorrocks and Cheatum !
Mr. Capias attorney at law ! Mr. Capias answer to
his name ! Mr. Sharp attorney at law ! Mr. Sharp's in
the jury room.—Then go fetch him directly,' from the
ushers and bailiffs of the court ; for though Tomkins
of Tomkins was slow himself, he insisted upon others
being quick, and was a great hand at prating about
saving the time of the suitors. At length the bustle
of counsel crossing the table, parties coming in and
others leaving court, bailiffs shouting, and ushers
responding, gradually subsided into a whisper of ' That's

---

[1] Magistrates always buy their hats about Session times, as
they have the privilege of keeping their hats on their *blocks* in
court.

Jorrocks ! that's Cheatum ! ' as the belligerent parties took their places by their respective counsel. Silence having been called and procured, Mr. Smirk, a goodish-looking man for a lawyer, having deliberately unfolded his brief, which his clerk had scored plentifully in the margin, to make the attorney believe he had read it very attentively, rose to address the court—a signal for half the magistrates to pull the newspapers out of their pockets, and the other half to settle themselves down for a nap, all the sport being considered over when the affiliation cases closed.

' I have the honour to appear on behalf of Mr. Jorrocks,' said Mr. Smirk, ' a gentleman of the very highest consideration—a fox-hunter—a shooter—and a grocer. In ordinary cases it might be necessary to prove the party's claim to respectability, but in this instance, I feel myself relieved from any such obligation, knowing, as I do, that there is no one in this court, no one in these realms,—I might almost add, no one in this world,—to whom the fame of my most respectable, most distinguished, and much injured client is unknown. Not to know JORROCKS is indeed to argue one-self unknown.

' This is a case of no ordinary interest, and I approach it with a deep sense of its importance, conscious of my inability to do justice to the subject, and lamenting that it has not been entrusted to abler hands. It is a case involving the commercial and the sporting character of a gentleman against whom the breath of calumny has never yet been drawn—of a gentleman who, in all the relations of life, whether as a husband, a fox-hunter, a shooter, or a grocer, has invariably preserved that character and reputation, so valuable in commercial life, so necessary in the sporting world, and so indispensable to a man moving in general society. Were I to look round London town in search of a bright specimen of a man combining the upright, sterling integrity of the honourable British merchant of former days with the ardour of the English fox-hunter of modern times, I would select my most respectable client, Mr. Jorrocks. He is a man for youth to imitate and revere ! Conceive, then, the horror of a man of his delicate sensibility—

of his nervous dread of depreciation—being compelled
to appear here this day to vindicate his character, nay
more, his honour, from one of the foulest attempts at
conspiracy that was ever directed against any individual.
I say that a grosser attack was never made upon the
character of any grocer, and I look confidently to the
reversion of this unjust, unprecedented conviction, and
to the triumphant victory of my most respectable and
public-spirited client. It is not for the sake of the few
paltry shillings that he appeals to this court—it is not
for the sake of calling in question the power of the
constituted authorities of this county—but it is for the
vindication and preservation of a character dear to all
men, but doubly dear to a grocer, and which once lost
can never be regained. Look, I say, upon my client as
he sits below the witness-box, and say if in that countenance there appears any indication of a lawless or rebellious
spirit ; look, I say, if the milk of human kindness is not
strikingly portrayed in every feature, and truly may I
exclaim in the words of the poet—

> ' If to his share some trifling errors fall,
> Look in his face, and you'll forget them all.'

I regret to be compelled to trespass upon the valuable
time of the court ; but, sir, this appeal is based on a
trespass, and one good trespass deserves another.'

The learned gentleman then proceeded to detail the
proceedings of the day's shooting, and afterwards to
analyse the enactments of the New Game Bill, which he
denounced as arbitrary, oppressive, and ridiculous, and
concluded a long and energetic speech by calling upon
the Court to reverse the decision of the magistrate, and
not support the preposterous position of fining a man for
a trespass committed by his toe.

After a few minutes had elapsed, Mr. Serjeant
Bumptious, a stiff, bull-headed little man, desperately
pitted with smallpox, rose to reply, and, looking round
the court, thus commenced :—

' Five-and-thirty years have I passed in Courts of
Justice, but never during a long and extensive practice
have I witnessed so gross a perversion of that sublimest

gift, called eloquence, as within the last hour,'—here he banged his brief against the table, and looked at Mr. Smirk, who smiled—' I lament, sir, that it has not been employed in a better cause—(bang again—and another look). My learned friend has, indeed, laboured to make the worst appear the better cause—to convert into a trifle one of the most outrageous acts that ever disgraced a human being or a civilized country. Well did he describe the importance of this case !—important as regards his client's character—important as regards this great and populous county—important as regards those social ties by which society is held together—important as regards a legislative enactment, and important as regards the well-being and prosperity of the whole nation—(bang, bang, bang). I admire the bombastic eloquence with which my learned friend introduced his *most distinguished* client—his *most* delicate-minded —sensitive client !—Truly, to hear him speaking, I should have thought he had been describing a lovely, blushing young lady, but when he comes to exhibit his paragon of perfection, and points out that great, red-faced, coarse, vulgar-looking, lubberly lump of humanity (here Bumptious looked at Jorrocks as though he would eat him) sitting below the witness-box, and seeks to enlist the sympathies of your worships on the Bench— of *you, gentlemen*, the high-minded, shrewd, penetrating judges of this important cause (and Bumptious smiled and bowed along the Bench upon all whose eyes he could catch) on behalf of such a monster of iniquity, it does make one blush for the degradation of the British bar —(bang—bang—bang—Jorrocks here looked unutter-able things). Does my learned friend think by display-ing his hero as a fox-hunter, and extolling his prowess in the field, to gain over the sporting magistrates on the Bench ? He knows little of the upright integrity—the uncompromising honesty—the undeviating, inflexible impartiality that pervades the breast of every member of this tribunal, if he thinks for the sake of gain, fear, favour, hope, or reward, to influence the opinion, much less turn the judgment of any one of them.' (Here Bumptious bowed very low to them all and laid his hand upon his heart. Tomkins nodded approbation.) 'Far, far be it from me to dwell with unbecoming asperity on the conduct of any one—we are all mortals—and alike liable to err ;—but when I see a man who has been guilty of an act which has brought him all but within the verge of the prisoners' dock ; I say, when I see a man who has been guilty of such an outrage on society as this ruffian Jorrocks, come forward with the daring effrontery that he has this day done, and claim redress where he himself is the offender, it does create a feeling in my mind divided between disgust and amazement ' —(bang).

Here Jorrocks's cauldron boiled over, and, rising from his seat with an outstretched shoulder-of-mutton fist, he bawled out, 'D—n you, sir, what do you mean ? '

The court was thrown into amazement, and even Bumptious quailed before the fist of the mighty Jorrocks. 'I claim the protection of the court,' he exclaimed. Mr. Tomkins interposed, and said he should certainly order Mr. Jorrocks into custody if he repeated his conduct, adding that it was 'most disrespectful to the justices of our Lord the King.'

Bumptious paused a little to gather breath and a fresh volume of venom wherewith to annihilate Jorrocks, and, catching his eye, he transfixed him like a rattle-snake, and again resumed.

'How stands the case ? ' said he—'This cockney grocer—for after all he is nothing else—who I dare say scarcely knows a hawk from a hand-saw, leaves his figs and raisins, and sets out on a marauding excursion into the county of Surrey, and regardless of property—of boundaries—of laws—of liberties—of life itself—strides over every man's land, letting drive at whatever comes in his way ! The hare he shot on this occasion was a *pet* hare !—For three successive summers had Miss Cheatum watched and fed it with all the interest and anxiety of a parent. I leave it to you, gentlemen, who have daughters of your own, with pets also, to picture to yourselves the agony of her mind on finding that her favourite had found its way down the throat of that great guzzling, gormandizing, cockney cormorant ; and then, forsooth, because he is fined for the outrageous trespass, he comes here as the injured party, and instructs his counsel to indulge in Billingsgate abuse that would disgrace the mouth of an Old Bailey practitioner ! I regret that instead of the insignificant fine imposed upon him, the law did not empower the worthy magistrate to send him to the treadmill, there to recreate himself for six or eight months, as a warning to the whole fraternity of lawless vagabonds.' Here he nodded his head at Jorrocks, as much as to say—' I'll *trounce* you, my boy ! ' He then produced maps and plans of the different estates, and a model of the shed, to show how it all happened, and, after going through the case in such a strain as would induce one to believe it was a trial for murder or high treason, concluded as follows :—

' The eyes of England are upon us—reverse this conviction, and you let loose a rebel band upon the country, ripe for treason, stratagem, or spoil—you overturn the finest order of society in the world ; henceforth no man's property will be safe, the laws will be disregarded, and even the upright, talented and independent magistracy of England brought into contempt. But I feel convinced that your decision will be far otherwise—that by it you will teach these hotheaded—rebellious—radical grocers that they cannot offend with impunity, and show them that there is a law which reaches even the lowest and meanest inhabitants of these realms, that amid these days of anarchy and innovation you will support the laws and aristocracy of this country, that you will preserve to our children, and our children's children, those rights and blessings which a great and enlightened administration have conferred upon ourselves, and raise for Tomkins of Tomkins and the magistracy of the proud county of Surrey, a name resplendent in modern times, and venerated to all eternity.'

Here Bumptious cast a parting frown at Jorrocks, and, banging down his brief, tucked his gown under his arm, turned on his heel, and left the court, to indulge in a glass of pale sherry and a sandwich, regardless which way the verdict went, so long as he had given him a good quilting. The silence that followed had the effect of rousing some of the dozing justices, who nudging those who had fallen asleep, they all began to stir themselves, and having laid their heads together, during which time they settled the dinner hour for that day, and the meets of the stag-hounds for the next fortnight, they began to talk of the matter before the court.

'I vote for reversing,' said Squire Jolthead, 'Jorrocks is such a capital fellow.' 'I *must* support Boreem,' said Squire Hicks, 'he gave me a turn when I made the mistaken commitment of Gipsy Jack.' 'What do you say, Mr. Giles?' inquired Mr. Tomkins. 'Oh, anything *you* like, Mr. Tomkins.' 'And you, Mr. Hopper?' who had been asleep all the time. 'Oh, *guilty*, I should say—three months at the treadmill—privately whipped, if you like,' was the reply. Mr. Petty always voted on whichever side Bumptious was counsel—the learned serjeant having married his sister,—and four others always followed the chair.

Tomkins then turned round, the magistrates resumed their seats along the bench, and, coming forward, he stood before the judge's chair, and, taking off his hat with solemn dignity and precision, laid it down exactly in the centre of the desk, amid cries from the bailiffs and ushers for '*Silence*, while the Justices of the Peace of our Sovereign Lord the King deliver the judgment of the Court.'

'The appellant in this case,' said Mr. Tomkins very slowly, 'seeks to set aside a conviction for trespass, on the ground, as I understand, of his not having committed one. The principal points of the case are admitted, as also the fact of Mr. Jorrocks's toe, or a part of his toe, having intruded upon the respondent's estate. Now, so far as that point is concerned, it seems clear to myself and to my brother magistrates, that it mattereth not how much or how little of the toe was upon the land, so long as any part thereof was there. "*De minimis non curat lex*"—the English of which is, 'the law taketh no cognizance of fractions'—is a maxim among the salaried judges of the inferior courts in Westminster Hall, which we, the unpaid, the in-cor-rup-ti-ble magistrates of the proud county of Surrey, have adopted in the very deep and mature deliberation that preceded the formation of our most solemn judgment. In the present great and important case, we, the unpaid magistrates of our Sovereign Lord the King, do not consider it necessary that there should be " a toe, a whole toe, and nothing but a toe," to constitute a trespass, any more than it would be necessary in the case of an assault to prove that the kick was given by the foot, the whole foot, and nothing but the foot. If any part of the toe was there, the law considers that it was there in *to-to*. Upon this doctrine, it is clear that Mr. Jorrocks was guilty of a trespass, and the conviction must be affirmed. Before I dismiss the case I must say a few words on the statute under which this decision takes place.

' This is the first conviction that has taken place since the passing of the Act, and will serve as a precedent throughout all England. I congratulate the country upon the efficacy of the tribunal to which it has been submitted. The Court has listened with great and becoming attention to the arguments of the counsel on both sides : and though one gentleman with a flippant ignorance has denounced this new law as inferior to the pre-existing system, and a curse to the country, we, the magistrates of the proud county of Surrey, must enter our protest against such a doctrine being promulgated. Peradventure, you are all acquainted with my prowess as a shooter ; I won two silver tankards at the Red House, Anno Domini, 1815. I mention this to show that I am a practical sportsman ; and as to the theory of the Game Laws, I derive my information from the same source that you may all derive yours—from the bright refulgent pages of the *New Sporting Magazine* ! '

MR. JORROCKS AND THE SURREY
STAG-HOUNDS

THE Surrey fox-hounds had closed their season—a
most brilliant one—but ere Mr. Jorrocks consigned
his boots and breeches to their summer slumber, he
bethought of having a look at the Surrey stag-hounds,
a pack now numbered among the things that were.

Of course he required a companion, were it only to
have some one to criticize the hounds with, so the
evening before the appointed day, as the Yorkshireman
was sitting in his old corner at the far end of the Piazza
Coffee-room in Covent Garden, having just finished his
second marrow-bone and glass of white brandy, George
—the only waiter in the room with a name—came
smirking up with a card in his hand, saying, that the
gentleman was waiting outside to speak with him. It
was a printed one, but the large round hand in which the
address had been filled up encroaching upon the letters,
had made the name somewhat difficult to decipher. At
length he puzzled out ' Mr. John Jorrocks—Coram
Street ' ; the name of the city-house or shop in the
corner (No. —, St. Botolph's Lane) being struck through
with a pen. ' Oh, ask him to walk in directly,' said the
Yorkshireman to George, who trotted off ; and presently
the flapping of the doors in the passage announced his
approach, and honest Jorrocks came rolling up the
room—not like a fox-hunter, or any other sort of hunter,
but like an honest wholesale grocer, fresh from the city.

' My dear fellow, I'm so glad to see you, you can't
think,' said he, advancing with both hands out, and
hugging the Yorkshireman after the manner of a Polar
bear, ' I have not time to stay one moment ; I have to
meet Mr. Wiggins at the corner of Bloomsbury Square
at a quarter to six, and it wants now only seven minutes
to,' casting his eye up at the clock over the side-board.
—' I have just called to say that as you are fond of
hunting, and all that sort of thing, if you have a mind
for a day with the stag-hounds to-morrow, I will mount

you same as before, and all that sort of thing—you understand, eh ? ' ' Thank you, my good friend,' said the
Yorkshireman ; ' I have nothing to do to-morrow, and
am your man for a stag-hunt.' ' That's right, my good
fellow,' said Jorrocks, ' then I'll tell you what do—
come and breakfast with me in Great Coram Street, at
half-past seven to a minute. I've got one of the first
'ams (hams) you ever clapt eyes on in the whole course
of your memorable existence.—Saw the hog alive myself
—sixteen score within a pound ; must come—know
you like a fork breakfast (*dejeuné à la fouchette*), as we
say in France, eh ? Like my Lord Mayor's fool, I guess,
love what's good ; well, all right too—so come without
any ceremony—*us* fox-hunters hates ceremony—where
there's ceremony there's no friendship.—Stay—I had
almost forgotten,' added he, checking himself as he
was on the point of departure, ' When you come, ring
the area bell, and then Mrs. J. won't hear ; know you
don't like Mrs. J. no more than myself.'

At the appointed hour the Yorkshireman reached
Great Coram Street, just as Old Jorrocks had opened
the door to look down the street for him. He was
dressed in a fine-flowing, olive-green frock (made like a
dressing-gown), with a black velvet collar, having a
gold embroidered stag on each side, gilt stag buttons,
with rich embossed edges ; an acre of buff waistcoat,
and a most antediluvian pair of bright yellow-ochre
buckskins, made by White of Tarporley, in the twenty-
first year of the reign of George the Third ; they were
double-lashed, back-stitched, front-stitched, middle-
stitched, and patched at both knees, with a slit up
behind. The coat he had won in a bet and the breeches
in a raffle, the latter being then second or third hand.
His boots were airing before the fire, consequently he
displayed an amplitude of calf in grey worsted stockings,
while his feet were thrust into green slippers. ' So glad
to see you,' said he ; ' here's a charming morning,
indeed—regular southerly wind and a cloudy sky—rare
scenting it will be—think I could almost run a stag
myself. Come in—never mind your hat, hang it anywhere, but don't make a noise. I stole away and left

Mrs. J. snoring, so won't do to awake her, you know.
By the way, you should see *my* hat ;—Batsey, *fatch* my
hat out of the back parlour. I've set up a new green
silk cord, with a gold frog to fasten it to my button-hole
—werry *illigant*, I think, and werry suitable to the dress
—quite my own idea—have a notion all the Surrey
chaps will get them ; for, between you and me, I set
the fashions, and what is more I sometimes set them at
a leap too. But now tell me, have you any objection
to breakfasting in the kitchen ?—more retired, you
know, besides which you get everything hot and hot,
which is what I call doing a bit of pl*i*sure.' ' Not at all,'
said the Yorkshireman, ' so lead the way ' ; and down
they walked to the lower regions.

It was a nice comfortable-looking place, with a
blazing fire, half the floor covered with an old oil-cloth,
and the rest exhibiting the cheerless aspect of the naked
flags. About a yard and a half from the fire was placed
the breakfast table ; in the centre stood a magnificent
uncut ham, with a great quartern loaf on one side and
a huge Bologna sausage on the other ; besides these
there were nine eggs, two pyramids of muffins, a great
deal of toast, a dozen ship-biscuits, and half a pork-pie,
while a dozen kidneys were spluttering on a spit before
the fire, and Betsy held a gridiron covered with mutton-
chops on the top ; altogether there was as much as
would have served ten people. ' Now, sit down,' said
Jorrocks, ' and let us be doing, for I am as hungry as a
hunter. Hope you are *peckish* too ; what shall I give
you ? tea or coffee ?—but take both—coffee first and
tea after a bit. If *I* can't give you them good, don't
know who can. You must pay your *devours*, as we say
in France, to the 'am, for it is an especial fine one, and
do take a few eggs with it ; there, I've not given you
above a pound of 'am, but you can come again you
know—" waste not, want not." Now take some muffins,
do, pray. Batsey, bring some more cream, and set the
kidneys on the table, the Yorkshireman is getting
nothing to eat. Have a chop with your kidney, werry
luxterous—I could eat an elephant stuffed with
grenadiers, and wash them down with a ocean of tea ;

but pray lay in to the breakfast, or I shall think you
don't like it. There, now take some tea and toast or
one of those biscuits, or whatever you like ; would a
little more 'am be agreeable ? Batsey, run into the larder
and see if your Missis left any of that cold chine of pork
last night—and hear, bring the cold goose, and any cold
flesh you can lay hands on, there are really no wittles
on the table. I am quite ashamed to set you down to
such a scanty fork breakfast ; but this is what comes of
not being master of your own house. Hope your hat
may long cover your family : rely upon it, it is " cheaper
to buy your bacon than to keep a pig." ' Just as
Jorrocks uttered these last words the side-door opened,
and without either ' with your leave or by your leave,'
in bounced Mrs. Jorrocks in an elegant dishabille (or
' dish-of-veal,' as Jorrocks pronounced it), with her hair
tucked up in papers, and a pair of worsted slippers on
her feet, worked with roses and blue lilies.

    ' Pray, *Mister* J.,' said she, taking no more notice
of the Yorkshireman than if he had been enveloped in
Jack the Giant-killer's coat of darkness, ' what is the
meaning of this card ? I found it in your best coat
pocket, which you had on last night, and I *do desire*,
sir, that you will tell me how it came there. Good
morning, sir (spying the Yorkshireman at last), perhaps
you know where Mr. Jorrocks was last night, and perhaps
you can tell me who this person is whose card I have
found in the corner of Mr. Jorrocks's best coat pocket ? '
' Indeed, madam,' replied the Yorkshireman, ' Mr.
Jorrocks's movements of yesterday evening are quite a
secret to me. It is the night that he usually spends at
the Magpie and Stump, but whether he was there or not
I cannot pretend to say, not being a member of the free
and easy club. As for the card, madam—' ' There, then,
take it and read it,' interrupted Mrs. J. ; and he took
the card accordingly—a delicate pale pink, with blue
borders, and gilt edge—and read—we would fain put it
all in dashes and asterisks—' Miss Juliana Granville,
John Street, Waterloo Road.'

    This digression giving Mr. Jorrocks a moment or two
to recollect himself, he pretended to get into a thundering

passion, and, seizing the card out of the Yorkshireman's
hand, he thrust it into the fire, swearing it was an application for admission into the Deaf and Dumb Institution,
where he wished he had Mrs. J. The Yorkshireman,
seeing the probability of a breeze, pretended to have
forgotten something at the Piazza, and stole away,
begging Jorrocks to pick him up as he passed. Peace
had soon been restored : for the Yorkshireman had not
taken above three or four turns up and down the coffee-
room, ere George the waiter came to say that a gentleman
waited outside. Putting on his hat and taking a coat
over his arm, he turned out ; when just before the door
he saw a man muffled up in a great military cloak and a
glazed hat, endeavouring to back a nondescript double-
bodied carriage (with lofty mail box-seats and red
wheels), close to the pavement. ' Who-ay, who-ay,'
said he, ' who-ay, who-ay, horse ! ' at the same time
jerking at his mouth. As the Yorkshireman made his
exit, a pair of eyes gleamed through the small aperture
between the high cloak collar and the flipe of the glazed
hat, which he instantly recognized to belong to Jorrocks.
' Why, what the deuce is this you are in ? ' said he, looking at the vehicle. ' Jump up,' said Jorrocks, ' and I'll
tell you all about it ' ; which having done, and the
machine being set in motion, he proceeded to relate the
manner in which he had exchanged his cruelty-van for it
—by the way, as arrant a bone-setter as ever unfortunate
got into, but which he, with the predilection all men have
for their own, pronounced to be a ' monstrous fine
carriage.' On their turning off the rough pavement on
to the quiet smooth macadamized road leading to
Waterloo Bridge, his dissertation was interrupted by a
loud horse-laugh raised by two or three toll-takers and
boys lounging about the gate.

' I say, Tom, twig this 'ere machine,' said one. ' Dash
my buttons, I never seed such a thing in all my life.'
' What's to pay,' inquired Jorrocks, pulling up with
great dignity, their observations not having penetrated
the cloak collar which encircled his ears. ' To pay ! '
said the toll-taker—' vy, vot do ye call your consarn ? '
' Why, a phaeton,' said Jorrocks. ' My eyes ! that's a

MR. JORROCKS INTRODUCES THE YORKSHIREMAN TO THE SURREY

SQUIRE CHEATUM'S KEEPER ATTACKS THE MURDERER OF OLD TOM

good un,' said another. ' I say, Jim,—he calls this 'ere thing a phe-a-ton ! ' ' A phe-a-ton !—vy, it's more like a fire-engine,' said Jim. ' Don't be impertinent,' said Jorrocks, who had pulled down his collar to hear what he had to pay—' but tell me what's to pay ? ' ' Vy, it's a phe-a-ton drawn by von or more 'orses,' said the toll-taker. ' And containing von or more asses,' said Tom. ' Sixpence-halfpenny, sir.' ' You are a saucy fellow,' said Jorrocks. ' Thank ye, master, you're another,' said the toll-keeper ; ' and now that you have had your say, vot do ye ax for your mouth ? ' ' I say, sir, do you belong to the Phœnix ? Vy don't you show your badge ? ' ' I say, Tom, that 'ere fire-engine has been painted by some house-painter, it's never been in the hands of no coach-maker. Do you shave by that 'ere glazed castor of yours ? ' ' I'm blowed if I wouldn't get you a shilling a week to shove your face in sand, to make moulds for brass knockers.' ' Ay, get away !— make haste, or the fire will be out,' bawled out another, as Jorrocks whipped on, and rattled out of hearing.

' Now, you see,' said he, resuming the thread of his discourse, as if nothing had happened, ' this back seat turns down and makes a box, so that when Mrs. J. goes to her mother's at Tooting, she can take all her things with her, instead of sending half of them by the coach as she used to do ; and if we are heavy, there is a pole belonging to it, so that we can have two horses ; and then there is a seat draws out here (pulling a stool from between his legs) which anybody can sit on.' ' Yes, anybody that is small enough,' said the Yorkshireman, ' but you would cut a queer figure on it, I reckon.' The truth was, that the ' fire-engine ' was one of those useless affairs built by some fool upon a plan of his own, with the idea of combining every possible comfort and advantage, and in reality not possessing one. Friend Jorrocks had seen it at a second-hand shop in Fore Street, and became the happy owner of it, in exchange for the cruelty-van and seventeen pounds. Their appearance on the road created no small sensation, and many were the jokes passed upon the ' fire-engine.' One said they were mountebanks ; another that it was a

3

horse-break ; a third asked if it was one of Gurney's steam carriages ; while a fourth swore it was a new convict-cart going to Brixton. Jorrocks either did not or would not hear their remarks, and kept expatiating upon the different purposes to which the machine might be converted, and the stoutness of the horse that was drawing it.

As they approached the town of Croydon, he turned his cloak over his legs in a very workmanlike manner, and was instantly hailed by some brother sportsmen ;— one complimented him on his looks, another on his breeches, a third praised his horse, a fourth abused the fire-engine, and a fifth inquired where he got his glazed hat. He had an answer for them all, and a nod or a wink for every pretty maid that showed at the windows ; for, though past the grand climacteric, he still has a spice of the devil in him, and, as he says, ' there is no harm in looking.' The Red Lion at Smitham Bottom was the rendezvous of the day. It is a small inn on the Brighton road, some three or four miles below Croydon. On the left of the road stands the inn, on the right is a small training ground, and the country about is open common and down. There was an immense muster about the inn, and also on the training ground, consisting of horse-men, gig-men, postchaise-men, foot-men ; Jorrocks and the Yorkshireman made the fire-men.

' Here's old Jorrocks, I do declare ! ' exclaimed one, as Jorrocks drove the fire-engine up at as quick a pace as his horse would go. ' Why, what a concern he's in,' said another, ' why, the old man's mad, surely.' ' He's good for a subscription,' added another, addressing him ; ' I say, Jorrocks, old boy, you'll give us ten pounds for our hounds, won't you ?—that's a good old fellow.' ' Oh, yes, Jorrocks promised us a subscription last year,' observed another, ' and he is a man of his word, aren't you, old leather-breeches ? ' ' *No*, gentlemen,' said Jorrocks, standing up in the fire-engine and sticking the whip into its nest, ' I really *can not*—I wish I could, but I really *can not* afford it. Times really are so bad, and I have my *own* pack to subscribe to, and I must be " just before I am generous." ' ' Oh, but ten pounds is nothing in your way, you know, Jorrocks,—adulterate a chest of tea. Old —— here will give you all the leaves off his ash-trees.' ' No,' said Jorrocks, ' I really *can not*—ten pounds *is* ten pounds, and I must cut my coat according to my cloth.' ' By Jove, but you must have had plenty of cloth when you cut that coat you've got on, old boy. Why, there's as much cloth in the laps as would make a pair of horse-sheets.' ' Never mind,' said Jorrocks, ' *I* wear it, and not you.' ' Now,' said Jorrocks in an under-tone to the Yorkshireman, ' you see what an unconscion-able set of dogs these stag-'unters are. They're *at* every man for a subscription, and talk about guineas as if they grew upon gooseberry bushes. Besides, they are such a rubbishing set—all drafts from the fox-'ounds. Now there's a chap on the piebald just by the trees,—he goes into the *Gazette reglarly* once in three years, and yet to see him out you'd fancy all the country round belonged to him. And there's a buck with his bearing rein so tight that he can hardly move his neck,' pointing to a gentleman in scarlet, with a tremendous stiff blue cravat,—' he lives by keeping a madhouse, and being a werry high, consequential sort of a cock, they calls him the " Lord *High* Keeper ! "—I'll tell ye a joke about that fellow,' he said, pointing to a man alighting from a red-wheeled buggy—' he's a werry shabby screw, and is always trying to save a penny. Well, he hires a young half-witted hawbuck for a servant, who didn't clean his boots to his liking, so he began by reading the Riot Act one day, and concluded by saying, " I'm blowed if I couldn't clean them better myself with a little pump water." The next day up came the boots duller than ever. " Bless my soul," exclaimed he, " why they are worse than before, how's this, sir ? " " Please, sir, you said you could clean them better with a little pump water, so I tried it, and I *do* think they are worse ! " Haw ! haw ! haw !—Yon chap in the black plush breeches and Hessians, standing by the ginger-pop tray, is the only man vot ever got the better of me in the 'oss-dealing line, and he certain*lie* did bite me uncommon 'andsomely. I gave him three-and-twenty pounds, a strong violin case with patent hinges, lined with superfine green baize,

and an uncut copy of Middleton's *Cicero*, for an 'oss that
the blacksmith really declared wasn't worth shoeing.
Howsomever, I paid him off, for I christened the 'oss
Barabbas—who, you knows, was a robber—and the seller
has gone by the name of Barabbas ever since.'

'Well, but tell me, gentlemen, where do we dine ? '
inquired Jorrocks, turning to a group who had just
approached the fire-engine. 'We don't know yet,'
said a gentleman in scarlet, ' the deer has not come yet ;
but yonder he is,' pointing up the road to a covered
cart, ' and there are the hounds just coming over the
hill at the back.' The covered cart approached, and
several went to meet it. The cry of, ' Oh, it's old
Tunbridge,' was soon heard. 'Well, we shall have a
good dinner,' said Jorrocks, ' if that is the case. Is it
Tunbridge ? ' inquired he eagerly of one of the party
who returned from the deer cart. 'Yes, it's old
Tunbridge, and Snooks has ordered dinner at the Wells
for sixteen at five o'clock, so the first sixteen that get
there had better look out.' ' Here, *bouy*,' said Jorrocks
in an undertone to his servant, who was leading his
screws about on the green, ' take this 'oss out of the
carriage, and give him a feed of corn, and then go on to
Tunbridge Wells and tell Mr. Pegg, at the Sussex Arms,
that I shall be there with a friend to the dinner, and bid
him write " Jorrocks " upon two plates and place them
together. Nothing like making sure,' said he, chuckling
at his own acuteness.

'Now to 'orse—to 'orse ! ' exclaimed he, suiting the
action to the word, and climbing on to his great chestnut,
leaving the Yorkshireman to mount the rat-tail brown.
'Let's have a look at the 'ounds,' turning his horse in
the direction in which they were coming. Jonathan
Griffin [1] took off his cap to Jorrocks as he approached,
who waved his hand in the most patronizing manner
possible, adding, ' How are you, Jonathan ? ' ' Pretty

[1] Poor Jonathan, one of the hardest riders and drinkers of his
day, exists, like his pack, but in the recollection of mankind. He
was long huntsman to the late Lord Derby, who, when he gave
up his stag-hounds, made Jonathan a present of them, and for
two or three seasons he scratched on in an indifferent sort of way,
until the hounds were sold to go abroad—to Hungary, we believe.

well, thank you, Mister Jorrocks, hope you're the same.'
' No, *not* the same, for I'm *werry* well, which makes all
the difference—haw ! haw ! haw ! You seem to have
but a shortish pack, I think—ten, twelve, fourteen
couple—'ow's that ? We always take nine-and-twenty
with the Surrey.' ' Why, you see, Mr. Jorrocks, stag-
hunting and fox-hunting are very different. The scent
of the deer is very ravishing, and then we have no
drawing for our game. Besides, at this season, there
are always bitches to put back,—but we have plenty of
hounds for sport,—I suppose we may be after turning
out,' added Jonathan, looking at his watch—' it's past
eleven.'

On hearing this, a gentleman off with his glove and
began collecting, or *capping*, prior to turning out—it
being the rule of the hunt to make sure of the money
before starting, for fear of accidents. ' Half a crown,
if you please, sir.' ' Now I'll take your half a crown.'
' Mr. Jorrocks, shall I trouble you for half a crown ? '
' Oh surely,' said Jorrocks, pulling out a handful of
great five-shilling pieces, ' here's for this gentleman
and myself,' handing one of them over, ' and I shan't
even *ask* you for discount for ready money.' The
capping went round, and a goodly sum was collected.
Meanwhile the deer cart was drawn to the far side of
a thick fence, and the door being opened, a lubberly-
looking animal as big as a donkey, blobbed out, and
began feeding very composedly. ' That won't do,' said
Jonathan Griffin, eyeing him—' ride on, Tom, and whip
him away.' Off went the whip, followed by a score of
sportsmen whose shouts, aided by the cracking of their
whips, would have frightened the devil himself ; and
these worthies, knowing the hounds would catch them
up in due time, resolved themselves into a hunt for the
present, and pursued the animal themselves. Ten
minutes having expired, and the hounds seeming likely
to break away, Jonathan thought it advisable to let
them have their wicked will, and accordingly they
rushed off in full cry to the spot where the deer had been
uncarted. Of course there was no trouble in casting for
the scent, indeed they were very honest, and did not

pretend to any mystery ; the hounds knew within an inch where it would be, and the start was pretty much like that for a hunter's plate in four-mile heats. A few dashing blades rode before the hounds at starting, but otherwise the field was tolerably quiet, and was considerably diminished after the first three leaps. The scent improved, as did the pace, and presently they got into a lane along which they rattled for five miles as hard as ever they could lay legs to the ground, throwing the mud into each other's faces, until each man looked as if he was rough-cast. A Kentish waggon, drawn by six oxen, taking up the whole of the lane, had obliged the *dear* animal to take to the fields again, where, at the first fence, most of our high-mettled racers stood still. In truth, it was rather a nasty place, a yawning ditch, with a mud bank, and a rotten landing. ' Now, who's for it ? Go it, Jorrocks, you're a fox-hunter,'[1] said one, who, erecting himself in his stirrups, was ogling the opposite side. ' I don't like it,' said Jorrocks,—' is never a gate near ? ' ' Oh, yes, at the bottom of the field,' and away they all tore for it. The hounds now had got out of sight, but were heard running in cover at the bottom of the turnip-field into which they had just passed, and also the clattering of horses' hoofs on the highway. The hounds came out several times on to the road, evidently carrying the scent, but as often threw up and returned into the cover. The huntsman was puzzled at last ; and quite convinced that the deer was not in the wood, he called them out, and proceeded to make a cast, followed by the majority of the field. They trotted about at a brisk pace, first to the right, then to the left, afterwards to the north, and then to the south, over grass, fallow, turnips, potatoes, and flints, through three farmyards, round two horse-ponds, and at the back of a small village or hamlet, without a note, save those of a few babblers. Every one seemed to consider it a desperate job. They were all puzzled ; at last they heard a terrible holloaing about a quarter of a mile to the south, and immediately after was espied a group of

[1] Fox-hunters always have the privilege of breaking their necks first, when they go out with other hounds.

horsemen, galloping along the road at full speed, in the centre of which was Jorrocks : his green coat wide open, with the tails flying a long way behind that of his horse, his right leg was thrust out, down the side of which he kept applying his ponderous hunting whip, making a most terrible clatter. As they approached, he singled himself out from the group, and was the first to reach the field. He immediately burst out into one of his usual hunting energetic strains. ' Oh, Jonathan Griffin ! Jonathan Griffin ! ' said he, ' here's a lamentable occur-rence—a terrible disaster ! Oh dear, oh dear—we shall never get to Tunbridge—that unfortunate deer has escaped us, and we shall never see nothing more of him —rely upon it, he's killed before this ! ' ' Why, how's that ? ' inquired Griffin, evidently in a terrible perturba-tion. ' Why,' said Jorrocks, slapping the whip down his leg again, ' there's a little girl tells me, that as she was getting water at the well just at the end of the wood, where we lost him, she saw what she took to be a donkey jump into a return post-chaise from the Bell, at Seven Oaks, that was passing along the road with the door swinging wide open ! and you may rely upon it, it was the deer. The landlord of the Bell will have cut his throat before this, for, you know, he vowed wengeance against us last year, because his wife's pony-chaise was upset, and he swore that we did it.' ' Oh, but that's a bad job,' said the huntsman ; ' what shall we do ? ' ' Here, Tom,' calling to the whipper-in, ' jump on to the Hastings coach (which just came up), and try if you can't overtake him, and bring him back, chaise and all, and I'll follow slowly with the hounds.' Tom was soon up, the coach bowled on, and Jonathan and the hounds trotted gently forward till they came to a public-house. Here, as they stopped lamenting over their unhappy fate, and consoling themselves with some cold sherry negus, the post-chaise appeared in sight, with the deer's head sticking out of the side window with all the dignity of a Lord Mayor. ' Huzza ! huzza ! huzza ! ' exclaimed Jorrocks, taking off his hat, ' here's old Tunbridge come again, huzza ! huzza ! ' ' But who's to pay me for the po-chay,' said the driver, pulling up ; ' I must be paid before I let him out.' ' How much ? ' says Jonathan. ' Why, eighteenpence a mile, to be sure, and threepence a mile to the driver ! ' ' No,' says Jorrocks, ' that won't do, yours is a return chay ; however, here's five shillings for you, and now, Jonathan, turn him out again—he's quite fresh after his ride—and see he's got some straw in the bottom.'

Old Tunbridge was again turned out, with his head towards the town from whence he took his name, and after a quarter of an hour's law, the pack was again laid on. He was not, however, in very good wind, and it was necessary to divide the second chase into two heats, for which purpose the hounds were whipped off about the middle, while the deer took a cold bath, after which he was again set a-going. By half-past three they had accomplished the run ; and Mr. Pegg, of the Sussex Arms, having mounted his Pegasus, found them at the appointed place by the Medway, where old Tunbridge's carriage was waiting, into which having handed him, they repaired to the inn, and at five o'clock eighteen of them sat down to a dinner consisting ' of every delicacy of the season ' : the Lord High Keeper in the chair. Being all ' hungry as hunters,' little conversation passed until after removal of the cloth, when, after the King and His Majesty's Ministers had been drunk, the President gave ' The noble, manly Sport of Stag-hunting,' which he eulogized as the most legitimate and exhilarating of all sports, and sketched its progress from its wild state of infancy, when the unhappy sportsman had to range the fields and forests for their uncertain game, to the present state of luxurious ease and elaborate refinement, when they not only brought their deer to the meet, but, by selecting the proper animal, could insure a finish at a place they most wished to dine at,—all of which was most enthusiastically applauded ; and on the speaker's ending, ' Stag-hunting,' and the ' Surrey stag-hounds,' and ' Long life to all stag-hunters,' were drunk in brimming and over-flowing bumpers. Fox-hunting, hare-hunting, rabbit-hunting, cat-hunting, rat-catching, badger-baiting,—all wild, seasonable, and legitimate sports followed ; and the chairman having run through his list, and thinking Jorrocks was getting rather mellow, resolved to try the *soothing* system on him for a subscription, the badgering of the morning not having answered. Accordingly, he called on the company to charge their glasses, as he would give them a bumper toast, which he knew they would have great pleasure in drinking.—' He wished to propose the health of his excellent friend on his right—MR. JORROCKS (applause), a gentleman whose name only required mentioning in any society of hunters to insure it a hearty and enthusiastic reception. He did not flatter his excellent friend when he said he was a man for the imitation of all, and he was sure that when the present company recollected the liberal support he gave to the Surrey fox-hounds, together with the keenness with which he followed that branch of amusement, they would duly appreciate, not only the honour he had conferred upon them by his presence in the field that morning, and at the table that day, but the disinterested generosity which had prompted him voluntarily to declare his intention of contributing to the future support of the Surrey stag-hounds (immense cheers) ;—he therefore thought the least they could do, was to drink the health of Mr. Jorrocks, and success to the Surrey fox-hounds, with three times three ' ; which was immediately responded to with deafening cheers.

Old Jorrocks, after the noise had subsided, got on his legs, and with one hand rattling the five-shilling pieces in his breeches-pocket, and the thumb of the other thrust into the arm-hole of his waistcoat, thus began to address them—' Gentlemen,' said he, ' I'm no orator, but I'm an honest man—(hiccup)—I feels werry (hiccup) much obliged to my excellent friend the Lord High Keeper (shouts of laughter), I begs his pardon—my friend Mr. Juggins—for the werry flat*ten*ing compliment he has paid me in coupling my name (hiccup) with the Surrey fox-'ounds—a pack, I may say, without wanity (hiccup), second to none. I'm a werry old member of the 'unt, and when I was a werry poor man (hiccup) I always did my best to support them (hiccup), and now that I'm a werry rich man (cheers) I shan't do no otherwise. About subscribing to the staggers, I doesn't

3*

recollect saying nothing whatsomever about it (hiccup), but as I'm werry friendly to sporting in all its ramifications (hiccup), I'll be werry happy to give ten pounds to your 'ounds,'—immense cheers followed this declaration, which lasted for some seconds—when they had subsided, Jorrocks put his finger on his nose, and with a knowing wink of his eye, added—'*prowided* my friend the Lord High Keep—I begs his pardon—Juggins—will give ten pounds to ours ! '

THE TURF : MR. JORROCKS AT NEWMARKET

'A MUFFIN—and the Post, sir,' said George to the Yorkshireman, on one of the fine fresh mornings that gently usher in the returning spring, and draw from the town-pent Cits sighs for the verdure of the fields,— as he placed the above-mentioned articles on his usual breakfast-table in the coffee-room of the Piazza.

With the calm deliberation of a man whose whole day is unoccupied, the Yorkshireman sweetened his tea, drew the muffins and a select dish of prawns to his elbow, and, turning sideways to the table, crossed his legs and prepared to con the contents of the paper. The first page as usual was full of advertisements.— Sales by Auction—Favour of your vote and interest— If the next of Kin—Reform your tailor's bills—Law— Articled Clerk—An absolute reversion—Pony phaeton —Artificial teeth—Messrs. Tattersall—Brace of pointers —Dog lost—Boy found—Great sacrifice—No advance in coffee—Matrimony—A single gentleman—Board and lodging in an airy situation—To Omnibus Proprietors —Steam to Leith and Hull—Stationery—Desirable investment for a small capital—The fire reviver or lighter.

Then turning it over, his eye ranged over a whole meadow of type, consisting of the previous night's debate, followed on by City News, Police Reports, Fashionable arrivals and departures, Dinners given, Sporting Intelligence, Newmarket Craven meeting. ' That's more in my way,' said the Yorkshireman to himself as he laid down the paper and took a sip of his tea. ' I've a great mind to go, for I may just as well be at Newmarket as here, having nothing particular to do in either place. I came to stay a hundred pounds in London, it's true, but if I stay ten of it at New-market, it'll be all the same, and I can go home from there just as well as from here ' ; so saying, he took another turn at the tea. The race list was a tempting one, Riddlesworth, Craven stakes, Column stakes, Oat-lands, Port, Claret, Sherry, Madeira, and all other sorts. A good week's racing, in fact ; for the saintly sinners who frequent the Heath had not then discovered any greater impropriety in travelling on a Sunday, than in cheating each other on the Monday. The tea was good, as were the prawns and eggs, and George brought a second muffin, at the very moment that the Yorkshire-man had finished the last piece of the first, so that by the time he had done his breakfast and drawn on his boots, which were drier and pleasanter than the recent damp weather had allowed of their being, he felt com-pletely at peace with himself and all the world, and putting on his hat, sallied forth with the self-satisfied air of a man who had eaten a good breakfast, and yet not too much.

Newmarket was still uppermost in his mind ; and as he sauntered along in the direction of the Strand, it occurred to him that perhaps Mr. Jorrocks might have no objection to accompany him. On entering that great thoroughfare of humanity, he turned to the East, and having examined the contents of all the caricature shops in the line, and paid threepence for a look at the *York Herald*, in the Chapter Coffee-house, St. Paul's Churchyard, about noon he reached the corner of St. Botolph Lane. Before Jorrocks & Co.'s warehouse, great bustle and symptoms of brisk trade were visible. With true city pride, the name on the door-post was in small dirty-white letters, sufficiently obscure to

render it apparent that Mr. Jorrocks considered his
house required no sign ; while, as a sort of contra-
diction, the covered errand-cart before it bore
' JORROCKS & CO.'S WHOLESALE TEA WAREHOUSE,' in
great gilt letters on each side of the cover, so large that
' he who runs might read,' even though the errand-cart
were running too. Into this cart, which was drawn
by the celebrated rat-tail hunter, they were pitching
divers packages for town delivery, and a couple of light
porters nearly upset the Yorkshireman, as they bustled
out with their loads. The warehouse itself gave evident
proof of great antiquity. It was not one of your fine,
light, lofty, mahogany-countered, banker-like establishments of modern times, where the stock in trade often
consists of books and empty canisters, but a large,
roomy, gloomy, dirty, dingy sort of cellar above-ground,
full of hogsheads, casks, flasks, sugar-loaves, jars, bags,
bottles, and boxes.

The floor was half an inch thick, at least, with dirt,
and was sprinkled with rice, currants, raisins, etc., as
though they had been scattered for the purpose of grow-
ing. A small corner seemed to have been cut off, like
the fold of a Leicestershire grazing ground, and made
into an office, in the centre of which was a square or
two of glass that commanded a view of the whole warehouse. ' Is Mr. Jorrocks in ? ' inquired the Yorkshireman of a porter, who was busy digging currants with a
wooden spade. ' Yes, sir, you'll find him in the count-
ing-house,' was the answer ; but on looking in, though
his hat and gloves were there, no Jorrocks was visible.
At the farther end of the warehouse a man in his shirt
sleeves, with a white apron round his waist and a brown
paper cap on his head, was seen under a very melancholy-
looking skylight, holding his head over something, as if
his nose were bleeding. The Yorkshireman groped his
way up to him, and asking if Mr. Jorrocks was in, found
he was addressing the grocer himself. He had been
leaning over a large tray full of little white cups—
with teapots to match—trying the strength, flavour, and
virtue of a large purchase of tea, and the beverage
was all smoking before him. ' My vig,' exclaimed he,

holding out his hand, ' who'd have thought of seeing you
in the city, this is something unkimmon ! However
you're werry welcome in St. Botolph Lane, and as this
is your first wisit, why, I'll make you a present of some
tea—wot do you drink ?—black or green, or perhaps
both—four pounds of one and two of t'other.—Here,
Joe ! ' summoning his foreman, ' put up four pounds of
that last lot of black that came in, and two pounds of
superior green, and this gentleman will tell you where to
leave it.—And when do you think of starting ? ' again
addressing the Yorkshireman—' egad, this is fine
weather for the country—have half a mind to have a
jaunt myself—makes one quite young—feel as if I'd
laid full fifty years aside, and were again a boy—when
did you say you start ? ' ' Why, I don't know exactly,'
replied the Yorkshireman, ' the weather's so fine that
I'm half tempted to go round by Newmarket. ' Newmarket ! ' exclaimed Jorrocks, throwing his arms in
the air, while his paper cap fell from his head with the
jerk—' by Newmarket ! why, what in the name of all
that's impure, have you to do at Newmarket ? '
    ' Why, nothing in particular ; only, when there's
neither hunting nor shooting going on, what is a man
to do with himself ?—I'm sure you'd despise me if I
were to go fishing.' ' True,' observed Mr. Jorrocks somewhat subdued, and jingling the silver in his breeches
pocket. ' Fox-'unting is indeed the prince of sports.
The image of war without its guilt, and only half its
danger. I confess that I'm a martyr to it—a perfect
wictim—no one knows wot I suffer from my ardour.
If ever I'm wisited with the last infirmity of noble minds,
it will be caused by my ungovernable passion for the
chase. The *sight* of a *saddle* makes me sweat. An
'ound makes me perfectly wild. A red coat throws me
into a scarlet fever. Never throughout life have I had a
good night's rest before an 'unting morning. But *werry*
little racing does for me ; Sadler's Wells is well enough
of a fine summer evening—especially when they plump
the clown over head in the New River cut, and the ponies
don't misbehave in the Circus—but oh ! *Newmarket's* a
dreadful place, the werry name's a sickener. I used to

hear a vast about it from poor Will Softly of Friday Street. It was the ruin of him—and wot a fine business his father left him, both wholesale and retail, in the tripe and cow-heel line—all went in two years, and he had nothing to show at the end of that time for upwards of twenty thousand golden sovereigns, but a hundredweight of children's lamb's-wool socks, and warrants for thirteen hogsheads of damaged sherry in the Docks. No, take my adwice, and have nothing to say to them—stay where you are, or, if you're short of swag, come to Great Coram Street, where you shall have a bed, wear-and-tear for your teeth, and all that sort of thing found you, and, if Saturday's a fine day, I'll treat you with a jaunt to Margate.'

'You are a regular old trump,' said the Yorkshire-man, after listening attentively until Mr. Jorrocks had exhausted himself, ' but, you see, you've never been at Newmarket, and the people have been hoaxing you about it. I can assure you from personal experience that the people there are quite as honest as those you meet every day on 'Change ; besides which, there is nothing more invigorating to the human frame— nothing more cheering to the spirits than the sight and air of Newmarket Heath on a fine fresh spring morning like the present. The wind seems to go by you at a racing pace, and the blood canters up and down the veins with the finest and freest action imaginable. A stranger to the racecourse would feel, and almost instinctively know, what turf he was treading, and the purpose for which that turf was intended.

'" There's a magic in the web of it." '

'Oh, I knows you are a most persuasive cock,' ob-served Mr. Jorrocks, interrupting the Yorkshireman, ' and would conwince the devil himself that black is white, but you'll never make me believe the Newmarket folks are honest, and as to the fine hair (air) you talk of, there's quite as good to get on Hampstead Heath, and if it doesn't make the blood canter up and down your weins, you can always amuse yourself by watching the donkeys cantering up and down with the sweet little children—haw, haw, haw!—But tell me what is there at Newmarket that should take a man there?' '*What is there?*' rejoined the Yorkshireman, 'why, there's everything that makes life desirable and constitutes happiness, in this world, except hunting. First there is the beautiful, neat, clean town, with groups of booted *professors*, ready for the rapidest march of intellect; then there are the strings of clothed horses—the finest in the world—passing indolently at intervals to their exercise—the flower of the English aristocracy residing in the place. You leave the town and stroll to the wide open heath, where all is brightness and space; the white rails stand forth against the clear blue sky—the brushing gallop ever and anon startles the ear and eye; crowds of stable urchins, full of silent importance, stud the heath; you feel elated, and long to bound over the well-*groomed* turf, and try the speed of the careering wine. *All* things at Newmarket train the mind to racing. Life seems on the start, and dull indeed were he who could rein in his feelings when such inspiriting objects meet together to madden them!'

'Bravo!' exclaimed Jorrocks, throwing his paper cap in the air as the Yorkshireman concluded; 'Bravo! —werry good indeed! You speak like ten Lord Mayors, —never heard nothing better. Dash my vig, if I won't go. By Jove, you've *done* it. Tell me one thing —is there a good place to feed at?'

'Capital!' replied the Yorkshireman; 'beef, mutton, cheese, ham, all the delicacies of the season, as the sailor said'; and thereupon the Yorkshireman and Jorrocks shook hands upon the bargain.

Sunday night arrived, and with it arrived, at the Belle Sauvage, in Ludgate Hill, Mr. Jorrocks's boy 'Binjimin,' with Mr. Jorrocks's carpet bag; and shortly after, Mr. Jorrocks, on his chestnut hunter, and the Yorkshireman, in a hack cab, entered the yard. Having consigned his horse to Binjimin, after giving him a very instructive lesson relative to the manner in which he would chastise him if he heard of his trotting or playing any tricks with the horse on his way home, Mr. Jorrocks proceeded to pay the remainder of his fare in the coach-

office. The mail was full inside and out ; indeed the
bookkeeper assured him he could have filled a dozen
more, so anxious were all London to see the Riddlesworth run. ' Inside,' said he, ' are you and your friend,
and if it weren't that the night air might give you cold,
Mr. Jorrocks ' (for all the bookkeepers in London know
him), ' I should have liked to have got you outsides,
and I tried to make an exchange with two blacklegs,
but they would hear of nothing less than two guineas
a head, which wouldn't do, you know. Here comes
another of your passengers—a great foreign nobleman,
they say—Baron something—though he looks as much
like a foreign pickpocket as anything else.'

' Vich be de voiture ? ' inquired a tall, gaunt-looking
foreigner, with immense moustache, a high conical hat
with a bright buckle, long loose blueish-blackish frock
coat, very short white waistcoat, baggy brownish
striped trousers, and long-footed Wellington boots,
with a sort of Chinese turn-up at the toe. ' Vich be de
Newmarket voiture ! ' said he, repeating the query, as
he entered the office and deposited a silk umbrella, a
camlet cloak, and a Swiss knapsack on the counter.
The porter, without any attempt at an answer, took
his goods and walked off to the mail, followed closely
by the Baron, and after depositing the cloak inside, so
that the Baron might ride ' with his face to the horses,'
as the saying is, he turned the knapsack into the hind
boot, and swung himself into the office till it was time
to ask for something for his exertions. Meanwhile the
Baron made a tour of the yard, taking a lesson in English
from the lettering on the various coaches, when on the
hind boot of one, he deciphered the word Cheapside—
' Ah, Cheapside ! ' said he, pulling out his dictionary,
and turning to the letter C, ' Chaste, chat, chaw,—*cheap*,
dat be it. Cheap,—to be had at a low price—small
value. Ah ! I hev (have) it,' said he, stamping and
knitting his brows, '*Sacr-r-r-r-é nom de Dieu*,' and the
first word being drawn out to its usual longitude, three
strides brought him and the conclusion of the oath
into the office together. He then opened out upon the
bookkeeper in a tremendous volley of French, English,

and Hanoverian oaths, for he was a cross between the
first and last named countries, the purport of which
was ' dat he had paid de best price, and he be dem if
he vod ride on de Cheapside of de coach.' In vain the
clerks and the bookkeepers tried to convince him he
was wrong in his interpretation. With the full conviction of a foreigner that he was about to be cheated,
he had his cloak shifted to the opposite side of the
coach, and the knapsack placed on the roof. The
fourth inside having cast up, the outside passengers
mounted, the insides took their places, threepences and
sixpences were pulled out for the porters, the guard
twanged his horn, the coachman turned out his elbow,
flourished his whip, caught the point, cried ' All right !
Sit tight ! ' and trotted out of the yard.

Jorrocks and the Yorkshireman sat opposite each
other, the Baron and old Sam Spring, the betting-man,
did likewise. Who doesn't know old Sam, with his
curious tortoiseshell-rimmed spectacles, his old drab
hat turned up with green, careless neckcloth, flowing
robe, and comical cut ? *He* knew Jorrocks, though—
tell it not in Coram Street—he didn't know his name ;
but concluding from the disparity of age between him
and his companion, that Jorrocks was either a shark or
a shark's jackal, and the Yorkshireman a victim, with
due professional delicacy he contented himself with
scrutinising the latter through his specs. The Baron's
choler having subsided, he was the first to break the ice
of silence. ' Foine noight,' was the observation, which
was thrown out promiscuously to see who would take it
up. Now, Sam Spring, though he came late, had learned
from the porter that there was a Baron in the coach, and
being a great admirer of the nobility, for whose use he
has a code of signals of his own, consisting of one finger
to his hat for a Baron-Lord, as he calls them, two for a
Viscount, three for an Earl, four for a Marquiss, and
the whole hand for a Duke, he immediately responded
with ' Yes, my Lord,' with a forefinger to his hat. There
is something sweet in the word ' Lord ' which finds its
way home to the heart of an Englishman. No sooner
did Sam pronounce it, than the Baron became trans-

formed in Jorrocks's eyes into a very superior sort of
person, and forthwith he commenced ingratiating
himself by offering him a share of a large paper of
sandwiches, which the Baron accepted with the greatest
condescension, eating what he could and stuffing the
remainder into his hat. His lordship was a better hand
at eating than speaking, and the united efforts of the
party could not extract from him the precise purport
of his journey. Sam threw out two or three feasible
offers in the way of bets, but they fell still-born to the
bottom of the coach, and Jorrocks talked to him about
hunting, and had the conversation all to himself, the
Baron merely replying with a bow and a stare, sometimes diversified with, or 'I tank you—vare good.'
The conversation by degrees resolved itself into a snore,
in which they were all indulging, when the raw morning
air rushed in among them, as a porter with a lantern
opened the door and announced their arrival at Newmarket. Forthwith they turned into the street, and the
outside passengers having descended, they all commenced straddling, yawning, and stretching their limbs,
while the guards and porters sorted their luggage. The
Yorkshireman, having an eye to a bed, speedily had
Mr. Jorrocks's luggage and his own on the back of a
porter on its way to the Rutland Arms, while that
worthy citizen followed in a sort of sleepy astonishment
at the smallness of the place, inquiring if they were sure
they had not stopped at some village by mistake. Two
beds had been ordered for two gentlemen who could not
get two seats by the mail, which fell to the lot of those
who did, and into these our heroes trundled, having
arranged to be called by the early exercising hour.

Whether it was from want of his usual night-cap of
brandy and water, or the fatigues of travelling, or what
else, remains unknown, but no sooner was Mr. Jorrocks
left alone with his candle, than all at once he was seized
with a sudden fit of trepidation, on thinking that he
should have been inveigled to such a place as Newmarket,
and the tremor increasing as he pulled four five-pound
bank notes out of his watch-pocket, besides a vast of
silver, and his great gold watch, he was resolved, should

an attempt be made upon his property, to defend it
with his life, and having squeezed the notes into the
toe of his boots, and hid the silver in the wash-hand
stand, he very deliberately put his watch and the poker
under the pillow, and set the heavy chest of drawers
with two stout chairs and a table against the door,
after all which exertions he got into bed and very soon
fell sound asleep.

Most of the inmates of the house were up with the
lark to the early exercise, and the Yorkshireman was as
early as any of them. Having found Mr. Jorrocks's
door, he commenced a loud battery against it without
awakening the grocer ; he then tried to open it, but
only succeeded in getting it an inch or two from the
post, and after several holloas of ' Jorrocks, my man !
Mr. Jorrocks ! Jorrocks, old boy ! holloa, Jorrocks ! '
he succeeded in extracting the word ' *Wot ?* ' from
the worthy gentleman as he rolled over in his bed.
' Jorrocks ! ' repeated the Yorkshireman, ' it's time to
be up.' ' Wot ? ' again was the answer. ' Time to get
up. The morning's breaking.' ' *Let it break,*' replied
he, adding in a mutter, as he turned over again, ' *it owes
me nothing.*'

Entreaties being useless, and a large party being on
the point of setting off, the Yorkshireman joined them,
and spent a couple of hours on the dew-bespangled
heath, during which time they not only criticized the
figure and action of every horse that was out, but got
up tremendous appetites for breakfast. In the meantime Mr. Jorrocks had risen, and having attired himself
with his usual care in a smart blue coat with metal
buttons, buff waistcoat, blue stocking-netted tights,
and Hessian boots, he turned into the main street of
Newmarket, when he was lost in astonishment at the
insignificance of the place. But wiser men than Mr.
Jorrocks have been similarly disappointed, for it enters
into the philosophy of few to conceive the fame and
grandeur of Newmarket compressed into the limits of
the petty, outlandish, Icelandish place that bears the
name. ' Dash my vig,' said Mr. Jorrocks, as he brought
himself to bear upon Rogers's shop-window, ' this is the

werry meanest town I ever did see. Pray, sir,' addressing
himself to a groomish-looking man in a brown cut-away
coat, drab shorts and continuations, who had just
emerged from the shop with a race list in his hand.
' Pray, sir, be this your principal street ? ' The man
eyed him with a mixed look of incredulity and contempt.
At length, putting his thumbs into the arm-holes of his
waistcoat, he replied, ' I bet a crown you know as well
as I do.' ' Done,' said Mr. Jorrocks, holding out his
hand. ' No—I won't do that,' replied the man, ' but
I'll tell you what I'll do with you,—I'll lay you two to
one in fives or fifties if you like, that you knew before
you axed, and that Thunderbolt don't win the Riddlesworth.' ' Really,' said Mr. Jorrocks, ' I'm not a betting
man.' ' Then, what the 'ell (hell) business have you at
Newmarket ? ' was all the answer he got. Disgusted
with such inhospitable impertinence, Mr. Jorrocks
turned on his heel and walked away. Before the White
Hart Inn was a smartish pony phaeton, in charge of a
stunted stable lad. ' I say, young chap,' inquired
Jorrocks, ' whose is that ? ' ' How did you know that
I was a young chap ? ' inquired the abortion, turning
round. ' Guessed it,' replied Jorrocks, chuckling at his
own wit. ' Then *guess* whose it is.'

' Pray, are your clocks here by London time ? ' he
asked of a respectable elderly-looking man whom he
saw turn out of the entry leading to the Kingston rooms,
and take the usual survey first up the town and then
down it, and afterwards compose his hands in his breeches-
pockets, there to stand to see the ' world.' [1] ' Come
now, *old un*—none o' your tricks here—you've got a
match on against time, I suppose,' was all the answer
he could get after the man (old R—n the ex-flagellator)
had surveyed him from head to foot.

We need hardly say after all these rebuffs, that when
Mr. Jorrocks met the Yorkshireman, he was not in the
best possible humour ; indeed, to say nothing of the
extreme sharpness and suspicion of the people, we know
of no place where a man, not fond of racing, is so

---

[1] Newmarket or London—it's all the same. ' The World ' is
but composed of *one's own* acquaintance.

completely out of his element as at Newmarket, for, with the exception of a little ' elbow shaking ' in the evening, there is literally and truly nothing else to do. It is ' Heath,' ' Ditch in,' ' Abingdon mile,' ' T.Y.C. Stakes,' ' Sweepstakes,' ' Handicaps,' ' Bet,' ' Lay,' ' Take,' ' Odds,' ' Evens,' morning, noon, and night.

Mr. Jorrocks made bitter complaints during the breakfast, and some invidious comparisons between racing-men and fox-hunters, which, however, became softer towards the close, as he got deeper in the delicacy of a fine Cambridge brawn. Nature being at length appeased, he again thought of turning out, to have a look, as he said, at the shows on the course, but the appearance of his friend the Baron opposite the window, put it out of his head, and he sallied forth to join him. The Baron was evidently incog. : for he had on the same short dirty-white waistcoat, Chinese boots, and conical hat, etc., that he travelled down in, and, being a stranger in the land, of course he was uncommonly glad to pick up Jorrocks, so after he had hugged him a little, called him a " bon garçon," and a few other endearing terms, he ran his great long arm through his, amd walked him down street, the whole peregrinations of Newmarket being comprised in the words ' up street ' and ' down.' He then communicated in most unrepresentable language, that he was on his way to buy ' an 'oss,' and Jorrocks informing him that he was a perfect connoisseur in the article, the Baron again assured him of his distinguished consideration. They were met by Joe Rogers the trainer with a ring key in his hand, who led the way to the stable, and, having unlocked a box in which was a fine slapping four-year-old, according to etiquette he put his hat in a corner, took a switch in one hand, laid hold of the horse's head with the other, while the lad in attendance stripped off its clothes. The Baron then turned up his wrists, and making a curious noise in his throat, proceeded to pass his hand down each leg, and along its back, after which he gave it a thump in the belly and squeezed its throat, when, being as wise as he was at starting, he stuck his thumb in his side, and took a mental survey of the whole—' Ah,'

said he at length—' foin 'oss,—foin 'oss ; vot ears he
has ? ' ' Oh,' said Rogers, ' they show breeding.'
' Non, non, *I say* vot ears he has ? ' ' Well, but he
carries them well,' was the answer. ' Non, non,' stamping, ' I say vot ears (*years*) he has ? ' ' Oh, hang it, I
twig—four years old.' Then the Baron took another
long look at him. At length he resumed, ' I vill my
wet.' ' What's that ? ' inquired Rogers, of Jorrocks.
' His *wet*—why, a drink to be sure,' and thereupon Rogers
went to the pump and brought a glass of pure water,
which the Baron refused with becoming indignation.
' Non, non,' said he stamping, ' *I vill my wet.*'
Rogers looked at Jorrocks, and Jorrocks looked at
Rogers, but neither Rogers nor Jorrocks understood
him. ' *I vill my wet,*' repeated the Baron, with
vehemence. ' He must want some brandy in it,' observed Mr. Jorrocks, judging of the Baron by himself,
and thereupon the lad was sent for three-penn'orth.
When it arrived, the Baron dashed it out of his hand
with a prolonged *sacr-r-r-r-é*— ! adding, ' I vill von
wet-tin-nin-na-ary surgeon.' The boy was despatched
for one, and on his arrival the veterinary surgeon went
through the process that the Baron had attempted, and
not being a man of many words, he just gave the Baron
a nod at the end. ' How moch ? ' inquired the Baron
of Rogers. ' Five hundred,' was the answer. ' Vot,
five hundred livre ? ' ' Oh, d—n it, you may take him or
leave him, just as you like, but you won't get him for
less.' The ' vet ' explained that the Baron wished to
know whether it was five hundred francs (French
tenpences), or five hundred guineas English money, and
being informed that it was the latter, he gave his conical
hat a thrust on his brow, and bolted out of the box.

But race hour approaches, and people begin to as-
semble in groups before the ' rooms,' while tax-carts,
pony-gigs, post-chaises, the usual aristocratical accom-
paniments of Newmarket, come dribbling at intervals
into the town. Here is old Sam Spring in a spring-cart,
driven by a plough-boy in fustian, there the Earl of ——
on a ten-pound pony, with the girths elegantly parted
to prevent the saddle slipping over its head, while

Miss ——, his jockey's daughter, dashes by him in a
phaeton with a powdered footman, and the postilion in
scarlet and leathers, with a badge on his arm. Old
Crockey puts on his greatcoat, Jem Bland draws the
yellow phaeton and greys to the gateway of the White
Hart to take up his friend Crutch Robinson ; Zac, Jack
and another have just driven in on a fly. In short, it's a
brilliant meeting ! [1] Besides four coroneted carriages
with post horses, there are three phaetons-and-pair ;
a thing that would have been a phaeton if they'd have
let it ; General Grosvenor's dog-carriage, that is to say,
his carriage with a dog upon it ; Lady Chesterfield and
the Hon. Mrs. Anson, in a pony phaeton with an out-
rider (Miss —— will have one next meeting instead
of the powdered footman) ; Tattersall in his double
carriage, driving without bearing reins ; Old Theobald in
leather breeches and a buggy ; five Bury butchers in
a tax-cart ; Young Dutch Sam on a pony ; ' Short-odds
Richards ' on a long-backed crocodile-looking rosinante ;
and no end of pedestrians.

But where is Mr. Jorrocks all this time ? Why, eating
brawn in the Rutland Arms with his friend the Baron,
perfectly unconscious that all these passers-by were
not the daily visibles of the place. ' Dash my vig,' said
he, as he bolted another half of the round. ' I see no
symptoms of a stir. Come, my Lord, do me the honour
to take another glass of sherry." His lordship was
nothing loth, so by mutual entreaties they finished the
bottle, besides a considerable quantity of porter. A
fine, fat, chestnut, long-tailed Suffolk punch-cart mare
—fresh from the plough—having been considerately
provided by the Yorkshireman for Mr. Jorrocks, with
a cob for himself, they proceeded to mount in the yard,
when Mr. Jorrocks was concerned to find that the Baron
had nothing to carry him. His lordship, too, seemed
disconcerted, but it was only momentary ; for walking
up to the punch mare, and resting his elbow on her hind
quarter to try if she kicked, he very coolly vaulted
up behind Mr. Jorrocks. Now Jorrocks, though proud

[1] The poverty both in numbers and appearance of a Newmarket
turn-out must have surprised many a beholder.

of the patronage of a lord, did not exactly comprehend whether he was in earnest or not, but the Baron soon let him know ; for thrusting his conical hat on his brow, he put his arm round Jorrocks's waist, and gave the old mare a touch in the flank with the Chinese boot, crying out—'Along, me brave garçon, along, ma cher ! ' and the owner of the mare living at Kentford, she went off at a brisk trot in that direction, while the Yorkshire-man slipped down the town unperceived. The sherry had done its business on them both ; the Baron, and who, perhaps, was the most ' cut ' of the two, chaunted the Marseillaise hymn of liberty with as much freedom as though he were sitting in the saddle. Thus they proceeded laughing and singing until the Bury pay-gate arrested their progress, when it occurred to the steersman to ask if they were going right. ' Be this the vay to Newmarket races ? ' inquired Jorrocks of the pike-keeper. The man dived into the small pocket of his white apron for a ticket, and very coolly replied, ' Shell out, old 'un.' ' How much ? ' said Jorrocks. ' Tup-pence ' ; which having got, he said, ' Now then, you may turn, for the Heath be over yonder,' pointing back, ' at least, it was there this morning, I know.' After a volley of abuse for his impudence, Mr. Jorrocks, with some difficulty, got the old mare pulled round, for she had a deuced hard mouth of her own, and only a plain snaffle in it ; at last, however, with the aid of a boy to beat her with a furze bush, they got her set agoing again, and, retracing their steps, they trotted ' down street,' rose the hill, and entered the spacious, wide-extending flat of Newmarket Heath. The races were going forward on one of the distant courses, and a slight, insignificant, black streak, swelling into a sort of oblong (for all the world like an overgrown tadpole) was all that denoted the spot, or interrupted the verdant aspect of the quiet, extensive plain. Jorrocks was horrified ; having through life pictured Epsom as a mere drop in the ocean compared with the countless multitude of Newmarket, whilst the Baron, who was wholly in-different to the matter, nearly had old Jorrocks pitched over the mare's head by applying the furze bush (which

he had got from the boy) to her tail while Mr. Jorrocks
was sitting loosely, contemplating the barrenness of the
prospect. The sherry was still alive, and being all for
fun, he shuffled back into the saddle as soon as the old
mare gave over kicking ; and giving a loud tally-ho,
with some minor ' hunting-noises,' which were responded
to by the Baron in notes not capable of being set to
music, and aided by an equally indescribable accompaniment from the old mare at every application of the bush,
she went off at score over the springy turf, and bore
them triumphantly to the betting-post just as the ring
was in course of formation, a fact which she announced
by a loud neigh on viewing her companion of the plough,
as well as by upsetting some half-dozen blacklegs as
she rushed through the crowd to greet her. Great was
the hubbub, shouting, swearing, and laughing,—for
though the Newmarketites are familiar with most
conveyances, from a pair of horses down to a pair of
shoes, it had not then fallen to their lot to see two men
ride into the ring on the same horse—certainly not
with such a hat between them as the Baron's.

The gravest and weightiest matters will not long
distract the attention of a blackleg, and the laughter
having subsided without Jorrocks or the Baron being
in the slightest degree disconcerted, the ring was again
formed ; horses' heads again turn towards the post,
while carriages, gigs, carts, etc., form an outer circle.
A solemn silence ensues. The legs are scanning the
list. At length one gives tongue. ' What starts ?
Does Lord Eldon start ? ' ' No, he don't,' replies the
owner. ' Does Trick, by Catton ? ' ' Yes, and Conolly
rides—but *mind*, three pounds over.' ' Does John
Bull ? ' ' No, John's struck out.' ' Polly Hopkins does,
so does Talleyrand, also O, Fy ! out of Penitence.
Beagle and Paradox also—and perhaps Pickpocket.'

Another pause, and the pencils are pulled from the
betting books. The legs and lords look at each other,
but no one likes to lead off. At length a voice is heard
offering to take nine to one he names the winner. ' It's
short odds, doing it cautiously.' ' I'll take eight, then,'
he adds—' *sivin !* ' but no one bites. ' What will any

one lay *about* Trick by Catton ? ' inquires Jem Bland.
' I'll lay three to two again him.'   ' I'll take two to one
—two ponies to one, and give you a suv for laying it.'
' Carn't,' is the answer.   ' I'll do it, Jem,' cries a voice.
' No, *you* won't,' from Bland, not liking his customer.
Now they are all at it, and what a hubbub there is !
' I'll back the field—I'll lay—I'll take—I'll bet—
ponies — fifties — hundreds — five hundred to two.'
' What do you want, my Lord ? '   ' Three to one
against Trick, by Catton.'   ' Carn't afford it—the odds
real*ly* aren't that in the ring.'   ' Take two—two hundred
to one.'   ' No.'   ' Crockford, you'll do it for me ? '
' Yes, my Lord.   Twice over if you like.   Done, done.'
' Do it again ? '   ' No, thank you.'

' Trick by Catton don't start ! ' cries a voice. ' *Impossible !* ' exclaim his backers.   ' Quite true, I'm just
from the weighing-house, and —— told me so himself.'
'*:Shame ! shame !* ' roar those who have backed him (it
being a play or pay day), and ' honour—rascals—rogues
—thieves—robbery — swindle — turf-ruined ' — fly from
tongue to tongue, but they are all speakers with never
a speaker to cry *order*.   Meanwhile the lads have
galloped by on their hacks with the horses' clothes to
the rubbing-house and the horses have actually started,
and are now visible in the distance sweeping over the
open heath, apparently without guide or beacon.

The majority of the ring rush to the white judge's
box, and have just time to range themselves along the
rude stakes and ropes that guard the run-in, and the
course-keeper in a shooting-jacket on a rough pony to
crack his whip, and cry to half a dozen stable lads to
' clear the course,' before the horses come flying towards
home.   Now all is tremor ; hope and fear vacillating
in each breast.   Silence stands breathless with expectation—all eyes are riveted—the horses come within
descrying distance—' beautiful ! ' three close together,
two behind.   ' Clear the course ! clear the course ! *pray*
clear the course ! '   ' Polly Hopkins ! Polly Hopkins ! '
roar a hundred voices as they near, ' O, Fy ! O, Fy ! '
respond an equal number.   ' The horse ! the *horse* ! '
bellow a hundred more, as though their yells would aid

his speed, as Polly Hopkins, O, Fy ! and Talleyrand
rush neck-and-neck along the cords and pass the judge's
box. A cry of ' dead heat ! ' is heard. The bystanders
see as suits their books, and immediately rush to the
judge's box, betting, bellowing, roaring, and yelling
the whole way. ' What's won ? what's won ? what's
won ? ' is vociferated from a hundred voices. ' Polly
Hopkins ! Polly Hopkins ! Polly Hopkins ! ' replies Mr.
Clark with judicial dignity. ' By how much ? by how
much ? ' ' Half a head—half a head,' replies the same
functionary. ' What's second ? ' ' O, Fy ! ' And so,
amid the song of ' Pretty, pretty Polly Hopkins,' from
the winners, and curses and execrations long, loud and
deep, from the losers, the scene closes.

The admiring winners follow Polly to the rubbing-
house, while the losing horses are left in the care of their
trainers and stable-boys, who condole themselves with
hopes of ' better luck next time.'

After a storm comes a calm, and the next proceeding is the wheeling of the judge's box, and removal of
the old stakes and ropes to another course on a different
part of the heath, which is accomplished by a few ragged
rascals, as rude and uncouth as the furniture they bear.
In less than half an hour the same group of anxious care-
worn countenances are again turned upon each other
at the betting-post, as though they had never separated.
But see ! the noble owner of Trick, by Catton, is in the
crowd, and Jem Bland eyeing him like a hawk. ' I
say, Waggey,' cries he (singling out a friend stationed
by his lordship), ' had you aught on Trick, by Catton ? '
' No, Jem,' roars Wagstaff, shaking his head, ' I knew my
man *too* well.' ' Why now, Waggey, do you know *I*
wouldn't have done such a thing for the world ! no, not
even to have been *made a Markiss* ! ' A horse-laugh
follows this denunciation, at which the newly-created
marquis bites his livid lips.

The Baron, who appears to have no taste for walking,
still sticks to the punch mare, which Mr. Jorrocks steers
to the newly-formed ring, aided by the Baron and the
furze bush. Here they come upon Sam Spring, whose
boy has just brought his spring-cart to bear upon the

ring formed by the horsemen, and thinking it a pity
that a nobleman of any country should be reduced to
the necessity of riding double, very politely offers to
take one into his carriage. Jorrocks accepts the offer,
and forthwith proceeds to make himself quite at home
in it. The chorus again commences, and Jorrocks
interrogates Sam as to the names of the brawlers.
' Who is that ? ' said he, ' offering to bet a thousand to
a hundred.' Spring, after eyeing him through his
spectacles, with a grin and a look of suspicion, replies,
' Come now—come—let's have no nonsense—you know
as well as I.' ' Really,' replies Mr. Jorrocks, most
earnestly, ' *I don't*,' ' Why, where have you lived all
your life ? ' ' First part of it with my grandmother at
Lisson Grove, afterwards at Camberwell, but now I
resides in Great Coram Street, Russell Square—a werry
fashionable neighbourhood.' ' Oh, I see,' replies Sam,
' you are one of the reg'lar city coves, then—now, what
brings you here ? ' ' Just to say I've been to Newmarket, for I'm blowed if ever you catch me here again.'
' That's a pity,' replied Sam, ' for you look like a
promising man—a handsome-bodied chap in the face—
don't you sport any ? ' ' Oh, a vast !—'unt regularly—
I'm a member of the Surrey 'unt—capital one it is, too
—best in England by far.' ' What do you hunt ? '
inquired Sam. ' Foxes, to be sure.' ' And are they
good eating ! ' ' Come,' replied Jorrocks, ' you know
as well as I do, we don't eat 'em.' The dialogue was
interrupted by someone calling to Sam to know what
he was backing.

' The Bedlamite colt, my Lord,' with a forefinger to
his hat. ' Who's that ? ' inquired Jorrocks. ' That's
my Lord L——, a baron-lord—and a very nice one—
best baron-lord I know—always bets with me—that's
another baron-lord next him, and the man next him is
a baron-knight, a stage below a baron-lord—something
between a nobleman and a gentleman.' ' And who be
that stout, good-looking man in a blue coat and velvet
collar next him, just rubbing his chin with the race-
card—he'll be a lord too, I suppose ? ' ' No,—that's Mr.
Gully, as honest a man as ever came here,—that's Crock-

ford before him. The man on the right is Mr. C——,
who they call the " Cracksman," because formerly he
was a professional house-breaker, but he has given up
that trade, and turned gentleman, bets, and keeps a
gaming-table. This little ugly, black-faced chap, that
looks for all the world like a bilious Scotch terrier, has
lately come among us. He was a tramping pedlar—
sold worsted stockings—attended country courses, and
occasionally bet a pair. Now he bets thousands of
pounds, and keeps race-horses. The chaps about him,
all covered with chains and rings and brooches, were in
the duffing-line—sold brimstoned sparrows for canary-
birds, Norwich shawls for real Cashmere, and dried
cabbage-leaves for cigars. Now each has a first-rate
house, horses and carriages, and a play-actress among
them. Yon chap, with an *ex*travagantly big mouth, is a
cabinetmaker at Cambridge. He'll bet you a thousand
pounds as soon as look at you.

' The chap on the right of the post, with the red tie,
is the son of an ostler. He commenced betting thousands
with a farthing capital. The man next him, all teeth
and hair, like a rat-catcher's dog, is an Honourable by
birth, but not very honourable in his nature.' ' But
see,' cried Mr. Jorrocks, ' Lord —— is talking to the
Cracksman.' ' To be sure,' replies Sam, ' that's the
beauty of the turf. The lord and the leg are reduced
to an equality. Take my word for it, if you have a
turn for good society, you should come upon the turf.—
I say, my Lord Duke ! ' with all five fingers up to his
hat, ' I'll lay you three to two on the Bedlamite colt.'
' Done, Mr. Spring,' replies his Grace, ' three ponies to
two.' ' *There !* ' cried Mr. Spring, turning to Jorrocks,
' didn't I tell you so ? ' The riot around the post
increases. It is near the moment of starting, and the
legs again become clamorous for what they want. Their
vehemence increases. Each man is *in extremis*. ' They
are off ! ' cries one. ' No, they are not,' replies another.
' False start,' roars a third. ' *Now* they come ! ' ' No,
they don't ! ' ' Back again.' They are off at last,
however, and away they speed over the flat. The horses
come within descrying distance. It's a beautiful race—

run at score the whole way, and only two tailed off within the cords. Now they set to—whips and spurs go, legs leap, lords shout, and amid the same scene of confusion—betting, galloping, cursing, swearing, and bellowing—the horses rush past the judge's box.

But we have run *our* race, and will not fatigue our readers with repetition. Let us, however, spend the evening, and then the ' Day at Newmarket ' will be done.

Mr. Spring, with his usual attention to strangers, persuades Mr. Jorrocks to make one of a most agreeable dinner-party at the White Hart, on the assurance of spending a delightful evening. Covers are laid for sixteen in the front room downstairs, and about six o'clock that number are ready to sit down. Mr. Badchild, the accomplished keeper of an oyster-room and minor hell in Pickering Place, is prevailed upon to take the chair, supported on his right by Mr. Jorrocks, and on his left by Mr. Tom Rhodes, of Thames Street, while the stout, jolly, portly Jerry Hawthorn fills—in the fullest sense of the word—the vice-chair. Just as the waiters are removing the covers, in stalks the Baron, in his conical hat, and reconnoitres the viands. Sam, all politeness, invites him to join the party. ' I tank you,' replies the Baron, ' but I have my *wet* in de next room.' ' But bring your wet with you,' rejoins Sam, ' we'll all have our *wet* together after dinner,' thinking the Baron meant his wine.

The usual inn grace—' For what we are going to receive the host expects to be paid,'—having been said with great feeling and earnestness, they all set to at the victuals, and little conversation passed until the removal of the cloth, when Mr. Badchild, calling upon his Vice, observed that as in all probability there were gentlemen of different political and other opinions present, perhaps the best way would be to give a comprehensive toast, and so get over any debatable ground, —he therefore proposed to drink in a bumper, ' The King, the Queen, and all the Royal Family, the Ministry, particularly the Master of the Horse, the Army, the Navy, the Church, the State, and after the excellent

dinner they had eaten, he would include the name of
the landlord of the White Hart ' (great applause). Song
from Jerry Hawthorn—' The King of the Cannibal
Islands.'—The chairman then called upon the company
to fill their glasses to a toast upon which there could be
no difference of opinion. ' It was a sport which they
all enjoyed, one that was delightful to the old and to
the young, to the peer and to the peasant, and open to
all. Whatever might be the merits of other amusements, he had never yet met any man with the hardi-
hood to deny that racing was at once the noblest and
most legitimate ' (loud cheers, and thumps on the table,
that set all the glasses dancing), ' not only was it the
noblest and most legitimate, but it was the most *profit-
'able* ; and where was the man of high and honourable
principle who did not feel, when breathing the pure
atmosphere of that Heath, a lofty self-satisfaction at
the thought that though he might have left those who
were near and dear to him in a less genial atmosphere,
still he was not selfishly enjoying himself, without a
thought for their welfare ; for racing, while it brought
health and vigour to the father, also brought what was
dearer to the mind of a parent—the means of promoting
the happiness and prosperity of his family ' (immense
cheers). ' With these few observations, he should
simply propose, " The Turf," and may we long be above
it '—(applause, and, on a motion of Mr. Spring, three
cheers for Mrs. Badchild and all the little Badchildren
were called for and given). When the noise had subsided, Mr. Jorrocks very deliberately got up, amid
whispers and inquiries as to who he was. ' Gentlemen,'
said he, with an indignant stare and a thump on the
table, ' Gentlemen, I say, in much of what has fallen
from our worthy chairman, I go-in-sides, save in what
he says about racing—I insists that *'unting* is the sport
of sports ' (immense laughter, and cries of ' Wot an old
fool ! ') ' Gentlemen yu may laugh, but I say it's a
fact, and though I doesn't wish to create no displeasancy
whatsomever, yet I should despise myself most con-
foundedly—should consider myself unworthy of the
great and distinguished 'unt to which I have the honour

to belong, if I sat quietly down without sticking up
for the Chase (laughter)—I say, it's one of the balances
of the Constitution (laughter)—I say, it's the sport of
kings ! the image of war without its guilt (hisses and
immense laughter). I will fearlessly propose a bumper
toast—I will give you " Fox-hunting." ' There was
some demur about drinking it, but on the interposition
of Sam Spring, who assured the company that Jorrocks
was one of the right sort, and with an addition proposed
by Jerry Hawthorn, which made the toast more compre-
hensible, they swallowed it, and the chairman followed
it up with ' The Sod,'—which was drunk with great
applause. Mr. Cox of Blue Hammerton returned
thanks. ' He considered cock-fighting the finest of all
fine amusements. Nothing could equal the rush
between two prime grey-hackles—that was his colour.
The chairman had said a vast for racing, and to cut
the matter short, he might observe that cock-fighting
combined all the advantages of making money, with
the additional benefit of not being interfered with by
the weather. He begged to return his best thanks for
himself and brother sods, and only regretted he had
not been taught speaking in his youth, or he would
certainly have convinced them all that " Cocking " was
the sport.' ' Coursing ' was the next toast, for which
Arthur Pavis, the jockey, returned thanks. ' He was
very fond of the " long dogs," and thought, after racing,
coursing was the *true* thing. He was no orator, and so
he drank off his wine to the health of the company.'
' Steeplechasing ' followed, for which Mr. Coalman of
St. Albans returned thanks, assuring the company that
it answered his purpose remarkably well. Then the
Vice gave the Chair, and the Chair gave the Vice ; and
by way of a finale, Mr. Badchild proposed the game of
Chicken-hazard, observing in a whisper to Mr. Jorrocks,
that perhaps he would like to subscribe to a joint-stock
purse [1] for the purpose of going to hell. To which Mr.
Jorrocks, with great gravity, replied, ' Sir, I'm d—d
if I do.'

[1] It is common for parties to club their money and appoint one
of their body to play the game.

MR JORROCKS DECLARES HIS INABILITY TO SUBSCRIBE TO THE SURREY STAG HOUNDS

THE BARON "VILLS HIS WET."

AQUATICS : MR. JORROCKS AT MARGATE

THE shady side of Cheapside had become a luxury, and footmen in red plush breeches objects of real commiseration, when Mr. Jorrocks, tired of the heat and ' ungrateful hurry of the town,' resolved upon undertaking an aquatic excursion. He was sitting, as is ' his custom always in the afternoon,' in the arbour at the farther end of his gravel walk, which he dignifies by the name of ' garden,' and had just finished a rough mental calculation as to whether he could eat more bread spread with jam or honey, when the idea of the jaunt entered his imagination. Being a man of great decision, he speedily winnowed the project over in his mind, and, producing a five-pound note from the fob of his small-clothes, passed it in review between his fingers, rubbed out the creases, held it up to the light, re-folded and restored it to his fob. ' Batsay,' cried he, ' bring my castor—the white one as hangs next the blue cloak ' ; and forthwith a rough-napped, unshorn-looking white hat was transferred from the peg to Mr. Jorrocks's head. This done, he proceeded to the Piazza, where he found the Yorkshireman exercising himself up and down the spacious coffee-room, and, grasping his hand with the firmness of a vice, he forthwith began unburthening himself of the object of his mission. ' '*Ow are you ?* ' said he, shaking his arm like the handle of a pump, ' 'Ow are you, I say ?—I'm so delighted to see you, ye carn't think—Isn't this charming weather ? It makes me feel like a butterfly—really think the 'air is sprouting under my vig.' Here he took off his wig and rubbed his hand over his bald head, as though he were feeling for the shoots.

' Now to business—Mrs. J. is away at Tooting, as you perhaps knows, and I'm all alone in Great Coram Street, with the key of the cellar, larder, and all that sort of thing, and I've a werry great mind to be off on a jaunt —what say you ? ' ' Not the slightest objection,' replied the Yorkshireman, ' on the old principle of you

4

finding cash and me finding company.' ' Why, now
I tell you, werry honestly, that I should greatly prefer
your paying your own shot ; but, however, if you've
a mind to do as I do, I'll let you stand in the half of a
five-pound note and whatever silver I have in my pocket,'
pulling out a great handful as he spoke, and counting
up thirty-two and sixpence. ' Very good,' replied the
Yorkshireman when he had finished, ' I'm your man ;
—and not to be behind-hand in point of liberality, I've
got threepence that I received in change at the cigar
divan just now, which I will add to the common stock,
so that we shall have six pounds twelve and ninepence
between us.' ' *Between* us ! ' exclaimed Mr. Jorrocks,
' now that's so *like* a Yorkshireman. I declare you
Northerns seem to think all the world are asleep except
yourselves ; howsomever, I von't quarrel with you—
you're a goodish sort of chap in your way, and so long
as I keep the swag, we carn't get far wrong. Well, then,
to-morrow, at two we'll start for Margate—the most
delightful place in all the world, where we will have
a rare jollification, and can stay just as long as the
money holds out. So now good-bye—I'm off home
again to see about wittles for the woyage.'

It were almost superfluous to mention that the
following day was a Saturday—for no discreet citizen
would think of leaving town on any other. It dawned
with uncommon splendour, and the cocks of Coram
Street and adjacent parts seemed to hail the morn with
more than their wonted energy. Never, save on a hunting morning, did Mr. Jorrocks tumble about in bed
with such restless anxiety as cock after cock took up
the crow, in every gradation of noise from the shrill
note of the free street-scouring chanticleer before the
door, to the faint response of the cooped and prisoned
victims of the neighbouring poulterer's, their efforts
being aided by the flutterings and impertinent chirrup-
ing of swarms of town-bred sparrows.

At length the boy, Binjimin, tapped at his master's
door, and, depositing his can of shaving-water on his
dressing-table, took away his coat and waistcoat under
pretence of brushing them, but in reality to feel if he

had left any pence in the pockets. With pleasure Mr.
Jorrocks threw aside the bed-clothes, and bounded
upon the floor with a bump that shook his own and
adjoining houses. On this day a few extra minutes
were devoted to his toilet, one or two of which were
expended in adjusting a gold foxhead pin in a conspicuous part of his white tie, and in drawing on a pair
of new dark-blue stocking-net pantaloons made so
excessively tight that at starting any of his Newmarket friends would have laid three to two against
his ever getting into them at all. When on, however,
they fully developed the substantial proportions of his
well-rounded limbs, while his large-tasselled Hessians
showed that the bootmaker had been instructed to
make a pair for a ' great calf.' A blue coat, with metal
buttons, ample laps, and pockets outside, with a handsome buff kerseymere waistcoat, formed his costume
on this occasion. Breakfast being over, he repaired to
St. Botolph Lane, there to see his letters and look after
his commercial affairs ; in which the reader not being
interested, we will allow the Yorkshireman to figure a
little.

About half-past one this enterprising young man
placed himself in Tommy Sly's wherry at the foot of
the Savoy Stairs, and, not agreeing in opinion with
Mr. Jorrocks that it is of ' no use keeping a dog and
barking oneself,' he took an oar and helped to row
himself down to London Bridge. At the wharf below
the bridge there lay a magnificent steamer, painted
pea-green and white, with flags flying from her masts,
and the deck swarming with smart bonnets and bodices.
Her name was the *Royal Adelaide*, from which the
sagacious reader will infer that this excursion was made
during the late reign. The Yorkshireman and Tom Sly
having wormed their way among the boats, were at
length brought up near one of the vessels, and, after
lying on their oars a few seconds, they were attracted
by ' Now, sir, are you going to sleep there ? ' addressed
to a rival nautical whose boat obstructed the way, and,
on looking up on deck, what a sight burst upon the
Yorkshireman's astonished vision !—Mr. Jorrocks with

his coat off, and a fine green velvet cap or turban, with a broad gold band and tassel, on his head, hoisting a great hamper out of the wherry, rejecting all offers of assistance, and treating the laughter and jeers of the porters and bystanders with ineffable contempt. At length he placed the load to his liking, and, putting on his coat, adjusted his hunting telescope, and advanced to the side, as the Yorkshireman mounted the step-ladder, and came upon deck. 'Werry near being over late,' said he, pulling out his watch, just at which moment the last bell rang, and a few strokes of the paddles sent the vessel away from the quay. 'A miss is as good as a mile,' replied the Yorkshireman; 'but pray what have you got in the hamper?'

'In the 'amper! Why, wittles, to be sure! You seem to forget we are going a woyage, and 'ow keen the sea hair is. I've brought a knuckle of weal, half a ham, beef, sarsingers, chickens, sherry white an all that sort of thing, and werry acceptable they'll be by the time we get to the Nore, or may be before.

'*Ease her! Stop her!*' cried the captain through his trumpet, just as the vessel was getting into her stride in midstream, and, with true curiosity, the passengers flocked to the side, to see who was coming, though they could not possibly have examined half they had on board. Mr. Jorrocks, of course, was not behindhand in inquisitiveness, and proceeded to adjust his telescope. A wherry was seen rowing among the craft, containing the boatman and a gentleman in a woolly white hat, with a bright pea-green coat, and a basket on his knee. 'By Jingo, here's Jemmy Green!' exclaimed Mr. Jorrocks, taking his telescope from his eye, and giving his thigh a hearty slap. 'How un-kimmon lucky! The werry man of all others I should most like to see. You know James Green, don't you?' addressing the Yorkshireman,—'*young* James Green, *junior*, of Tooley Street—everybody knows him—most agreeable young man in Christendom—fine warbler—beautiful dancer—everything that a young man should be.'

'How are you, James?' cried Jorrocks, seizing him

by the hand as his friend stepped upon deck ; but
whether it was the nervousness occasioned by the
rocking of the wherry, or the shaking of the step-ladder
up the side of the steamer, or Mr. Jorrocks's new turban
cap, but Mr. Green, with an old-maidish reserve, drew
back from the proffered embrace of his friend. ' You
have the adwantage of me, sir,' said he, fidgeting back
as he spoke, and eyeing Mr. Jorrocks with unmeasured
surprise—' Yet stay,—if I'm not deceived it's Mr.
Jorrocks,—so it is ! ' and thereupon they joined hands
most cordially, amid exclamations of ' 'Ow are you, J. ? '
' 'Ow are you, G. ? ' ' 'Ow are you, J. ? ' ' So glad
to see you, J.' ' So glad to see you, G.' ' So glad to
see you, J.' ' And pray what may you have in your
basket ? ' inquired Mr. Jorrocks, putting his hand to
the bottom of a neat little green-and-white willow
woman's-basket, apparently for the purpose of ascer-
taining its weight. ' Only my clothes, and a little
prowision for the woyage. A baked pigeon, some cold
maccaroni, and a few pectoral lozenges. At the bottom
are my Margate shoes, with a comb in one, and a razor
in t'other ; then comes the prog, and at the top I've a
dickey and a clean front for to-morrow. I abominates
travelling with much luggage. Where, I ax, is the use
of carrying nightcaps, when the innkeepers always
prowide them, without extra charge ? The same with
regard to soap. Shave, I say, with what you find in
your tray. A wet towel makes an excellent tooth-
brush, and a penknife both cuts and cleans your nails.
Perhaps you'll present your friend to me ? ' added he in
the same breath, with a glance at the Yorkshireman,
upon whose arm Mr. Jorrocks was resting his telescope
hand. ' Much pleasure,' replied Mr. Jorrocks, with his
usual urbanity, ' Allow me to introduce Mr. Stubbs,
Mr. Green, Mr. Green, Mr. Stubbs ; now pray shake
hands,' added he, ' for I'm sure you'll be werry fond of
each other ' ; and thereupon Jemmy, in the most
patronizing manner extended his two forefingers to the
Yorkshireman, who presented him with one in return.
For the information of such of our readers as may never
have seen Mr. James Green, senior junior, either in

Tooley Street, Southwark, where the patronymic name
abounds, or at Messrs. Tattersall's, where he generally
exhibits on a Monday afternoon, we may premise, that
though a little man in stature, he is a great man in
mind, and a great swell in costume. On the present
occasion, as already stated, he had on a woolly
white hat, his usual pea-green coat, with a fine, false,
four-frilled front to his shirt, embroidered, pleated,
and puckered, like a lady's habit-skirt. Down the front
were three or four different sorts of studs, and a butterfly
brooch, made of various coloured glasses, sat in the
centre. His cravat was of a yellow silk with a flowered
border, confining gills sharp and pointed that looked
up his nostrils ; his double-breasted waistcoat was of
red and yellow tartan with blue glass post-boy buttons ;
and his trousers, which were very wide and cut out over
the foot of rusty-black chamois-leather opera-boots,
were of a broad blue stripe upon a white ground. A
curly, bushy, sandy-coloured wig protruded from the
sides of his woolly white hat, and shaded a vacant
countenance, which formed the frontispiece of a great
chuckle head. Sky-blue gloves and a stout cane, with
large tassels, completed the rigging of this Borough
dandy. Altogether he was as fine as any peacock, and
as vain as the proudest.

    ' And 'ow is Mrs. J. ? ' inquired Green, with the
utmost affability—' I hope she's uncommon well—
pray, is she of your party ? ' looking round. ' Why
no,' replied Mr. Jorrocks, ' she's off at Tooting at her
mother's and I'm just away, on the sly, to stay a five-
pound at Margate this delightful weather. 'Ow long
do you remain ? ' ' Oh, only till Monday morning—
I goes every Saturday ; in fact,' added he, in an undertone, ' I've a season ticket, so I may just as well use it,
as stay poking in Tooley Street with the old folks, who
really are so uncommon glumpy, that it's quite refresh-
ing to get away from them.'

    ' That's a pity,' replied Mr. Jorrocks, with one of his
benevolent looks. ' But 'ow comes it, James, you are
not married ? You are not a *bouy* now, and should be
looking out for a home of your own.' ' True, my dear

J., true,' replied Mr. Green ; ' and I tell you wot, our principal bookkeeper and I have made many calculations on the subject, and being a man of literature like yourself, he gave it as his opinion the last time we talked the matter over, that it would only be avoiding Silly and running into Crab-beds ; which, I presume, means Quod or the Bench. Unless he can have a wife " made to order," he says he'll never wed. Besides, the women are such a bothersome, encroaching set. I declare I'm so pestered with them that I don't know vich vay to turn. They are always tormenting of me. Only last week one sent me a specification of what she'd marry me for, and I declare her dress, alone, came to more than I have to find myself in clothes, ball and concert tickets, keep an 'oss, go to theatres, buy lozenges, letter-paper, and everything else with. There were bumbazeens, and challies, and merinoes, and crape, and gauze, and dimity, and caps, bonnets, stockings, shoes, boots, rigids, stays, ringlets ; and, would you believe it, she had the unspeakable audacity to include a bustle ! It was the most monstrous specification and proposal I ever read, and I returned it by the twopenny post, axing her if she hadn't forgotten to include a set of false teeth. Still, I confess, I am tired of Tooley Street. I feel that I have a soul above hemp, and was intended for a brighter sphere ; but vot can von do, cooped up at home without men of henergy for companions ? No prospect of improvement either ; for I left our old gentleman alarmingly well just now, pulling about the flax and tow, as though his dinner depended upon his exertions. I think if the women would let me alone, I might have some chance, but it worries a man of sensibility and refinement to have them always tormenting of one. I've no objections to be led, but, dash my buttons, *I won't be driven!*' 'Certainly not,' replied Mr. Jorrocks, with great gravity, jingling the silver in his breeches' pocket. 'It's an old saying, James, and time proves it true, that you may take an 'oss to the water, but you carn't make him drink—and, talking of 'osses, pray, how are you off in *that* line ? ' ' Oh, werry well—uncommon, I may say—a thorough-

bred, bang tail down to the hocks, by Phantom, out
of Baron Munchausen's dam—gave a hatful of money
for him at Tatt.'s—five fives—a deal of tin as times go.
But he's a perfect 'oss, I assure you—bright bay with
four black legs, and never a white hair upon him. He's
touched in the vind, but that's nothing—I'm not a fox-
hunter, you know, Mr. Jorrocks ; besides, I find the
music he makes werry useful in the streets, as a warning
to the old happle women to get out of the way. Pray,
sir,' turning to the Yorkshireman with a jerk, ' do you
dance ? '—as the boat-band, consisting of a harp, a
flute, a lute, a long horn, and a short horn, struck up a
quadrille,—and, without waiting for a reply, our hero
sidled past, and glided among the crowd that covered
the deck.

' A fine young man, James,' observed Jorrocks, eyeing Jemmy as he elbowed his way down to the boat—
' fine young man—wants a little of his father's ballast,
but there's no putting old heads on young shoulders.
He's a beautiful dancer,' added Mr. Jorrocks, putting
his arm through the Yorkshireman's, ' let's go and see
him foot it.' Having worked their way down, they at
length got near the dancers, and, mounting a ballast
box, had a fine view of the quadrille. There were eight
or ten couple at work, and Jemmy had chosen a fat,
dumpy, red-faced girl, in a bright orange-coloured
muslin gown, with black velvet Vandyked flounces, and
green boots—a sort of walking sunflower, with whom he
was pointing his toe, kicking out behind, and pirouetting
with great energy and agility. His male *vis-à-vis* was
a waistcoatless young Daniel Lambert, in white ducks
and a blue dress-coat, with a carnation in his mouth,
who, with a damsel in ten colours, reel'd to and fro in
humble imitation. ' Green for ever ! ' cried Mr. Jorrocks,
taking off his velvet cap and waving it encouragingly
over his head : ' Green for ever ! *Go it, Green !* ' and
accordingly Green went it with redoubled vigour.
' Wiggins for ever ! ' responded a female voice opposite,
' *I say, Wiggins !* ' which was followed by a loud clapping
of hands, as the fat gentleman made an astonishing
step. Each had his admiring applauders, though

Wiggins ' had the call ' among the ladies—the opposition voice that put him in nomination proceeding from the mother of his partner, who, like her daughter, was a sort of walking pattern-book. The spirit of emulation lasted throughout the quadrille, after which, Sunflower in hand, Green traversed the deck to receive the compliments of the company. *8 0 4 4 2*

' You must be 'ungry,' observed Mr. Jorrocks, with great politeness to the lady, ' after all your exertions,' as the latter stood mopping herself with a coarse linen handkerchief. ' Pray, James, bring your partner to our 'amper, and let me offer her some refreshment,' which was one word for the Sunflower and two for himself, the sea-breeze having made Mr. Jorrocks what he called ' unkimmon peckish.' The hamper was speedily opened, the knuckle of weal, the half ham, the aitch bone of beef, the Dorking sausages (made in Drury Lane), the chickens, and some dozen or two of plover's eggs, were exhibited, while Green, with disinterested generosity, added his baked pigeon and ccld maccaroni to the common stock. A vigorous attack was speedily commenced, and was kept up, with occasional interruptions by Green running away to dance, until they hove in sight of Herne Bay, which caused an interruption to a very interesting lecture on wines that Mr. Jorrocks was in the act of delivering, which went to prove that port and sherry were the parents of all wines, port the father, and sherry the mother ; and that *Bluecellas*, Hock, Burgundy, Claret, Teneriffe, Madeira, were made by the addition of water, vinegar, and a few chemical ingredients, and that of all ' humbugs,' pale sherry was the greatest, being neither more nor less than brown sherry watered. Mr. Jorrocks then set to work to pack up the leavings in the hamper, observing, as he proceeded, that wilful waste brought woeful want, and that ' waste not, want not,' had ever been the motto of the Jorrocks family.

It was nearly eight o'clock ere the *Royal Adelaide* touched the point of the far-famed Margate jetty, a fact that was announced as well by the usual bump and scuttle to the side to get out first, as by the band striking up ' God save the King,' and the mate demanding the

4*

tickets of the passengers. The sun had just dropped beneath the horizon, and the gas-lights of the town had been considerately lighted to show him to bed, for the day was yet in the full vigour of life and light.

Two or three other cargoes of cockneys having arrived before, the whole place was in commotion, and the beach swarmed with spectators as anxious to watch this last disembarkation as they had been to see the first. By a salutary regulation of the sages who watch over the interests of the town, 'all manner of persons' are prohibited from walking upon the jetty during this ceremony, but the platform of which it is composed being very low, those who stand on the beach, outside the rails, are just about on a right level to shoot their impudence cleverly into the ears of the new-comers, who are paraded along two lines of gaping, quizzing, laughing, joking, jeering citizens, who fire volleys of wit and satire upon them as they pass. 'There's *lee*tle Jemmy Green again!' exclaimed a nursery-maid, with two fat, ruddy children in her arms, 'he's a beauty without paint!' 'Holloa, Jorrocks, my hearty! lend us your hand!' cried a brother member of the Surrey Hunt. Then there was a pointing of fingers and cries of 'That's Jorrocks! That's Green! That's Green! That's Jorrocks!' and a murmuring titter, and exclamations of 'There's Simpkins! how pretty he is!' 'But there's Wiggins, who's much nicer.' 'My eye, what a cauliflower hat Mrs. Thompson's got!' 'What a buck young Snooks is!' 'What gummy legs that girl in green has!' 'Miss Trotter's bustle's on crooked!' from the young ladies at Miss Trimmer's seminary, who were drawn up to show the numerical strength of the academy, and act the part of walking advertisements. These observations were speedily drowned by the lusty lungs of a fly-man bellowing out, as Green passed, 'Holloa! my young brockley-sprout, are you here again?—now then for the tizzy [1] you owe me,—I have been waiting here for it ever since last Monday morning.' This salute produced an irate look and a shake of his cane from Green, with a mutter of something about '*imperance*,' and a wish that he had

[1] 'Tizzy'—Margate for sixpence.

his big fighting foreman there to thrash him. When
they got to the gate at the end, the tide of fashion became
obstructed by the kissings of husbands and wives, the
greetings of fathers and sons, the officiousness of porters,
the cries of fly-men, the importunities of innkeepers, the
cards of bathing-women, the salutations of donkey-
drivers, the programmes of librarians, and the rush and
push of the inquisitive ; and the waters of ' comers ' and
' stayers ' mingled in one common flood of indescribable
confusion.

Mr. Jorrocks, who, hamper in hand, had elbowed his
way with persevering resignation, here found himself so
beset with friends all anxious to wring his digits, that,
fearful of losing either his bed or his friends, he besought
Green to step on to the ' White Hart ' and see about
accommodation. Accordingly Green ran his fingers
through the bushy sides of his yellow wig, jerked up his
gills, and with a négligé air strutted up to that inn, which,
as all frequenters of Margate know, stands near the
landing place, and commands a fine view of the harbour.
Mr. Creed, the landlord, was airing himself at the door,
or as Shakespeare has it, ' taking his ease at his inn,'
and knowing Green of old to be a most unprofitable
customer, he did not trouble to move his position
further than just to draw up one leg so as not wholly to
obstruct the passage, and looked at him as much as to
say, ' I prefer your room to your company.' ' Quite
full here, sir,' said he, anticipating Green's question.
' Full, indeed ? ' replied Jemmy, pulling up his gills—
' that's werry awkward. Mr. Jorrocks has come down
with myself and a friend, and we want accommodation.'
' Mr. Jorrocks, indeed ! ' replied Mr. Creed, altering his
tone and manner ; ' I'm sure I shall be delighted to
receive Mr. Jorrocks—he's one of the oldest customers
I have—and one of the best—none of your " glass of
water and toothpick " gentleman—real, downright
black-strap man, likes it hot and strong from the wood
—always pays like a gentleman—never fights about
threepences, like *some people I know*,' looking at Jemmy.
' Pray, what rooms may you require ? '   ' Vy there's
myself, Mr. Jorrocks, and Mr. Jorrocks's other friend—

three in all, and we shall want three good hairy bed-rooms.' 'Well, I don't know,' replied Mr. Creed, laughing, 'about their *hairi*ness, but I can rub them with bear's grease for you.' Jemmy pulled up his gills and was about to reply, when Mr. Jorrocks's appearance interrupted the dialogue. Mr. Creed advanced to receive him, blowing up his porters for not having been down to carry up the hamper, which he took himself and bore to the coffee-room, amid protestations of his delight at seeing his worthy visitor.

Having talked over the changes of Margate, of those that were there, those that were not, and those that were coming, and adverted to the important topic of supper, Mr. Jorrocks took out his yellow and white spotted handkerchief and proceeded to flop his Hessian boots, while Mr. Creed, with his own hands, rubbed him over with a long billiard-table brush. Green, too, put himself in form by the aid of the looking-glass, and these preliminaries being adjusted, the trio sallied forth arm in arm, Mr. Jorrocks occupying the centre. It was a fine, balmy summer evening, the beetles and moths still buzzed and flickered in the air, and the sea rippled against the shingly shore, with a low indistinct murmur that scarcely sounded among the busy hum of men. The shades of night were drawing on—a slight mist hung about the hills, and a silvery moon shed a broad brilliant ray upon the quivering waters 'of the dark blue sea,' and an equal light over the wide expanse of the troubled town. How strange that man should leave the quiet scenes of nature to mix in myriads of those they profess to quit cities to avoid! One turn to the shore, and the gas-lights of the town drew back the party like moths to the streets, which were literally swarming with the population. 'Cheapside, at three o'clock in the afternoon,' as Mr. Jorrocks observed, was never fuller than Margate streets that evening. All was lighted up—all brilliant and all gay—care seemed banished from every countenance, and pretty faces and smart gowns reigned in its stead. Mr. Jorrocks met with friends and acquaintances at every turn, most of whom asked 'when he came?' and 'when he was going

away ? ' Having perambulated the streets, the sound
of music attracted Jemmy Green's attention, and our
party turned into a long, crowded, and brilliantly·
lighted bazaar, just as the last notes of a barrel organ
at the far end faded away, and a young woman in a
hat and feathers, with a swan's down muff and tippet,
was handed by a very smart young man in dirty-white
Berlin gloves, and an equally soiled white waistcoat,
into a sort of orchestra above, where, after the plaudits
of the company had subsided, she struck up—

> ' If I had a donkey vot vouldn't go.'

At the conclusion of the song, and before the company
had time to disperse, the same smart young gentleman,—
having rehanded the young lady from the orchestra and
pocketed his gloves,—ran his fingers through his hair,
and announced from that eminence, that the spirited
proprietors of the bazaar were then going to offer for
public competition, in the enterprising shape of a
raffle, in tickets at one shilling each, a most magnifi-
cently genteel, rosewood, general perfume-box, fitted
up with cedar and lined with red silk velvet, adorned
with cut-steel clasps at the sides, and a solid, massive
silver name-plate at the top, with a best patent Bramah
lock, and six chaste and beautifully rich cut-glass bottles,
and a plate-glass mirror at the top—a box so splendidly
perfect, so beautifully unique, as alike to defy the powers
of praise and the critiques of the envious ; and thereupon
he produced a flashy sort of thing that might be worth
three-and-sixpence, for which he modestly required ten
subscribers, at a shilling each, adding, ' that even with
that number the proprietors would incur a werry heavy
loss, for which nothing but a boundless sense of gratitude
for favours past could possibly recompense them.' The
youth's eloquence and the glitter of the box, reflecting,
as it did, at every turn, the gas-lights both in its steel
and glass, had the desired effect—shillings went down,
and tickets went off rapidly, until only three remained.
' Four, five, and ten, are the only numbers now remaining,' observed the youth, running his eye up the
list and wetting his pencil in his mouth. ' Four, five, and

ten ! ten, four, five ! five, four, ten ! are the only
numbers now vacant for this werry genteel and magnificent rosewood perfume-box, lined with red velvet, cut-
steel clasps, a silver plate for the name, best patent
Bramah lock, and six beautiful rich cut-glass bottles,
with a plate-glass mirror in the lid—and only, four, five,
and ten now vacant ! ' ' I'll take ten,' said Green,
laying down a shilling. ' Thank you, sir—only four and
five now wanting, ladies and gentlemen—pray be in
time—pray be in time ! This is without exception the
most brilliant prize ever offered for public competition.
There were only two of these werry elegant boxes made,
—the unfortunate mechanic who executed them being
carried off by that terrible malady the cholera morbus—
and the other is now in the possession of his most
Christian Majesty the King of the French. Only four
and five wanting to commence throwing for this really
perfect specimen of human ingenuity—only four and
five ? ' ' I'll take them,' cried Green, throwing down
two shillings more—and then the table was cleared—
the dice box produced, and the crowd drew round.
' Number one !—who holds number one ? ' inquired the
keeper, arranging the paper, and sucking the end of his
pencil. A young gentleman in a blue jacket and white
trousers owned the lot, and accordingly led off the
game. The lottery-keeper handed the box, and put in
the dice—rattle, rattle, rattle, rattle, rattle, rattle, plop,
and lift up—' seven and four are eleven '—' now again,
if you please, sir,' putting the dice into the box—rattle,
rattle, rattle, rattle, rattle, rattle,plop, and lift up—a
loud laugh—' one and two make three '—the youth bit
his lips ;—rattle, rattle, rattle, rattle, rattle, rattle, rattle,
plop—a pause—and lift up—' threes ! '—' six, three,
and eleven are twenty.' ' Now who holds number two ?
—what lady or gentleman holds number two ? Pray
step forward ! ' The Sunflower drew near—Green
looked confused—she fixed her eye upon him, half in
fear, half in entreaty—would he offer to throw for her ?
No, by Jove, Green was not so *green* as all that came to,
and he let her shake herself. She threw twenty-two,
thereby putting an extinguisher on the boy, and raising

Jemmy's chance considerably. 'Three' was held by a youngster in nankeen petticoats, who would throw for himself, and shook the box violently enough to be heard at Broadstairs. He scored nineteen, and, beginning to cry immediately, was taken home. Green was next, and all eyes were turned upon him, for he was a noted hand. He advanced to the table with great *sangfroid*, and turning back the wrists of his coat, exhibited his beautiful sparkling paste shirt buttons, and the elegant turn of his taper hand, the middle finger of which was covered with massive rings. He took the box in a négligé manner, and without condescending to shake it, slid the dice out upon the table by a gentle side-way motion—'sixes!' cried all, and down the marker put twelve. At the second throw he adopted another mode. As soon as the dice were in, he just chucked them up in the air like as many half-pence, and down they came five and six—'eleven,' said the marker. With a look of triumph Green held the box for the third time, which he just turned upside down, and lo, on uncovering, there stood two—'ones!' A loud laugh burst forth, and Green looked confused. 'I'm *so glad!*' whispered a young lady, who had made an unsuccessful 'set' at Jemmy the previous season, in a tone loud enough for him to hear. 'I *hope* he'll lose,' rejoined a female friend rather louder, '*That* Jemmy Green is my *absolute abhorrence,*' observed a third. ''Orrible man, with his nasty vig,' observed the mamma of the first speaker, 'shouldn't have my darter not at no price.' Green, however, headed the poll, having beat the Sunflower, and had still two lots in reserve. For number five he threw twenty-five, and was immediately outstripped, amid much laughter and clapping of hands from the ladies, by number six, who in his turn fell a prey to number seven. Between eight and nine there was a very interesting contest who should be lowest, and hopes and fears were at their altitude when Jemmy Green again turned back his coat-wrist to throw for number ten. His confidence had forsaken him a little, as indicated by a slight quivering of the under-lip, but he managed to conceal it from all except the ladies, who kept too scrutinizing an eye upon him. His first throw brought sixes, which raised his spirits amazingly ; but on their appearance a second time he could scarcely contain himself, backed as he was by the plaudits of his friend Mr. Jorrocks. Then came the deciding throw—every eye was fixed on Jemmy, he shook the box, turned it down, and lo, there came seven.

' Mr. James Green is the fortunate winner of this magnificent prize ! ' exclaimed the youth, holding up the box in mid-air, and thereupon all the ladies crowded round Green, some to congratulate him, others to compliment him on his looks, while one or two of the least knowing tried to coax him out of his box. Jemmy, however, was too old a stager, and pocketed the box and other compliments at the same time.

Another grind of the organ, and another song followed from the same young lady, during which operation Green sent for the manager, and, after a little beating about the bush, proposed singing a song or two if he would give him lottery-tickets gratis. He asked three shilling tickets for each song, and finally closed for five tickets for two songs, on the understanding that he was to be announced as a distinguished amateur, who had come forward by most particular desire.

Accordingly the manager—a roundabout, red-faced, consequential little cockney—mounted the rostrum, and begged to announce to the company that that ' celebrated wocalist, Mr. James Green, so well known as a distinguished amateur and conwivialist, both at Bagnigge Wells, and Vite Conduit House, LONDON, had werry kindly consented, in order to promote the hilarity of the evening, to favour the company with a song immediately after the drawing of the next lottery,' and after a few high-flown compliments, which elicited a laugh from those who were up to Jemmy's mode of doing business, he concluded by offering a ' papier-maché ' tea-caddy for public competition, in shilling lots as before.

As soon as the drawing was over, they gave the organ a grind, and Jemmy popped up with a hop, skip, and a jump, with his woolly white hat under his arm, and presented himself with a scrape and a bow to the company. After a few preparatory 'hems and haws,' he pulled up his gills and spoke as follows : ' Ladies and gentlemen ! hem '—another pull at his gills—' ladies and gentlemen—my walued friend, Mr. Kitey Graves, has announced that I will entertain the company with a song ; though nothing, I assure you—hem—could be farther from my idea—hem—when my excellent friend asked me,'—' Hookey Walker ! ' exclaimed some one who had heard Jemmy declare the same thing half a dozen times—' and, indeed, ladies and gentlemen— hem—nothing but the werry great regard I have for Mr. Kitey Graves, who I have known and loved ever since he was the height of sixpenn'orth of copper ' ; a loud laugh followed this allusion, seeing that eighteen pennyworth would almost measure out the speaker. On giving another ' hem,' and again pulling up his gills, an old Kentish farmer, in a brown coat and mahogany-coloured tops, holloaed out, ' I say, *sir* ! I'm afear'd you'll be catching cold ! ' ' I 'opes not,' replied Jemmy in a fluster, ' is it raining ? I've no umbrella, and my werry best coat on ! ' ' No ! raining no ! ' replied the farmer, ' only you've pulled at your shirt so long that I think your *behind* must be bare ! Haw ! haw ! haw ! " at which all the males roared with laughter, and the females hid their faces in their handkerchiefs, and tittered and giggled, and tried to be shocked. ' ORDER ! ORDER ! ' cried Mr. Jorrocks, in a loud and sonorous voice, which had the effect of quelling the riot and drawing all eyes upon himself. ' Ladies and gentlemen,' said he, taking off his cap with great gravity, and extending his right arm—

> ' Immodest words admit of no defence,
> For want of decency is want of sense ' ;

a couplet so *apropos*, and so well delivered, as to have the immediate effect of restoring order, and making the farmer look foolish. Encouraged by the voice of his great patron, Green once more essayed to finish his speech, which he did by a fresh assurance of the surprise by which he had been taken by the request of his friend,

Kitey Graves, and an exhortation for the company to make allowance for any deficiency of ' woice,' inasmuch as he was labouring under ' a wiolent 'orseness,' for which he had long been taking pectoral lozenges. He then gave his gills another pull, felt if they were even, and struck up—

'Bid me discourse,'

in notes compared to which the screaming of a peacock would be perfect melody. Mr. Jorrocks having taken a conspicuous position, applauded long, loudly, and warmly, at every pause—approbation the more deserved and disinterested, inasmuch as the worthy gentleman suffers considerably from music and only knows two tunes, one of which, he says, ' *is* God save the King, and the other *isn't*.'

Having seen his protégé fairly under way, Mr. Jorrocks gave him a hint that he would return to the White Hart, and have supper ready by the time he was done ; accordingly the Yorkshireman and he withdrew along an avenue politely formed by the separation of the company, who applauded as they passed.

An imperial quart and a half of Mr. Creed's stoutest draught port, with the orthodox proportion of lemon, cloves, sugar, and cinnamon, had almost boiled itself to perfection under the skilful superintendence of Mr. Jorrocks on the coffee-room fire, and a table had been handsomely decorated with shrimps, lobsters, broiled bones, fried ham, poached eggs, when just as the clock had finished striking eleven, the coffee-room door opened with a rush, and in tripped Jemmy Green, with his hands crammed full of packages, and his trousers' pockets sticking out like a Dutch burgomaster's. ' Vell, I've done 'em brown to-night, I think,' said he, depositing his hat and half a dozen packages on the sideboard, and running his fingers through his curls to make them stand up. ' I've won nine lotteries, and left one un-drawn when I came away, because it did not seem likely to fill. Let me see,' said he, emptying his pockets,— ' there is the beautiful rosewood box that I won, ven you was there ; the next was a set of crimping-irons,

vich I von also ; the third was a jockey vip, which I did
not vant, and only stood one ticket for and lost ; the
fourth was this elegant box, with a view of Margate
on the lid ; then came these six sherry labels with silver
rims ; a snuff-box with an inwisible mouse ; a coral
rattle with silver bells ; a silk yard-measure in a walnut
shell ; a couple of West India beetles ; a humming-
bird in a glass case, which I lost ; and then these dozen
bodkins with silver eyes—so that altogether I have
made a pretty good night's work of it. Kitey Graves
wasn't in great force, so after I had sung " Bid me discourse," and " I'd be a butterfly," I cut my stick, and
went to the hopposition shop, where they used me much
more genteelly ; giving me three tickets for a song, and
introducing me in more flattering terms to the company
—I don't like being considered one of the nasty ' reglars,'
and they should make a point of explaining that one
isn't. Besides, what business had Kitey to say anything about Bagnigge Vells ? a hass !—Now, perhaps,
you'll favour me with some supper ? '
    ' Certainly,' replied Mr. Jorrocks, patting Jemmy
approvingly on the head—' you deserve some. It's
only *no* song, no supper, and you've been singing like
a nightingale ' ; thereupon they set-to with vigorous
determination.
    A bright Sunday dawned, and the beach at an early
hour was crowded with men in dressing-gowns of every
shape, hue, and material, with buff slippers—the
' regulation Margate shoeing,' both for men and women.
As the hour of eleven approached, and the church
bells began to ring, the town seemed to awaken suddenly from a trance, and bonnets the most superb, and
dresses the most extravagant, poured forth from lodgings
the most miserable. Having shaved and dressed himself with more than ordinary care and attention, Mr.
Jorrocks walked his friends off to church, assuring them
that no one need hope to prosper throughout the week
who did not attend it on the Sunday, and he marked
his own devotion throughout the service by drowning
the clerk's voice with his responses. After this spiritual
ablution, Mr. Jorrocks bethought himself of having a

bodily one in the sea ; and the day being excessively
hot, and the tide about the proper mark, he pocketed
a couple of towels out of his bedroom and went away
to bathe, leaving Green and the Yorkshireman to amuse
themselves at the White Hart.

This house, as we have already stated, faces the
harbour, and is a corner one, running a considerable
way up the next street, with a side door communicating,
as well as the front one, with the coffee-room. This
room differs from the generality of coffee-rooms, inasmuch as the windows range the whole length of the
room, and, being very low, they afford every facility
for the children and passers-by to inspect the interior.
Whether this is done to show the Turkey carpet, the
pea-green cornices, the bright mahogany slips of tables,
the gay trellised geranium-papered room, or the aristo-
cratic visitors who frequent it, is immaterial—the
description is as accurate as if George Robins had drawn
it himself. In this room, then, as the Yorkshireman
and Green were lying dozing on three chairs apiece, each
having fallen asleep to avoid the trouble of talking to
the other, they were suddenly roused by loud yells and
hootings at the side door, and the bursting into the
coffee-room of what at first brush they thought must be
a bull. The Yorkshireman jumped up, rubbed his eyes,
and lo ! before him stood Mr. Jorrocks, puffing like a
stranded grampus, with a bunch of seaweed under
his arm and the dress in which he had started, with the
exception of the dark blue stocking-net pantaloons, the
place of which was supplied by a flowing white linen
kilt, commonly called a shirt, in the four corners of
which were knotted a few small pebbles—producing,
with the Hessian boots and one thing and another, the
most laughable figure imaginable. The blood of the
Jorrockses was up, however, and, throwing his hands
in the air, he thus delivered himself : ' O gentlemen !
gentlemen !—here's a lamentable occurrence—a terrible
disaster—oh dear ! oh dear ! —I never thought I
should come to this. You know, James Green,' appealing to Jemmy, ' that I never was the man to raise
a blush on the cheek of modesty ; I have always said

that " want of decency is want of sense," and see how
I am rewarded ! Oh dear ! oh dear ! that I should
ever have trusted my pantaloons out of my sight.'
While all this, which was the work of a moment, was
going forward, the mob, which had been shut out at the
side door on Jorrocks's entry, had got round to the
coffee-room window, and were all wedging their faces
in to have a sight of him. It was principally composed of children, who kept up the most discordant yells,
mingled with shouts of, ' There's old cutty shirt ! '—
' who's got your breeches, old cock ? '—' make a
scramble ! '—' turn him out for another hunt ! '—
' turn him again ! ' until, fearing for the respectability
of his house, the landlord persuaded Mr. Jorrocks to
retire into the bar to state his grievances. It then
appeared that having travelled along the coast as far as
the first preventive station-house on the Ramsgate side
of Margate, the grocer had thought it a convenient place
for performing his intended ablutions, and accordingly
proceeded to do what all people of either sex agree
upon in such cases—namely, to divest himself of his
garments ; but before he completed the ceremony,
observing some females on the cliffs above, and not being
(as he said) a man ' to raise a blush on the cheek of
modesty,' he advanced to the water's edge in his afore-
said unmentionables, and forgetting that it was not yet
high tide, he left them there, when they were speedily
covered, and the pockets being full of silver and copper,
of course they were ' swamped.' After dabbling about
in the water and amusing himself with picking up seaweed for about ten minutes, Mr. Jorrocks was horrified,
on returning to the spot where he thought he had left
his stocking-net pantaloons, to find that they had disappeared ; and, after a long and fruitless search, the
unfortunate gentleman was compelled to abandon the
pursuit, and render himself an object of chase to all
the little boys and girls who chose to follow him into
Margate on his return without them.

Jorrocks, as might be expected, was very bad about
his loss, and could not get over it—it stuck in his
gizzard, he said—and there it seemed likely to remain.

In vain Mr. Creed offered him a pair of trousers—he never had worn a pair. In vain he asked for the loan of a pair of white cords and top-boots, or even drab shorts and continuations. Mr. Creed was no sportsman, and did not keep any. The bellman could not cry the lost unmentionables because it was Sunday, and even if they should be found on the ebbing of the tide, they would take no end of time to dry. Mr. Jorrocks declared his pleasure at an end, and forthwith began making inquiries as to the best mode of getting home. The coaches were all gone, steam-boats there were none, save for every place but London, and posting, he said, was 'cruelly expensive.' In the midst of his dilemma, 'Boots,' who is always the most intelligent man about an inn, popped in his curly head, and informed Mr. Jorrocks that the *Unity* hoy, a most commodious vessel, neat, trim, and watertight, manned by his own maternal uncle, was going to cut away to London at three o'clock, and would land him before he could say 'Jack Robinson.' Mr. Jorrocks jumped at the offer, and forthwith attiring himself in a pair of Mr. Creed's loose inexpressibles, over which he drew his Hessian boots, he tucked the hamper containing the knuckle of veal and other etcæteras under one arm, and the bunch of seaweed he had been busy collecting, instead of watching his clothes, under the other, and, followed by his friends, made direct for the vessel.

Everybody knows, or ought to know, what a hoy is —it is a large sailing boat, sometimes with one deck, sometimes with none ; and the *Unity*, trading in bulky goods, was of the latter description, though there was a sort of dog-hole at the stern, which the master dignified by the name of a 'state cabin,' into which he purposed putting Mr. Jorrocks, if the weather should turn cold before they arrived. The wind, however, he said, was so favourable, and his cargo—'timber and fruit,' as he described it, that is to say, broom-sticks and potatoes— so light, that he warranted landing him at Blackwall at least by ten o'clock, where he could either sleep, or get a short stage or an omnibus on to Leadenhall Street. The vessel looked anything but tempting, neither was the captain's appearance prepossessing, still Mr. Jorrocks, all things considered, thought he would chance it ; and depositing his hamper and seaweed, and giving special instructions about having his pantaloons cried in the morning—recounting that, besides the silver and eighteenpence in copper, there was a steel pencil-case with J. J. on the seal at the top, an anonymous letter, and two keys—he took an affectionate leave of his friends, stepped on board, the vessel was shoved off and stood out to sea.

Monday morning drew the cockneys from their roosts betimes, to take their farewell splash and dive in the sea. As the day advanced the bustle and confusion on the shore and in the town increased, and every one seemed on the move. The ladies paid their last visits to the bazaars and shell shops, and children extracted the last ounce of exertion from the exhausted leg-weary donkeys. Meanwhile the lords of the creation strutted about, some in dressing-gowns, others, ' full puff,' with bags and boxes under their arms—while sturdy porters were wheeling barrows full of luggage to the jetty. The bellman went round dressed in a blue and red cloak, with a gold hat-band. Ring-a-ding, ring-a-ding, ring-a-ding, dong, went the bell, and the gaping cockneys congregated around. He commenced—' To be sould in the market-place a quantity of fresh ling.' Ring-a-ding, ring-a-ding, dong : ' The *Royal Adalaide*, fast and splendid steam-packet, Capt. Whittingham, will leave the pier this morning at nine o'clock precisely, and land the passengers at London Bridge Steam-Packet Wharf —fore-cabin fares and children four shillings—saloon five shillings.' Ring-a-ding, ring-a-ding, dong : ' The superb and splendid steam-packet, the *Magnet*, will leave the pier this morning at nine o'clock precisely, and land the passengers at the St. Catherine Docks—fore-cabin fares and children four shillings—saloon five shillings.' Ring-a-ding, ring-a-ding, dong : ' Lost at the back of James Street—a lady's black silk—black lace wale—whoever has found the same, and will bring it to the crier, shall receive one shilling reward.' Ring-a-ding, ring-a-ding, dong : ' Lost, last night, between the jetty and the York

Hotel, a little boy, as answers to the name of *Spot*. Whoever has found the same, and will bring him to the crier, shall receive a reward of half a crown.' Ring-a-ding, ring-a-ding, dong : ' Lost, stolen, or strayed, or otherwise conveyed, a brown and white King Charles's setter, as answers to the name of *Jacob Jones*. Whoever has found the same, or will give such information as shall lead to the detection and conversion of the offender or offenders, shall be handsomely rewarded.' Ring-a-ding, ring-a-ding, dong : ' Lost, below the prewentive-service station, by a gentleman of great respectability— a pair of blue-knit pantaloons, containing eighteen pennyworth of copper—a steel pencil-case—a werry anonymous letter, and two keys. Whoever will bring the same to the crier shall receive *a* reward.—God save the King ! '

Then, as the hour of nine approached, what a con-course appeared ! There were fat and lean, and short and tall, and middling, going away, and fat and lean, and short and tall, and middling, waiting to see them off ; Green, as usual, making himself conspicuous, and canvassing every one he could lay hold of for the *Magnet* steamer. At the end of the jetty, on each side, lay the *Royal Adelaide* and the *Magnet*, with as fierce a contest for patronage as ever was witnessed. Both decks were crowded with anxious faces—for the Monday's steam-boat race is as great an event as a Derby, and a cockney would as lieve lay on an outside horse as patronize a boat that was likely to let another pass her. Nay, so high is the enthusiasm carried, that books are regularly made on the occasion, and there is as much clamour for bets as in the ring at Epsom or Newmarket. ' Tomkins, I'll lay you a dinner—for three—*Royal Adelaide* against the *Magnet*,' bawled Jenkins from the former boat. ' Done,' cries Tomkins. ' The *Magnet* for a bottle of port,' bawled out another. ' A white-bait dinner for two, the *Magnet* reaches Greenwich first.' ' What should you know about the *Magnet ?* ' inquires the mate of the *Royal Adelaide*. ' Vy, I think I should know something about nauticals too, for Lord St. Wincent was my god-father.' ' I'll bet five shillings on the *Royal Adelaide*.'

' I'll take you,' says another. ' I'll bet a bottom of brandy on the *Magnet*,' roars out the mate. ' Two goes of Hollands, the *Magnet's* off Herne Bay before the *Royal Adelaide*.' ' I'll lay a pair of crimping-irons against five shillings, the *Magnet* beats the *Royal Adelaide*,' bellowed out Green, who, having come on board had mounted the paddle-box. ' I say, Green, I'll lay you an even five if you like.' ' Well, five pounds,' cries Green. ' No, shillings,' says his friend. ' Never bet shillings,' replies Green, pulling up his shirt collar. ' I'll bet fifty pounds,' he adds, getting valiant. ' I'll bet a hundred pounds—a thousand pounds—a million pounds—half the national debt, if you like.'

Precisely as the jetty-clock finishes striking nine, the ropes are slipped, and the rival steamers stand out to sea with beautiful precision, amid the crying, the kissing of hands, the raising of hats, the waving of handkerchiefs, from those who are left for the week, while the passengers are cheered by adverse tunes from the respective bands on board. The *Magnet*, having the outside, gets the breeze first hand, but the *Royal Adelaide* keeps well alongside, and both firemen being deeply interested in the event, they boil up a tremendous gallop, without either being able to claim the slightest advantage for upwards of an hour and a half, when the *Royal Adelaide* manages to shoot ahead for a few minutes, amid the cheers and exclamations of her crew. The *Magnet's* fireman, however, is on the alert, and a few extra pokes of the fire presently bring the boats together again, in which state they continue, nose and nose, until the stiller water of the side of the Thames favours the *Magnet*, and she shoots ahead amid the cheers and vociferations of her party, and is not neared again during the voyage.

This excitement over, the respective crews sink into a sort of melancholy sedateness, and Green in vain endeavours to kick up a quadrille. The men were exhausted, and the women dispirited, and altogether they were a very different set of beings to what they were on the Saturday. Dull faces and dirty-white ducks were the order of the day.

The only incident of the voyage was that, on approach-

ing the mouth of the Medway, the *Royal Adelaide* was
hailed by a vessel, and the Yorkshireman, on looking
overboard, was shocked to behold Mr. Jorrocks sitting
in the stern of his hoy in the identical position he had
taken up the previous day, with his bunch of seaweed
under his elbow, and the remains of the knuckle of veal,
ham, and chickens spread on the hamper before him.
Stop her ! ' cried the Yorkshireman ; and then hailing
' Mr. Jorrocks, he holloaed out, ' In the name of the
prophet, Figs, what are you doing there ? ' ' O gentleman ! gentleman ! ' exclaimed Mr. Jorrocks, brighten-
ing up as he recognized the boat, ' take compassion on a
most misfortunate individual—here have I been in this
'orrid 'oy ever since three o'clock yesterday afternoon,
and here I seem likely to end my days,—for blow me
tight if I couldn't swim as fast as it goes.' ' Look sharp,
then,' cried the mate of the steamer, and chuck us up
your luggage.' Up went the seaweed, the hamper, and
Mr. Jorrocks ; and before the hoyman awoke out of a
nap, into which he had composed himself on resigning
the rudder to his lad, our worthy citizen was steaming
away a mile before his vessel, bilking him of his
fare.

Who does not recognize in this last disaster, the truth
of the old adage :

' Most haste, least speed.'

THE ROAD : ENGLISH AND FRENCH

' JORROCKS'S France, in three volumes, would sound
werry well,' observed our worthy citizen one afternoon to his confidential companion the Yorkshireman, as they sat in the verandah in Coram Street, eating
red currants and sipping cold whiskey-punch ; ' and I
thinks I could make something of it. They tells me that
at the " West End " the booksellers will give forty

pounds [1] for anything that will run into three wolumes,
and one might soon pick up as much matter as would
stretch into that quantity.'

The above observation was introduced in a long
conversation between Mr. Jorrocks and his friend,
relative to an indignity that had been offered him by
the rejection by the Editor of a sporting periodical of
a long treatise on Eels, which, independently of the
singularity of diction, had become so attenuated in the
handling, as to have every appearance of filling three
whole numbers of the work ; and Mr. Jorrocks had
determined to avenge the insult by turning author on
his own account. The Yorkshireman, ever ready for
amusement, cordially supported Mr. Jorrocks in his
views, and a bargain was soon struck between them,
the main stipulations of which were that Mr. Jorrocks
should find cash, and the Yorkshireman should procure
information.

Accordingly, on the Saturday after, the nine o'clock
Dover heavy drew up at the Bricklayers' Arms with
Mr. Jorrocks on the box seat, and the Yorkshireman
imbedded among the usual heterogeneous assembly—
soldiers, sailors, Frenchmen, fishermen, ladies' maids,
and footmen—that compose the cargo of these coaches.
Here they were assailed with the usual persecution from
the tribe of Israel, in the shape of a hundred *merchants*,
proclaiming the virtue of their wares ; one with black-
lead pencils, twelve a shilling, with an invitation to
' cut 'em and try 'em ' ; another with a good pocket-
knife, ' twelve blades and a saw, sir ' ; a third with a
tame squirrel and a piping bullfinch that could whistle
' God save the King ' and ' The White Cockade '—to be
given for an old coat. ' Buy a silver guard chain for
your vatch, sir ! ' cried a dark-eyed urchin, mounting the
fore-wheel, and holding a bunch of them in Mr. Jorrocks's
face ; ' Buy pocket-book, memorandum book ! ' whined
another. ' Keepsake—Forget-me-not—all the last year's
annuals at half-price ! ' ' Sponge cheap, sponge ! take

[1] It is a fact that such an impression prevails among many of
the *non*-writing portion of the population, and wiser men than
Mr. Jorrock's have run away with the notion.

a piece, sir,—take a piece.' 'Patent leather straps.'
'Barcelona nuts. Slippers. *Morning Hurl* (*Herald*).
Rhubarb. 'Andsome dog-collar, sir, cheap!—do to
fasten your wife up with!'

'Stand clear, ye warmints!' cries the coachman,
elbowing his way among them—and, remounting the box,
he takes the whip and reins out of Mr. Jorrocks's hands,
cries, 'All right behind? sit tight!' and off they go.

The day was fine, and the hearts of all seemed light
and gay. The coach, though slow, was clean and smart,
the harness bright and well-polished, while the sleek
brown horses poked their heads about at ease, without
the torture of the bearing-rein. The coachman, like his
vehicle, was heavy, and had he been set on all fours, a
party of six might have eat off his back. Thus they
proceeded at a good steady substantial sort of pace;
trotting on level ground, walking up hills and dragging
down inclines. Nor among the whole party was there a
murmur of discontent at the pace. Most of the passengers seemed careless which way they went, so long
as they did but move, and they rolled through the garden
of England [1] with the most stoical indifference. We
know not whether it has ever struck the reader, but the
travellers by Dover coaches are less captious about pace
than those on most others.

And now let us fancy our friends up and down
Shooter's Hill, through Dartford, Northfleet, and
Gravesend—at which latter place, the first foreign
symptom appears, in the words 'Poste aux Chevaux,'
on the door-post of the inn; and let us imagine them
bowling down Rochester Hill at a somewhat amended
pace, with the old castle, by the river Medway, the towns
of Chatham, Stroud, and Rochester full before them,
and the finely-wooded country extending round in
pleasing variety of hill and dale. As they reach the
foot of the hill, the guard commences a solo on his bugle,
to give notice to the innkeeper to have the coach dinner
on the table, all huddled together, inside and out, long

[1] Kent has long been honoured with this title—why, we are at
a loss to discover, unless it be the 'kitchen garden' for supplying
London with vegetables, etc.

passengers and short ones, they cut across the bridge, rattle along the narrow street, sparking the mud from the newly-watered streets on the shop windows and passengers on each side, and pull up at the Pig and Cross-bow, with a jerk and a dash as though they had been travelling at the rate of twelve miles an hour. Two other coaches are ' dining,' while some few passengers, whose ' hour is not yet come,' sit patiently on the roof, or pace up and down the street with short and hurried turns, anxious to see the horses brought out that are to forward them on their journey. And what a commotion this new arrival creates ! From the arched doorway of the inn issue two chamber-maids, one in curls, the other in a cap ; boots, with both curls and a cap, and a ladder in his hand ; a knock-kneed waiter, with a dirty duster, to count noses ; while the neat landlady, in a spruce black silk gown and clean white apron, stands smirking, smiling, and rubbing her hands down her sides, inveigling the passengers into the house, where she will turn them over to the waiters to take their chance the instant she gets them in. About the door the usual idlers are assembled. A coachman out of place, a beggar out at the elbows, a sergeant in uniform, and three recruits with ribbons in their hats ; a captain with his boots cut for corns, the coachman that is to drive to Dover, a youth in a straw hat and a rowing shirt, the little inquisitive old man of the place—who sees all the mid-day coaches change horses, speculates on the passengers, and sees who the parcels are for— and though last not lease, Mr. Bangup, the ' varmint ' man, the height of whose ambition is to be taken for a coachman. As the coach pulled up he was in the bar taking a glass of cold sherry ' without ' and a cigar, which latter he brings out lighted in his mouth, with his shaved white hat stuck knowingly on one side, and the thumbs of his brown hands thrust into the armholes of his waistcoat, throwing back his single-breasted fancy-buttoned green coat, and showing a cream-coloured cravat, fastened with a gold coach-and-four pin, which, with a buff waistcoat and tight drab trousers buttoning over the boot, complete his ' toggery ' as he would call it. His whiskers are large and riotous in the extreme, while his hair is clipped as close as a charity-school boy's. The coachman and he are on the best of terms, as the outward twist of their elbows and jerks of the head on meeting testify. His conversation is short and slangy, accompanied with the correct nasal twang. After standing and blowing a few puffs, during which time the passengers have all alighted, and the coachman has got through the thick of his business, he takes the cigar out of his mouth, and, spitting on the flags, addresses his friends with, ' Y've got the old near-side leader back from Joe, I see.' ' Yes, Mr. Bangup, yes,' replies his friend, ' but I had some work first—our gov'rnor was all for the change— at last, says I to our 'oss-keeper, says I, it ar'n't no use your harnessing that 'ere roan for me any more, for as how I von't drive him, so it's not to no use harnessing of him, for I von't be gammon'd out of my team not by none on them, therefore it ar'n't to never no use harnessing of him again for me.' ' So you did em,' observes Mr. Bangup. ' Lord bless ye, yes ! it warn't to no use aggravizing about it, for, says I, I *von't* stand it, so it warn't to no manner of use harnessing of him again for me.' ' Come, Smith, what are you chaffing there about ? ' inquires the landlord, coming out with the wide-spread way-bill in his hands, ' have you two insides ? ' ' No, gov'rnor I has but von, and that's precious empty, haw ! haw ! haw ! ' ' Well, but now get Brown to blow his horn early, and you help to hurry the passengers away from my grub, and maybe I'll give you your dinner for your trouble,' replies the landlord, reckoning he would save both his meat and his horses by the experiment. ' Ay, there goes the dinner ! ' added he, just as Mr. Jorrocks's voice was heard inside the Pig and Cross-bow, giving a most tremendous roar for his food. ' Pork at the top, and pork at the bottom,' the host observes to the waiter in passing, ' and *mind*, put the joints before the women—they are slow carvers.'

While the foregoing scene was enacting outside, our travellers had been driven through the passage into a little dark dingy room at the back of the house, with a dirty, rain-bespattered window, looking against a white-washed, blank wall. The table, which was covered with a thrice-used cloth, was set out with lumps of bread, knives, and two and three-pronged forks laid alternately. Altogether it was anything but inviting, but coach passengers are very complacent ; and on the Dover road it matters little if they are not. The bustle of preparation was soon over. Coats No. 1, No. 2, and No. 3 are taken off in succession, for some people wear top-coats to keep out the ' heat ' ; chins are released from their silken jeopardy, hats are hid in corners, and fur caps thrust into the pockets of the owners. Inside passengers eye outside ones with suspicion, while a deaf gentleman, who has left his trumpet in the coach, meets an acquaintance whom he has not seen for seven years, and can only shake hands and grin to the movements of the lips of the speaker. ' You find it very warm inside, I should think, sir ? ' ' Thank ye, thank ye, my good friend ; I'm *ray*ther deaf, but I presume you're inquiring after my wife and daughters—they are very well, I thank ye.' ' Where will you sit at dinner ? ' rejoins the first speaker, in hopes of a more successful hit. ' It is two years since I saw him.' ' No ; where will you sit, sir ? I said.' ' Oh, John ? I beg your pardon—I'm *ray*ther deaf—he's in Jamaica with his regiment.' ' Come, waiter, BRING DINNER ! ' roared Mr. Jorrocks, at the top of his voice, being the identical shout that was heard outside ; and presently the two dishes of pork, a couple of ducks, and a lump of half-raw, sadly-mangled, cold roast beef, with waxy potatoes and overgrown cabbages, were scattered along the table. ' What a beastly dinner ! ' exclaims an inside dandy, in a sable-collared frock— ' the whole place reeks with onions and vulgarity. Waiter, bring me a silver fork ! ' ' Allow me to *duck* you, ma'am ? ' inquires an outside passenger, in a facetious tone, of a female in a green silk cloak, as he turns the duck over in the dish. ' Thank you, sir, but I've some pork coming.' ' Will you take some of this thingum-bob ? ' turning a questionable-looking pig's countenance over in its pewter bed. ' You are in considerable

danger, my friend—you are in considerable danger,'
drawls forth the superfine insider to an outsider opposite.
' How's that ? ' inquires the former in alarm. ' Why,
you are eating with your knife, and you are in considerable danger of cutting your mouth.'—What is the matter
at the far end of the table ?—a lady in russet brown,
with a black velvet bonnet and a feather, in convulsions.
She's choking, by Jove ! hit her on the back—gently,
gently—she's swallowed a fish-bone. ' I'll lay five to
two she dies,' cried Mr. Bolus, the sporting doctor of
Sittingbourne. She coughs—up comes a couple of
tooth-picks, she having drunk off a green glass of them
in mistake.

' Now hark'e, waiter ! there's the guard blowing his
horn, and we have scarcely had a bite apiece,' cries Mr.
Jorrocks, as that functionary sounded his instrument
most energetically in the passage ; ' blow me tight, if
I stir before the half-hour's up, so he may blow till he's
black in the face.' ' Take some cheese, sir ? ' inquires
the waiter. ' No, surely not, some more pork and then
some tarts.' ' Sorry, sir, we have no tarts we can
recommend. Cheese is partiklar good.' [Enter coachman, peeled down to a more moderate-sized man.]

' Leaves ye here, if you please, sur.' ' With all my
heart, my good friend.' ' Please to remember the
coachman—driv ye thirty miles.' ' Yes, but you'll
recollect how saucy you were about my wife's bonnet-
box—there's sixpence between us for you.' ' Oh, sur !
I'm sure I didn't mean no unpurliteness. I 'opes you'll
forget it ; it was very aggravizing, certainly, but driv
ye thirty miles. 'Opes you'll give a trifle more, thirty
miles.' ' No, no, no more ; so be off.' ' Please to
remember the coachman, ma'am, thirty miles ! '
' Leaves ye here, sur, if you please ; goes no farther,
sur ; thirty miles, ma'am ; all the vay from Lunnun,
sur.'

A loud flourish on the bugle caused the remainder
of the gathering to be made in dumb show, and having
exhausted his wind the guard squeezed through the
door, and with an extremely red face, assured the
company that ' time was h'up ' and the ' coach quite

MR. JORROCKS MAKES HIS ENTREE INTO THE NEWMARKET BETTING RING

"OH GENTLEMEN! GENTLEMEN! HERE'S A LAMENTABLE OCCURRENCE!"

ready.' Then out came the purses, brown, green,
and blue, with the usual inquiry—' What's dinner,
waiter ? ' ' Two-and-six, dinner beer, three—two-and-
nine yours,' replied the knock-kneed caitiff to the first
inquirer, pushing a blue-and-white plate under his nose ;
' yours is three-and-six, ma'am ;—two glasses of brandy-
and-water, four shillings, if you please, sir—a bottle
of real Devonshire cider.'—' You must change me a
sovereign,' handing one out. ' Certainly, sir,' upon
which the waiter, giving it a loud ring upon the table,
ran out of the room. ' Now, gentlemen and ladies ;
pray, come, time's h'up—carn't wait—*must* go '—roars
the guard, as the passengers shuffle themselves into their
coats, cloaks, and cravats, and Joe ' Boots ' runs up the
passage with the ladder for the lady. ' Now, my dear
Mrs. Sprat, good-bye—God bless you, and remember
me most kindly to your husband and dear little ones—
and pray, write soon,' says an elderly lady, as she hugs
and kisses a youngish one at the door, who has been
staying with her for a week, during which time they
have quarrelled regularly every night. ' Have you all
your things, dearest ? three boxes, five parcels, an
umbrella, a parasol, the cage for Tommy's canary, and
the bundle in the red silk handkerchief—then good-bye,
my beloved, step up—and now, Mr. Guard, you know
where to set her down.' ' Good-bye, dearest Mrs.
Jackson, all right, thank you,' replies Mrs. Sprat,
stepping up the ladder, and adjusting herself in the
gammon board opposite the guard, the seat the last
comer generally gets—' but stay ! I've forgot my
reticule—it's on the drawers in the bedroom—stop,
coachman ! I say, guard ! ' ' *Carn't* wait, ma'am—
time's hup,'—and just at this moment a two-horse
coach is heard stealing up the street, upon which the
coachman calls to the horsekeepers to ' stand clear with
their cloths, and take care no one pays them twice over,'
gives a whistling hiss to his leaders, the double thong to
his wheelers, and starts off at a trot, muttering something about ' cuss'd pair-'oss coach,—convict-looking
passengers,' observing confidentially to Mr. Jorrocks,
as he turned the angle of the street, ' that he would

5

rather be hung off a long stage, than die a natural death
on a short one,' while the guard drowns the voices of the
lady who has left her reticule, and of the gentleman who
has got no change for his sovereign, in a hearty puff
of—

> ' Rule, Britannia,—Britannia, rule the waves,
>   Britons, never, never, never, shall be slaves ! '

Blithely and merrily, like all coach passengers after
feeding, our party rolled steadily along, with occasional
gibes at those they met or passed, such as telling
waggoners their linch-pins were out,—carters' mates,
there were nice pocket-knives lying on the road,—
making urchins follow the coach for miles by holding
up shillings and mock parcels, or simple equestrians
dismount in a jiffy on telling them their horses' shoes
were not all on ' before.' [1]   Towards the decline of the
day, Dover heights appeared in view, with the stately
castle guarding the channel, which, seen through the
clear atmosphere of an autumnal evening, with the
French coast conspicuous in the distance, had more the
appearance of a wide river than a branch of the sea.

The coachman mended his pace a little, as he bowled
along the gentle descents or rounded the base of some
lofty hill, and, pulling up at Lydden, took a glass of
soda-water and brandy, while four strapping greys,
with highly-polished, richly-plated harness, and holly-
hocks at their heads, were put to, to trot the last few
miles into Dover. Paying-time being near, the guard
began to do the amiable—hoped Mrs. Sprat had ridden
comfortable ; and the coachman turned to the gentleman
whose sovereign was left behind to assure him he would
bring his change the next day, and was much comforted
by the assurance that he was on his way to Italy for the
winter. As the coach approached Charlton gate, the
guard flourished his bugle and again struck up ' Rule
Britannia,' which lasted the whole breadth of the market-
place and length of Snargate Street, drawing from
Mr. Muddle's shop the few loiterers who yet remained,

---

[1] This is more of a hunting-field joke than a real one. ' Have
I all my shoes on ? ' ' They are not all on before.'

and causing Mr. Le Plastrier, the patriotic moth
impaler, to suspend the examination of the bowels of a
watch, as they rattled past his window.

At the door of the Ship Hotel, the canary-coloured
coach of Mr. Wright, the landlord, with four piebald
horses, was in waiting for him to take his evening
drive, and Mrs. Wright's pony phaeton, with a neat
tiger in a blue frock-coat and leathers, was also stationed
behind, to convey her a few miles on the London Road.
Of course the equipages of such important personages
could not be expected to move for a common stage-
coach, consequently it pulled up a few yards from the
door. It is melancholy to think that so much spirit
should have gone unrewarded, or in other words, that
Mr. Wright should have gone wrong in his affairs—Mrs.
Ramsbottom said she never understood the meaning
of the term, ' The Crown, and Bill of Rights (Wright's),'
until she went to Rochester. Many people, we doubt
not, retain a lively recollection of the ' *bill* of Wright's of
Dover.' But to our travellers.

' Now, sir ! *this* be Dover, *that* be the Ship, I be the
coachman, and we goes no farther,' observed the am-
phibious-looking coachman, in a pea-jacket and top-
boots, to Mr. Jorrocks, who still kept his seat on the box,
as if he expected, that because they booked people
' through to Paris ' at the coach-office in London, that
the vehicle crossed the channel and conveyed them on
the other side. At this intimation, Mr. Jorrocks
clambered down, and was speedily surrounded by touts
and captains of vessels soliciting his custom. ' Bon jour,
me Lor',' said a gaunt French sailor in ear-rings, and a
blue-and-white Jersey shirt, taking off a red night-cap
with mock politeness, ' you shall be cross.' ' What's
that about ? ' inquires Mr. Jorrocks—' cross ! what
does the chap mean ? ' ' Ten shillin', just, me Lor',' replied the man. ' Cross for ten shillings,' muttered Mr.
Jorrocks, ' vot *does* the Mouncheer mean ? Hope he
hasn't picked my pocket.' ' I—you—vill,' said the
sailor slowly, using his fingers to enforce his meaning,
' take to France,' pointing south, ' for ten shillin' in
my batteau, me Lor',' continued the sailor, with a

grin of satisfaction, as he saw Mr. Jorrocks began to comprehend him. 'Ah! I twig—you'll take me across the water,' said our citizen, chuckling at the idea of understanding French and being called a Lord—' for ten shillings—a half-sovereign, in fact.' 'Don't go with him, sir,' interrupted a Dutch-built English tar ; ' he's got nothing but a lousy lugger that will be all to-morrow in getting over, if it ever gets at all ; and the *Royal George*, superb steamer, sails with a king's messenger and despatches for all the foreign courts at half-past ten, and must be across by twelve, whether it can or not.' 'Please take a card for the *Brocklebank*— quickest steamer out of Dover—winds made expressly to suit her, and she can beat the *Royal George* like winking. Passengers never sick in the most uproarious weather,' cried another tout, running the corner of his card into Mr. Jorrocks's eye to engage his attention. Then came the captain of the French mail-packet, who was dressed much like a new policeman, with an em- broidered collar to his coat, and a broad red band round a forage-cap which he raised with great politeness, as he entreated Mr. Jorrocks's patronage of his high-pressure engine, 'vich had beat a balloon, and vod take him for half less than noting.' A crowd collected, in the centre of which stood Mr. Jorrocks perfectly unmoved, with his wig awry and his carpet-bag under his arm. 'Gentlemen,' said he, extending his right hand, 'you seem to me to be desperately civil—your *pur*liteness appears to know no bounds—but, to be candid with you, I beg to say that whoever will carry me across the herring pond *cheapest* shall have my custom, so now begin and bid downwards.' 'Nine shillings,' said an Englishman, directly—' eight,' replied a Frenchman— ' seven-and-sixpence '—' seven shillings '—' six-and-six- pence '—' six shillings '—' five-and-sixpence ' ; at last it came down to five shillings, at which there were two bidders, the French captain and the tout of the *Royal George*,—and Mr. Jorrocks, like a true-born Briton, promised his patronage to the latter, at which the French- men shrugged up their shoulders and burst out a laugh- ing, one calling him 'my Lor' Rosbif,' and the other

'Monsieur God-dem,' as they walked off in search of other victims.

None but the natives of Dover can tell what the weather is, unless the wind comes directly off the sea, and it was not until Mr. Jorrocks proceeded to embark, after breakfast the next morning, that he ascertained there was a heavy swell on, so quiet had the heights kept the gambols of Boreas.   Three steamers were simmering into action on the London Hotel side of the harbour, in one of which—the *Royal George*—two britchkas and a barouche were lashed ready for sea, while the custom-house porters were trundling barrows full of luggage under the personal superintendence of a little shock-headed French commissionnaire of Mr. Wright's in a gold-laced cap, and the other gentry of the same pro-fession from the different inns.   As the *Royal George* lay nearly level with the quay, Mr. Jorrocks stepped on board without troubling himself to risk his shins among the steps of a ladder that was considerately thrust into the place of embarkation ; and as soon as he set foot upon deck, of course he was besieged by the usual myriad of landsharks.   First came Monsieur the com-missionnaire with his book, out of which he enumerated two portmanteaus and two carpet-bags, for each of which he made a specific charge, leaving his own gratuity optional with his employer ; then came Mr. Boots to ask for something for showing them the way ; after him the porter of the inn for carrying their cloaks and great-coats, all of which Mr. Jorrocks submitted to, most philosophically, but when the interpreter of the deaf-and-dumb ladderman *demanded* something for the use of the ladder, his indignation got the better of him, and he exclaimed, loud enough to be heard by all on deck, ' Surely you wouldn't charge a man for what he has not enjoyed ! '

A voyage is to many people like taking an emetic—they look at the medicine and wish it well over, and look at the sea and wish *themselves* well over.   Every-thing looked bright and gay at Dover—the cliff seemed whiter than ever—the sailors had on clean trousers, and the few people that appeared in the streets were dressed in their Sunday best. The cart-horses were seen feeding leisurely on the hills, and there was a placid calmness about everything on shore, which the travellers would fain have extended to the sea. They came slowly and solemnly upon deck, muffled up in cloaks and coats, some with their passage-money in their hands, and took their places apparently with the full expectation of being sick.

The French packet-boat first gave symptoms of animation, in the shape of a few vigorous puffs from the boiler, which were responded to by the *Royal George*, whose rope was slipped without the usual tinkle of the bell, and she shot out to sea, closely followed by the Frenchman, who was succeeded by the other English boat. Three or four tremendous long protracted dives, each followed by a majestic rise on the bosom of the waves, denoted the crossing of the bar ; and just as the creaking of the cordage, the flapping of the sails, and the nervous quivering of the paddles, as they lost their hold of the water, were in full vigour, the mate crossed the deck with a large white basin in his hand, the sight of which turned the stomachs of half the passengers. Who shall describe the misery that ensued ? The groans and moans of the sufferers increasing every minute, as the vessel heaved and dived, and rolled and creaked, while hand-basins multiplied as half-sick passengers caught the green countenance and fixed eye of some prostrate sufferer, and were overcome themselves.

Mr. Jorrocks, what with his Margate trips and a most substantial breakfast of beef-steaks and porter, tea, eggs, muffins, prawns, and fried ham, held out as long as anybody—indeed, at one time the odds were that he would not be sick at all ; and he kept walking up and down deck like a true British tar. In one of his turns he was observed to make a full stop.—Immediately before the boiler, his eye caught a cadaverous-looking countenance that rose between the top of a blue camlet cloak and the bottom of a green travelling-cap, with a large patent-leather peak ; he was certain that he knew it, and, somehow or other, he thought not favourably. The passenger was in that happy

mood just debating whether he should hold out against
sickness any longer or resign himself unreservedly to its
horrors, when Mr. Jorrocks's eye encountered his, and
the meeting did not appear to contribute to his happiness. Mr. Jorrocks paused and looked at him steadily
for some seconds, during which time his thoughts made
a rapid cast over his memory. ‘ *Sergeant Bumptious*, by
gum ! ’ exclaimed he, giving his thigh a hearty slap, as
the deeply-indented pockmarks on the learned gentleman’s face betrayed his identity. ‘ Sergeant,’ said he,
going up to him, ‘ I’m werry ’appy to see ye—maybe in
the course of your practice at Croydon you’ve heard
that there are more times than one to catch a thief.’
‘ Who are you ? ’ inquired the sergeant with a growl,
just at which moment the boat gave a roll, and he
wound up the inquiry by a donation to the fishes.
‘ Who am I ? ’ replied Mr. Jorrocks as soon as he was
done, ‘ I’ll soon tell ye that—I’m Mr. JORROCKS !—
Jorrocks *wersus* Cheetum, in fact—and now that you
have got your bullying toggery off, I’ll be ’appy to fight
ye either by land or sea.’
   ‘ Oh-h-h-h ! ’ groaned the sergeant at the mention
of the latter word, and thereupon he put his head over
the boat and paid his second subscription. Mr. Jorrocks
stood eyeing him, and when the sergeant recovered,
he observed with apparent mildness and compassion,
‘ Now, my dear sergeant, to show ye that I can return
good for evil, allow me to fatch you a nice ’ot mutton-
chop ! ’ ‘ *Oh-h-h-h-h !* ’ groaned the sergeant, as though
he would die. ‘ Or perhaps you’d prefer a cut of boiled
beef with yellow fat, and a dab of cabbage ? ’ an altern-
ative which was too powerful for the worthy citizen
himself—for, like Sterne with his captive, he had drawn
a picture that his own imagination could not sustain—
and, in attempting to reach the side of the boat, he
cascaded over the sergeant, and they rolled over each
other, senseless and helpless, upon deck.
   ‘ Mew, mew,’ screamed the sea-gulls ;—‘ creak, creak,’
went the cordage ;—‘ flop, flop,’ went the sails ; round
went the white basins, and the steward with the mop ;
and few passengers would have cared to have gone

overboard, when at the end of three hours' misery, the
captain proclaimed that they were running into still
water off Boulogne. This intimation was followed by
the collection of the passage-money by the mate, and
the jingling of a tin box by the steward, under the
noses of the party, for perquisites for the crew.   Jorrocks
and the sergeant lay together like babes in the wood until
they were roused by this operation, when, with a parting
growl at his companion, Mr. Jorrocks got up ; and
though he had an idea in his own mind that a man had
better live abroad all his life than encounter such misery
as he had undergone, for the purpose of returning to
England, he recollected his intended work upon France,
and began to make his observations upon the town of
Boulogne, towards which the vessel was rapidly steaming. ' Not half so fine as Margate,' said he ; ' the
houses seem all afraid of the sea, and turn their ends
to it instead of fronting it, except yon great white
place which I suppose is the baths ' ; and, taking his
hunting telescope out of his pocket, he stuck out his
legs and prepared to make an observation. ' How the
people are swarming down to see us ! ' he exclaimed.
' I see such a load of petticoats—glad Mrs. J. an't with
us ; may have some fun here, I guess. Dear me, wot
lovely women ! wot ankles ! beat the English, hollow—
would give something to be a single man ! '   While he
made these remarks, the boat ran up the harbour in
good style, to the evident gratification of the multitude
who lined the pier from end to end, and followed her in
her passage. ' Ease her ! stop her ! ' at last cried the
Captain, as she got opposite a low wooden guard-house,
midway down the port.   A few strokes of the paddles
sent her up to the quay, some ropes were run from
each end of the guard-house down to the boat, within
which space no one was admitted except about a dozen
soldiers or custom-house officers—in green coats, white
trousers, black sugar-loaf ' caps,' and having swords by
their sides—and some thick-legged fisherwomen, with
long gold ear-rings, to lower the ladder for disembarkation.   The idlers, that is to say, all the inhabitants of
Boulogne, range themselves outside the ropes, on foot,

horseback, in carriages, or anyhow, to take the chance
of seeing some one they know, to laugh at the melancholy looks of those who have been sick, and to criticize
the company, who are turned into the guarded space
like a flock of sheep before them.

Mr. Jorrocks, having scaled the ladder, gave himself
a hearty and congratulatory shake on again finding himself on *terra firma*, and, sticking his hat jauntily on one
side, as though he didn't know what sea-sickness was,
proceeded to run his eye along the spectators on one
side of the ropes ; when presently he was heard to
exclaim, ' My vig, there's Thompson ! He owes us a
hundred pounds, and has been doing these three years.'
And thereupon he bolted up to a fine-looking young
fellow—with mustachios, in a hussar foraging-cap
stuck on one side of his head, dressed in a black velvet
shooting-jacket, and with half a jeweller's shop about
him in the way of chains, brooches, rings, and buttons
—who had brought a good-looking bay-horse to bear
with his chest against the cords.   ' Thompson,' said Mr.
Jorrocks, in a firm tone of voice, ' how are you ? ' ' How
do ye do, *Mister* Jorrocks,' drawled out the latter, taking
a cigar from his mouth, and puffing a cloud of smoke over
the grocer's head.   ' Well, I'm werry well, but I should
like to have a few moments' conversation with you.'
' Would ye ? ' said Thompson, blowing another cloud.
' Yes, I would ; you remember that 'ere little bill you
got Simpkins to discount for you one day when I was
absent ; we have had it by us a long time now, and
it is about time you were taking it up.'   ' You think
so, do you, Mister Jorrocks ; can't you renew it ? I'll
give you a draft on Aldgate pump for the amount.'
' Come, none of your funning with me, I've had enough
of your nonsense ; give me my pewter, or I'll have that
horse from under you ; for though it has got the hair
rubbed off its near knee, it will do werry well to carry
me with the Surrey occasionally.'   ' You old fool,' said
Thompson, ' you forget where you are ; if I could pay
your little bill, do you suppose I would be here ? You
can't squeeze blood out of a turnip, can ye ? But I'll
tell you what, my covey, if I can't give you satisfaction
5*

in money, you shall give me the satisfaction of a gentleman if you don't take care what you are about, you
old tinker. By Jove, I'll order pistols and coffee for
two to-morrow morning at Napoleon's column, and let
the daylight through your carcass, if you utter another
syllable about the bill. Why, now, you stare as Balaam
did at his ass, when he found it capable of holding an
argument with him.'

And, true enough, Jorrocks was dumbfoundered at
this sort of reply from a creditor, it not being at all
in accordance with the 'Lex mercatoria,' or law of
merchants, and quite unknown on 'Change. Before,
however, he had time to recover his surprise, all the
passengers having entered the roped area, one of the
green-coated gentry gave him a polite twist by the
coat-tail, and with a wave of the hand and bend of his
body, beckoned him to proceed with the crowd into
the guard-house. After passing an outer room, they
entered the bureau by a door in the middle of a wooden
partition, where two men were sitting with pens ready
to enter the names of the arrivers in ledgers.

'Votre nom et désignation?' said one of them to
Mr. Jorrocks—who, with a bad start, had managed to
squeeze in first—to which Mr. Jorrocks shook his head.
'Sare, what's your name, sare?' inquired the same
personage. 'JORROCKS,' was the answer, delivered
with great emphasis, and thereupon the secretary wrote
'Shorrock.'—'Monsieur Shorrock,' said he, looking
up, 'votre profession, Monsieur? Vot you are, sir?'
'A grocer,' replied Mr. Jorrocks, which caused a titter
from those behind who meant to sink the shop. 'Mar-
chand-Epicier,' wrote the bureau-keeper. 'Quel âge
avez-vous, Monsieur? How old you are, sare?' 'Two
pound twelve,' replied Mr. Jorrocks, surprised at his
inquisitiveness. 'No, sare, not vot monnay you have,
sare, bot how old you are, sare?' 'Well, two pound
twelve, fifty-two in fact.' Mr. Jorrocks was then
passed out, to take his chance among the touts and
commissionnaires of the various hotels, who are enough
to pull passengers to pieces in their solicitations for
custom. In Boulogne, however, no man with money

is ever short of friends ; and Thompson having given
the hint to two or three acquaintances as he rode up
street, there were no end of broken-down sportsmen,
levanters, and gentlemen who live on the interest of
what they owe other people, waiting to receive Mr.
Jorrocks. The greetings on their parts were most
cordial and enthusiastic, and even some who were in his
books did not hesitate to hail him ; the majority of the
party, however, was composed of those with whom he
had at various times and places enjoyed the sports of
the field, but whom he had never missed until they met
at Boulogne.

Their inquiries were business-like and familiar !—
' How are ye, Jorrocks ? ' cried one, holding out both
hands ; ' How are ye, my lad of wax ? Do you still play
billiards ?—Give you nine, and play you for a Nap.'
' Come to my house this evening, old boy, and take a
hand at whist for old acquaintance' sake,' urged the
friend on his left ; ' got some rare cognac, and a box
of beautiful Havannahs.' ' No, Jorrocks, — dine with
me,' said a third, ' and play chicken-hazard.' ' *Don't*,'
said a fourth, confidentially, ' he'll fleece ye like fun.'
' Let me put your name down to our Pigeon Club ; only
a guinea entrance and a guinea subscription—nothing
to a rich man like you.' ' Have you any coin to lend
on unexceptionable personal security, with a power of
killing and selling your man if he don't pay ? ' inquired
another. ' Are they going to abolish the law of arrest ?
'twould be very convenient if they did.' ' Will you
discount me a bill at three months ? ' ' Is B— out of
the Bench yet ? ' ' Who do they call Nodding Homer
in your hunt ? ' ' O gentlemen, gentlemen ! ' cried
Mr. Jorrocks, ' go it gently, go it gently ! Consider
the day is 'ot, I'm almost out of breath, and faint for
want of food. I've come all the way from Angletear,
as we say in France, and lost my breakfast on the
woyage. Where is there an inn where I can recruit
my famished frame ? What's this ? ' looking up at a
sign, ' " *Done a boar in a manger*," what does this mean ?
—where's my French dictionary ? I've heard that
boar is very good to eat.' ' Yes, but this *boar* is to

drink,' said a friend on the right ; ' but you must not put up at a house of that sort ; come to the Hôtel d'Orléans, where all the *best* fellows and men of consequence go, a celebrated house in the days of the Boulogne Hunt. Ah, that was the time, Mr. Jorrocks ! we lived liked fighting-cocks then ; you should have been among us, such a rollicking set of dogs ! could hunt all day, race maggots and drink claret all night, and take an occasional by-day with the hounds on a Sunday. Can't do that with the Surrey, I guess. There's the Hôtel d'Orléans,' pointing to it as they turned the corner of the street ; ' splendid house it is. I've no interest in taking you there, don't suppose so ; but the sun of its greatness is fast setting—there's no such shaking of elbows as there used to be—the I O U system knocked that up. Still, you'll be very comfortable ; a bit of carpet by your bedside, curtains to your windows, a pie-dish to wash in, a clean towel every third day, and as many friends to dine with you as ever you like—no want of company in Boulogne, I assure you. Here, Mr. W.,' addressing the innkeeper who appeared at the door, ' this is the very celebrated Mr. Jorrocks, of whom we have all heard so much,—take him and use him as you would your own son ; and, hark ye (aside), *don't forget I brought him.*'

' Gar*soon*,' said Jorrocks, after having composed himself a little, during which time he was also composing a French speech from his dictionary and Madame de Genlis's [1] *Manuel du Voyageur* ; ' A che hora [ora] si pranza ? ' looking at the waiter, who seemed astonished. ' Oh, stop ! ' said he, looking again, ' *that's* Italian— I've got hold of the wrong column. ' A quelle heure *dine* '—hang me if I know how to call this chap—*dine* [spelling it], t'on ? ' ' What were you wishing to say, sir ? ' inquired the waiter, interrupting his display of

---

[1] For the benefit of our ' tarry-at-home ' readers, we should premise that Madame de Genlis's work is arranged for the convenience of travellers who do not speak any language but their own ; and it consists of dialogues on different necessary subjects, with French and Italian translations opposite the English.

the language. ' Wot, do you speak English ? ' asked
Jorrocks in amazement. ' I hope so, sir,' replied the
man, ' for I'm an Englishman.' ' Then why the devil
did you not say so, you great lout, instead of putting
me into a sweat this 'ot day by speaking French to you ? '
' Beg pardon, sir, thought *you* were a Frenchman.'
' Did you, indeed ? ' said Jorrocks, delighted ; ' then,
by Jove, I *do* speak French ! Somehow or other I
thought I could, as I came over. Bring me a thundering beaf-steak, and a pint of stout, directly ! ' The
Hôtel d'Orléans being a regular roast-beef and plum-
pudding sort of house, Mr. Jorrocks speedily had an
immense strip of tough beef and boiled potatoes placed
before him, in the well-windowed ' *Salle à manger* ' ;
and the day being fine, he regaled himself at a table at
an open window, whereby he saw the smart passers-by,
and let them view him in return.

Sunday is a gay day in France, and Boulogne equals
the best town in smartness. The shops are better set
out, the women are better dressed, and there is a holiday
brightness and air of pleasure on every countenance.
Then instead of seeing a sulky husband trudging behind
a pouting wife with a child in her arms, an infallible sign
of a Sunday evening in England, they trip away to the
rural *fête champêtre*, where with dancing, lemonade, and
love, they pass away the night in temperate if not
innocent hilarity. ' Happy people ! that once a week
at least, lay down their cares, and dance and sing, and
sport away the weights of grievance, which bow down
the spirit of other nations to the earth.'

The voyage, though short, commenced a new era
in Mr. Jorrocks's life, and he entirely forgot all about
Sunday and Dover dulness the moment he set foot on
sprightly France, and he no more recollected it was
Sunday, than if such a day had ceased to exist in the
calendar. Having bolted his steak, he gave his Hessians
their usual flop with his handkerchief, combed his
whiskers, pulled his wig straight, and sallied forth,
dictionary in hand, to translate the signs, admire the
clever little children *talking French*, quiz the horses, and
laugh at everything he didn't understand ; to spend

his first afternoon, in short, as nine-tenths of the English who ' go abroad ' are in the habit of doing.

Early the next morning, Mr. Jorrocks and the York-shireman, accompanied by the commissionnaire of the Hôtel d'Orléans, repaired to the upper town, for the purpose of obtaining passports, and as they ascended the steep street called La Grande Rue, which connects the two towns, they held a consultation as to what the former should be described. A ' Marchand Epicier ' would obtain Mr. Jorrocks no respect, but, then, he objected to the word ' Rentier.' ' What is the French for fox-'unter ? ' said he, after a thoughtful pause, turning to his dictionary. There was no such word. ' Sportsman, then ? Aye, Chasseur ! How would that read ? John Jorrocks, Esq., Chasseur,—not *bad*, I think,' said he. ' That will *do*,' replied the Yorkshire-man, ' but you must sink the Esquire now, and tack " Monsieur " before your name, and a very pretty, euphonious sound " Monsieur Jorrocks " will have ; and when you hear some of the little Parisian grisettes lisp it out as you turn the garters over on their counters, while they turn their dark flashing eyes over upon you, it will be enough to rejuvenate your old frame. But suppose we add to " Chasseur "—" Member of the Surrey Hunt " ? ' ' By all means,' replied Mr. Jorrocks, de-lighted at the idea, and ascending the stairs of the Consulate three steps at a time.

The Consul, Mons. De Horter, was in attendance, sitting in state, with a gendarme at the door and his secretary at his elbow. ' Bon jour, Monsieur,' said he, bowing, as Mr. Jorrocks passed through the lofty folding-door ; to which our traveller replied, ' The top of the morning to you, sir,' thinking something of that sort would be right. The Consul, having scanned him through his green spectacles, drew a large sheet of thin printed paper from his portfolio, with the arms of France placed under a great petticoat at the top, and proceeded to fill up a request from His Most Christian Majesty to all the authorities, both civil and military, of France, and also of all the allied ' pays,' ' de laisser libre-ment passer,' Monsieur John Jorrocks, Chasseur and member of the *Hont* de Surrey, and plusieurs other *Honts* ; and also, Monsieur Stubbs, native of Angleterre, going from Boulogne to Paris, and to give them aid and protection, ' en cas de besoin,' all of which Mr. Jorrocks—like many travellers before him—construed into a most flattering compliment and mark of respect, from His Most Christian Majesty to himself.

Under the word ' signalement ' in the margin, the Consul also drew the following sketch of our hero, in order, as Mr. Jorrocks supposed, that the King of the Mouncheers might know him when he saw him.

> ' Age de 52 ans
> Taille d'un metre 62 centimetres
> Perruque brun
> Front large
> Yeux gris-sanguin
> Nez moyen
> Barbe grisâtre
> Visage ronde
> Teint rouge.'

He then handed it over to Mr. Jorrocks for his signature, who, observing the words, ' Signature du Porteur ' at the bottom, passed it on to the porter of the inn, until put right by the Consul, who, on receiving his fee, bowed him out with great politeness.

Great as had been the grocer's astonishment at the horses and carts that he had seen stirring about the streets, his amazement knew no bounds when the first Paris diligence came rolling into town with six horses, spreading over the streets as they swung about in all directions — covered with bells, sheep-skins, worsted balls, and foxes' brushes, driven by one solitary postilion on the off-wheeler. ' My vig,' cried he, ' here's Wombwell's wild-beast show ! What the deuce are *they* doing in France ? I've not heard of them since last Bartlemy fair, when I took my brother Joe's children to see them fed. But stop—this is full of men ! My eyes, so it is. It's what young Dutch Sam would call a *male* coach, because there are no females about it. Well, I declare, I am almost sorry I did not bring Mrs. J. Wot would they think to see such a concern in Cheapside ? Why,

it holds half a township—a perfect willage on wheels.
My eyes, wot a curiosity ! Well, I never thought to
live to see such a sight as this !—wish it was going our
way that I might have a ride in it. Hope ours will be
as big.' Shortly after theirs did arrive, and Mr. Jorrocks
was like a perfect child with delight. It was not a *male*
coach, however, for in the different compartments were
five or six ladies. ' Oh, wot elegant creatures,' cried he,
eyeing them ; ' I could ride to Jerusalem with them
without being tired ; wot a thing it is to be a bachelor ! '

The conducteur—with the usual frogged, tagged,
embroidered jacket, and fur-bound cap—having hoisted
their luggage on high, the passengers who had turned
out of their respective compartments to stretch their
legs after their cramping from Calais, proceeded to
resume their places. There were only two seats vacant
in the interior, or, as Mr. Jorrocks called it, the ' middle
house,' consequently the Yorkshireman and he crossed
legs. The other four passengers had corner seats,
things much coveted by French travellers. On Mr.
Stubbs's right sat an immense Englishman, enveloped
in a dark blue camlet cloak, fastened with bronze lion-
head clasps, a red neckcloth, and a shabby, napless,
broad-brimmed, brown hat. His face was large, round,
and red, without an atom of expression, and his little
pig eyes twinkled over a sort of a mark that denoted
where his nose should have been ; in short, his head
was more like a barber's wig-block than anything else,
and his outline would have formed a model of the dome
of St. Paul's. On the Yorkshireman's left was a chatter-
ing young red-trousered dragoon, in a frock-coat and
flat foraging cap with a flying tassel. Mr. Jorrocks
was more fortunate than his friend, and rubbed sides
with two women ; one was English, either an upper
nursery-maid or an under-governess, but who might
be safely trusted to travel by herself. She was dressed
in a black beaver bonnet lined with scarlet silk, a
nankeen pelisse with a blue ribbon, and pea-green boots,
and she carried a sort of small fish-basket on her knee,
with a ' *plain* Christian's prayer-book ' on the top.
The other was French, approaching to middle age, with

a nice smart plump figure, good hazel-coloured eyes, a beautiful foot and ankle, and very well dressed. Indeed, her dress very materially reduced the appearance of her age, and she was what the milliners would call remarkably well ' got up.' Her bonnet was a pink satin, with a white blonde *ruche* surmounted by a rich blonde veil, with a white rose placed elegantly on one side, and her glossy auburn hair pressed down the sides of a milk-white forehead, in the Madonna style. Her pelisse was of ' violet-des-bois ' figured silk, worn with a black velvet pelerine and a handsomely-embroidered collar. Her boots were of a colour to match the pelisse ; and a massive gold chain round her neck, and a solitary pearl ring on a middle finger, were all the jewellery she displayed. Mr. Jorrocks caught a glimpse of her foot and ankle as she mounted the steps to resume her place in the diligence ; and, pushing the Yorkshireman aside, he bundled in directly after her, and took up the place we have described.

The vehicle was soon in motion, and its ponderous roll enchanted the heart of the grocer. Independently of the novelty, he was in a humour to be pleased, and everything with him was *couleur de rose*. Not so the Yorkshireman's right-hand neighbour, who lounged in the corner, muffled up in his cloak, muttering and cursing at every jolt of the diligence, as it bumped across the gutters and jolted along the streets of Boulogne. At length, having got off the pavement, after crushing along at a trot through the soft road that immediately succeeds, they reached the little hill near Mr. Gooseman's farm, and the horses gradually relaxed into a walk, when he burst forth with a tremendous oath, swearing that he had ' travelled three hundred thousand miles, and never saw horses walk up such a bit of a bank before.' He looked round the diligence in the expectation of someone joining him, but no one deigned a reply, so, with a growl and a jerk of his shoulders, he again threw himself into his corner. The dragoon and the French lady then began narrating the histories of their lives, as the French people always do, and Mr. Jorrocks and the Yorkshireman sat looking at each other. At length

Mr. Jorrocks, pulling his dictionary and Madame de Genlis out of his pocket, observed, ' I quite forgot to ask the guard at what time we dine—a most important consideration, for I hold it unfair to take one's stomach by surprise, and a man should have due notice, that he may tune his appetite accordingly. I have always thought that there's as much dexterity required to bring an appetite to table in the full bloom of perfection, as there is in training an 'oss to run on a particular day. Let me see,' added he, turning over the pages of De Genlis—' it will be under the head of eating and drinking, I suppose.—Here it is—(opens and reads)—" I have a good appetite—I am hungry—I am werry hungry—I am almost starved "—that won't do—" I have eaten enough "—that won't do either—" To breakfast "—no. But here it is, by Jingo—" Dialogue before dinner "— capital book for us travellers, this Mrs. de Genlis—(reads) " Pray take dinner with us to-day, I shall give you plain fare."—That means rough and enough, I suppose,' observed Mr. Jorrocks to the Yorkshireman. ' " What time do we dine to-day ? French : A quelle heure dinons-nous aujourd'hui ?—Italian : A che hora (ora) si prancey (pranza) oggi ? " ' ' Ah, Monsieur, vous parlez Français à merveille,' said the French lady, smiling with the greatest good nature upon him. ' A marble ! ' said Mr. Jorrocks, ' wot does that mean ? ' preparing to look it out in the dictionary. ' Ah, Monsieur, I shall you explain—you speak French like a natif.' ' Indeed ! ' said Mr. Jorrocks, with a bow, ' I feel werry proud of your praise ; and your English is quite delightful. By Jove,' said he to the Yorkshireman, with a most self-satisfied grin, ' you were right in what you told me about the gals calling me *Monsieur*. I declare she's driven right home to my 'art—transfixed me at once, in fact.'

Every one who has done a little ' voyaging,' as they call it in France, knows that a few miles to the south of Samer rises a very steep hill, across which the route lies, and that diligence travellers are generally invited to walk up to it. A path which strikes off near the foot of the hill, across the open, cuts off the angle, and—

diligences being anything but what the name would
imply—the passengers, by availing themselves of the
short cut, have ample time for striking up confabs, and
inquiring into the comforts of the occupiers of the various
compartments. Our friends of the 'interior' were all
busy jabbering and talking—some with their tongues,
others with their hands and tongues—with the exception
of the monster in the cloak, who sat like a sack in the
corner, until the horses, having reached the well-known
breathing-place, made a dead halt, and the conducteur
proceeded to invite the party to descend and ' promenade'
up the hill. ' What's happened now ? ' cried the monster,
jumping up as the door opened ; ' surely they don't
expect us to walk up this mountain ; I've travelled
three hundred thousand miles, and was never asked to
do such a thing in all my life before. *I won't do it ;* I
paid for riding, and ride I will. You are all a set of
infamous cheats,' said he to the conducteur in good plain
English ; but the conducteur, not understanding the
language, shut the door as soon as all the rest were out,
and let him roll on by himself. Jorrocks stuck to his
woman, who had a negro boy in the rotonde, dressed
in baggy slate-coloured trousers, with a green waistcoat
and a blue coat, with a coronet on the button, who came
to hand her out, and was addressed by the heroic name
of ' Agamemnon.' Jorrocks got a glimpse of the button,
but, not understanding foreign coronets, thought it
was a crest ; nevertheless, he thought he might as well
inquire who his friend was, so, slinking back as they
reached the foot of the hill, he got hold of the nigger, and
asked what they called his missis. Massa did not understand, and Mr. Jorrocks, sorely puzzled how to explain,
again had recourse to the *Manual du Voyageur* ; but
Madame de Genlis had not anticipated such an occur-
rence, and there was no dialogue adapted to his situation.
There was a conversation with a lacquey, however,
commencing with—' Are you disposed to enter into my
service ? ' and, in the hopes of hitting upon something
that would convey his wishes, he ' hark'd forward,' and
passing by—' Are you married ? ' arrived at—' What
is your wife's occupation ? ' ' Que fait votre femme ? '

said he, suiting the action to the word, and pointing to
Madame. Agamemnon showed his ivories, as he laughed
at the idea of Jorrocks calling his mistress his wife, and
by signs and words conveyed to him some idea of the
importance of the personage to whom he alluded. This
he did most completely, for before the diligence came
up, Jorrocks pulled the Yorkshireman aside, and asked
if he was aware that they were travelling with a real
live Countess ; ' Madame la Countess Ben*wolio*, the
nigger informs me,' said he ; ' a werry *grande femme*,
though what that means I don't know.' ' Oh, countesses
are common enough here,' replied the Yorkshireman.
' I dare say she's a stay-maker. I remember a paint-maker
who had a German Baron for a colour-grinder once.'
' Oh,' said Jorrocks, ' you are jealous—you always try
to run down my *friends* : but that won't do, I'm wide
awake to your tricks ' ; so saying, he shuffled off, and,
getting hold of the Countess, helped Agamemnon to
hoist her into the diligence. He was most insinuating
for the next two hours, and jabbered about love and
fox-hunting, admiring the fine, flat, open country, and
the absence of hedges and flints ; but as neither youth
nor age can subsist on love alone, his confounded appetite
began to trouble him, and got quite the better of him
before they reached Abbeville. Every mile seemed
a league, and he had his head out of the window at least
twenty times before they came in sight of the town.
At length the diligence got its slow length dragged not
only to Abbeville, but to the sign of the ' Fidèle Berger,'
—or ' Fiddle Burgur,' as Mr. Jorrocks pronounced it—
where they were to dine. The door being opened, out
he jumped, and with his *Manual du Voyageur* in one
hand, and the Countess Ben*wolio* in the other, he pushed
his way through the crowd of ' pauvres misérables '
congregated under the gateway, who exhibited every
species of disease and infirmity that poor human nature
is liable or heir to, and entered the hotel. The *Sally
Manger*, as he called it, was a long brick-floored room
on the basement, with a white stove at one end, and the
walls plentifully decorated with a panoramic view of
the *Grand Nation* walloping the Spaniards at the siege

of Saragossa. The diligence being a *leetle* behind time
as usual, the soup was on the table when they entered.
The passengers quickly ranged themselves round, and,
with his mouth watering as the female *garçon* lifted the
cover from the tureen, Mr. Jorrocks sat in the expectation of seeing the rich contents ladled into the plates.
His countenance fell fifty per cent. as the first spoonful
passed before his eyes,—' My vig, why, it's water ! '
exclaimed he—' water, I do declare, with worms [1] in
it—I can't eat such stuff as that—it's not man's meat
—oh dear, oh dear, I fear I've made a terrible mistake
in coming to France ! Never saw such stuff as this at
Bleaden's or Birch's, or anywhere in the city.' ' I've
travelled three hundred thousand miles,' said the fat
man, sending his plate from him in disgust, ' and never
tasted such a mess as this before.' ' I'll show them up
in *Bell's Life*,' cried Mr. Jorrocks ; ' and, look what stuff
is here—beef boiled to rags !—well, I never, *no never*,
saw anything like this before. Oh, I wish I was in Great
Coram Street again !—I'm sure I can't live here—I
wonder if I could get a return chaise—waiter—gar*soon*
—cuss ! Oh dear ! I see Madame de Genlis is of no use
in a pinch—and yet what a dialogue here is ! O Heavens !
grant your poor Jorrocks but one request, and that is
the contents of a single sentence. ' I want a roasted
or boiled leg of mutton, beef, hung beef, a quarter of
mutton, mutton chops, veal cutlets, stuffed tongue,
dried tongue, hog's pudding, white sausage, meat sausage,
chicken with rice, a nice fat roast fowl, roast chicken
with cressy, roast or boiled pigeon, a fricassee of chicken,
sweetbread, goose, lamb, calf's cheek, calf's head, fresh
pork, salt pork, cold meat, hash.—But where's the use
of titivating one's appetite with reading of such luxteries ?
Oh, what a wife Madame de Genlis would have made
for me ! Oh dear, oh dear, I shall die of hunger, I see—
I shall die of *absolute* famine—my stomach thinks my
throat's cut already ! ' In the height of his distress in
came two turkeys and a couple of fowls, and his countenance shone forth like an April sun after a shower.
' Come, this is better,' said he ; ' I'll trouble you, sir,

[1] Macaroni soup.

for a leg and a wing, and a bit of the breast, for I'm really
famished—oh hang! the fellow's a Frenchman, and I
shall lose half the day in looking it out in my dictionary.
Oh dear, oh dear, where's the dinner dialogue!—well,
here's something to the purpose. " I will send you a
bit of this fowl." " A little bit of the fowl cannot hurt
you."—No, nor a great bit either.—" Which do you
like best, a leg or a wing ? " " *Qu'aimez-vous le mieux, la
cuisse ou l'aile ?* " ' Here the Countess Benvolio, who
had been playing a good knife and fork herself, pricked
up her ears, and, guessing at Jorrocks's wants, inter-
ceded with her countryman, and got him a plateful of
fowl. It was soon disposed of, however, and half a dish
of hashed hare or cat, that was placed within reach of
him shortly after, was quickly transferred into his plate.
A French dinner is admirably calculated for leading the
appetite on by easy stages to the grand consummation
of satiety. It begins meagrely, as we have shown, and
proceeds gradually through the various gradations of
lights, savories, solids, and substantials. Presently there
was a large dish of stewed eels put on. ' What's that ? '
asked Jorrocks of the man. ' Poisson,' was the reply.
' *Poison !* why, you infidel, have you no conscience ? '
' *Fishe,*' said the Countess. ' Oh, aye, I smell—eels—
just like what we have at the Eel-pie house at Twicken-
ham—your ladyship, I am thirsty—*ge* soif, in fact.' ' Ah,
bon ! ' said the Countess, laughing, and giving him a
tumbler of claret. ' I've travelled three hundred thousand miles,' said the fat man, ' and never saw claret
drunk in that way before.' ' It's not werry good, I
think,' said Mr. Jorrocks, smacking his lips ; ' if it was
not claret, I would sooner drink port.' Some wild ducks
and *fricandeau de veau* which followed were cut up and
handed round, Jorrocks helping himself plentifully to
both, as also to *pommes de terre à la maître d'hôtel* and
bread at discretion. ' Faith, but this is not a bad dinner
after all's said and done, when one gets fairly into it.'
' Fear it will be very expensive,' [1] observed the fat man.
Just when Jorrocks began to think he had satisfied
nature, in came a roast leg of mutton, a beef-steak, ' à

[1] The Rochester dinner and this were exactly the same price.

la G—d-dam,' [1] and a dish of larks and snipes. ' Must
have another tumbler of wine before I can grapple with
these chaps,' said he, eyeing them, and looking into
Madame de Genlis's book : ' " Gar*soon*, donnez-moi un
verre de vin," ' holding up the book and pointing to
the sentence. He again set to, and ' went a good one '
at both mutton and snipes, but on pulling up he appeared
somewhat exhausted. He had not got through it all yet,
however. Just as he was taking breath, a *garçon* entered
with some custards and an enormous *omelette soufflée*,
whose puffy brown sides bagged over the tin dish that
contained it. ' There's a tart ! ' cried Mr. Jorrocks.
' Oh, my eyes, what a swell !—Well, I suppose I must
have a shy at it.—" In for a penny, in for a pound ! "
as we say at the Lord Mayor's feed. Know I shall be
sick, but, however, here goes,' sending his plate across
the table to the *garçon* who was going to help it. The
first dive of the spoon undeceived him as he heard it
sound at the bottom of the dish. ' Oh lauk, what a go !
All puff, by Jove !—a regular humbug—a balloon
pudding, in short ! I won't eat such stuff—give it to
Mouncheer there,' rejecting the offer of a piece. ' I like
the solids ;—will trouble you for some of that cheese,
sir, and don't let it taste of the knife. But what do they
mean by setting the dessert on before the cloth is removed ? And here comes tea and coffee—may as well
have some, I suppose it will be all the same price. And
what's this ? ' eyeing a lot of liqueur glasses full of *eau
de vie*. ' Chasse-café, Monsieur,' said the *garçon*. ' Chasse
calf—chasse calf—what's that ? Oh, I twig—what we
call " shove in the mouth " at the Free-and-easy. Yes,
certainly, give me a glass.' ' You shall take some
dessert,' said the Countess, handing him over some
peaches and biscuits. ' Well, I'll try my hand at it, if it
will ob*lege* your ladyship, but I really have had *almost*
enough.' ' And some abricot,' said she, helping him

[1] When the giraffe mania prevailed in Paris, and gloves,
handkerchiefs, gowns, reticules, etc., were ' à la Giraffe,' an
Englishman asked a waiter if they had any beef-steaks ' à la
Giraffe.' ' No, Monsieur, but we have them à la G—d-dem,'
was the answer.

to a couple of fine juicy ones. ' Oh, thank you, my lady, thank you, my lady, I'm *nearly* satisfied.' ' Vous ne mangez pas,' said she, giving him half a plate of grapes. ' Oh, my lady, you don't understand me—I *can't* eat any more—I am regularly high and dry—chock full— *bursting, in fact.*' Here she handed him a plate of sponge cakes mixed with bon-bons and macaroons, saying, ' Vous êtes un pauvre mangeur—vous ne mangez *rien*, Monsieur.' ' Oh, dear, she does not understand me, I see.—Indeed, my lady, I *can not* eat any more.—Ge *would*-era, se ge *could*-era, mais ge *can*-ne-ra pas ! ' ' Well, now, I've travelled three hundred thousand miles, and never heard such a bit of French as that before,' said the fat man, chuckling.

MR. JORROCKS IN PARIS

AS the grey morning mist gradually dispersed, and daylight began to penetrate the cloud that dimmed the four squares of glass composing the windows of the diligence, the Yorkshireman, half asleep and half awake, took a mental survey of his fellow-travellers. Before him sat his worthy friend, snoring away with his mouth open, and his head, which kept bobbing over on the shoulder of the Countess, enveloped in the ample folds of a white cotton nightcap. She too was asleep, and, disarmed of all her daylight arts, dozed away in tranquil security. Her mouth was also open, exhibiting rather a moderate set of teeth, and her Madonna *front* having got a twist, exposed a mixture of brown and iron-grey hairs at the parting place. Her bonnet swung from the roof of the diligence, and its place was supplied by a handsome lace cap, fastened under her chin by a broad-hemmed cambric handkerchief. Presently the sun rose, and a bright ray shooting into the Countess's corner, awoke her with a start, and after a hurried glance at the passengers, who appeared to be all asleep, she drew a small ivory-cased looking-glass from her bag and proceeded to examine her features. Mr. Jorrocks awoke shortly after, and with an awful groan exclaimed that his backbone was fairly worn out with sitting. ' Oh dear ! ' said he, ' my behind aches as if I had been kicked all the way from Holkley Hole to Marylebone. Are we near Paris ? for I'm sure I can't find *seat* any longer, indeed I can't. I'd rather ride two hundred miles in nine hours, like H'osbaldiston, than be shut up in this woiture another hour. It really is past bearing, and that's the long and short of the matter.' This exclamation roused all the party, who began yawning and rubbing their eyes, and looking at their watches. The windows were also lowered to take in fresh air, and, on looking out, they found themselves rolling along a sandy road, lined on each side with apple trees, whose branches were ' groaning ' with fruit. They break-fasted at Beaumont, and had a regular spread of fish, beef-steak, mutton-chops, a large joint of hot roast veal, roast chickens, several yards of sour bread, grapes, peaches, pears, and plums with *vin ordinaire* and coffee *au lait* ; but Mr. Jorrocks was off his feed, and stood all the time to ease his haunches.

Towards three in the afternoon they caught the first glimpse of the gilded dome of the Hospital of Invalids, which was a signal for all the party to brush up and make themselves agreeable. Even the three-hundred-thousand miler opened out, and began telling some wonderful anecdotes, while the Countess and Mr. Jorrocks carried on a fierce flirtation, or whatever else they pleased to call it. At last, after a deal of jargon, he broke off by appealing to the Yorkshireman to know what ' inn ' they should ' put up at ' at Paris.

' I don't know, I'm sure,' said he ; ' it depends a good deal upon how you mean to live. As you pay my shot, it does not do for beggars to be choosers ; but suppose we try Meurice's ? ' ' Oh no,' replied Mr. Jorrocks, ' her ladyship tells me it is werry expensive, for the English always pay through the nose if they go to English houses in Paris ; and as *we* talk French, we can put up at a French one, you know.' ' Well, then, we can try some of the French ones in the Rue de la

Paix." " Rue de la Pay ; no, by Jove, that won't do for me—the werry name is enough—no Rue de la *Pays* for me, at least if I have to *pay* the shot.' ' Well, then, you must get your friend there to tell you of some place, for I don't care twopence, as long as I have a bed, where it is.' The Countess and he then laid their heads together again, and when the diligence stopped to change horses at St. Denis, Mr. Jorrocks asked the Yorkshireman to alight, and, taking him aside, announced with great glee that her ladyship, finding they were strangers in the land, had most kindly invited them to stay with her, and that she had a most splendid house in the Rue des Mauvais-Garçons, ornamented with mirrors, musical clocks, and he didn't know what, and kept the best company in all France, marquesses, barons, viscounts, authors, etc. Before the Yorkshireman had time to reply, the conducteur came and hurried them back into the diligence, and closed the door with a bang, to be sure of having his passengers there while he and the postilion shuffled the cards and cut for a glass of eau-de-vie apiece.

The Countess, suspecting what they had been after, resumed the conversation as soon as Mr. Jorrocks was seated. ' You shall manger cinque fois every day,' said she ; ' cinque fois,' she repeated.—' Humph ! ' said Mr. Jorrocks to himself, ' What can that mean ?—cank four —four times five's twenty—eat twenty times a day— not possible ! ' ' Oui, Monsieur, cinque fois,' repeated the Countess, telling the number off on her fingers— ' Café at nine of the matin, déjeûner à la fourchette at onze o'clock, dîner at cinque heure, café at six hour, and souper at neuf hour.' ' Upon my word,' replied Mr. Jorrocks, his eyes sparkling with pleasure, ' your offer is werry inwiting. My lady,' said he, bowing before her, ' Je suis—I am much flattered.' ' And Monsieur ? ' said she, looking at the Yorkshireman. He too assured her that he was very much flattered, and was beginning to excuse himself, when the Countess interrupted him somewhat abruptly by turning to Mr. Jorrocks and saying, ' He sall be your son—n'est-ce pas ? ' ' No, my lady, I've no children,' replied he, and the

Countess's eyes in their turn underwent a momentary illumination.

The Parisian barrier was soon reached, and the man taken up to kick about the jaded travellers' luggage at the journey's end. While this operation was going on in the diligence yard, the Countess stuck close to Mr. Jorrocks, and having despatched Agamemnon for a fiacre, bundled him in, luggage and all, and desiring her worthy domestic to mount the box, and direct the driver, she kissed her hand to the Yorkshireman, assuring him she would be most happy to see him, in proof of which, she drove away without telling him her number, or where the Rue de Mauvais-Garçons was.

Paris is a charming place after the heat of the summer has passed away, and the fine, clear, autumnal days arrive. Then is the time to see the Tuileries gardens to prefection, when the Parisians have returned from their châteaus, and emigrating English and those homeward bound halt to renovate on the road ; then is the time that the gayest plants put forth their brightest hues, and drooping orange flowers scent the air which silvery fountains lend their aid to cool.

On a Sunday afternoon, such as we have described, our friend Mr. Stubbs (who since his arrival had been living very comfortably at the Hôtel d'Hollande, in expectation of Mr. Jorrocks paying his bill) indulged in six sous worth of chairs—one to sit upon and one for each leg—and, John Bull-like, stretched himself out in the shade beneath the lofty trees, to view the gay groups who promenaded the alleys before him. First, there came a helmeted cuirassier, with his wife in blue satin, and a little boy in his hand in uniform, with a wooden sword, a perfect miniature of the father, then a group of short-petticoated, shuffling French women, each with an Italian greyhound in slips, followed by an awkward Englishman with a sister on each arm, all stepping out like grenadiers ; then came a ribbon'd chevalier of the Legion of Honour, whose hat was oftener in his hand than on his head, followed by a non-descript-looking militaire with fierce mustachios, in shining jack-boots, white leathers, and a sort of Italian military cloak, with one side thrown over the shoulder, to exhibit the wearer's leg, and the bright scabbard of a large sword, while on the hero's left arm hung a splendidly-dressed woman. ' What a figure ! ' said the Yorkshireman to himself, as they came before him, and he took another good stare—' Yet, stay—no, impossible ! — Gracious Heaven ! it can't be — and yet it is—by Jove, it's Jorrocks ! '

' Why, now, you old imbecile,' cried he, jumping off his chair and running up to him, ' what are you after ? ' bursting into a loud laugh, as he looked at Mr. Jorrock's mustachios (a pair of great false ones). ' Is there no piece of tomfoolery too great for you ? What's come across you now ? Where the deuce did you get these things ? ' taking hold of the curls at one side of his mustachios.

' How now ? ' roared Mr. Jorrocks, with rage and astonishment. ' How now ! ye young scaramouch, vot do you mean by insulting a gentleman sportsman in broad daylight, in the presence of a lady of quality ? By Jingo,' added he, his eyes sparkling with rage, ' if you are not off before I can say " dumpling," I'll run you through the gizzard and give your miserable carcass to the dogs,' suiting the action to the word, and groping under his cloak for the hilt of his sword.—A crowd collected, and the Yorkshireman, perceiving symptoms of a scene, slunk out of the mêlée, and Mr. Jorrocks, after an indignant shake or two of his feathers and curl of his mustachios, pursued his course up the gardens.

This was the first time they had met since their arrival, which was above a week before ; indeed, it was nine days, for the landlord of the house where the Yorkshireman lived had sent his ' little bill ' two days before this, it being an established rule of his house, and one which was conspicuously posted in all the rooms, that the bills were to be settled weekly ; and Mr. Stubbs had that very morning observed that the hat of Monsieur l'Hôte was not raised half so high from his head, nor his body inclined so much towards the ground as it was wont to be,—a pretty significant hint that he wanted his cash. Now the Yorkshireman, among his other

accomplishments, had a turn for play, and unfortunately had been at the *Salon* the night before, when,
after a continuous run of ill luck, he came away twelve
francs below the amount of the hotel-keeper's bill,
consequently a rumpus with Mr. Jorrocks could not
have taken place at a more unfortunate moment.
Thinking, however, a good night's rest or two might
settle him down and put all matters right, he let things
alone until the Tuesday following, when again finding
Monsieur's little ' mémoire ' on one side of his coffee-
cup, and a framed copy of the ' rules and regulations '
of the house on the other, he felt constrained to take
some decisive step towards its liquidation. Accordingly,
having breakfasted, he combed his hair straight over
his face, and, putting on a very penitential look, called
a cab, and desired the man to drive him to the Rue
des Mauvais-Garçons. After zigzagging, twisting, and
turning about in various directions, they at last jingled
to the end of a very narrow, dirty-looking street, whose
unswept pavement had not been cheered by a ray of
sunshine since the houses were built. It was excessively
narrow, and there were no flags on either side ; but
through the centre ran a dribbling stream, here and
there obstructed by oyster-shells, or vegetable refuse,
as the water had served as a plaything for children, or
been stopped by servants for domestic purposes. The
street being extremely old, of course the houses were
very large, forming, as all houses do in Paris, little
squares entered by folding doors, at one side of which,
in a sort of lodge, lives the porter—' Parlez au portier '
—who receives letters, parcels, and communications for
the several occupiers, consisting sometimes of twenty
or thirty different establishments in one house. From
this functionary may be learned the names of the
different tenants. Having dismissed his cab, the Yorkshireman entered the first gateway on his left, to take
the chance of gaining some intelligence of the Countess.
The porter—a cobbler by trade—was hammering away,
last on knee, at the sole of a shoe, and, with a grin on
his countenance, informed the Yorkshireman that the
Countess lived next door but one. A thrill of fear came

over him on finding himself so near the residence·of his
indignant friend, but it was of momentary duration,
and he soon entered the courtyard of No. 3—where he
was directed by an unshaved, grisly-looking porter, to
proceed ' *au troisième*,' and ring the bell at the door
on the right-hand side.   Obedient to his directions, the
Yorkshireman proceeded to climb a wide but dirty stone
staircase, with carved and gilded balusters, whose wall
and steps had known no water for many years, and at
length found himself on the landing opposite the very
apartment which contained the redoubtable Jorrocks.
Here he stood for a few seconds, breathing and cooling
himself after his exertions, during which time he pictured
to himself the worthy citizen immersed in papers,
deeply engaged in the preparation of his France in three
volumes, and wished that the first five minutes of their
interview was over.   Al length he mustered courage to
grasp a greasy-looking red tassel, and give a gentle
tinkle to the bell.   The door was quickly opened by
Agamemnon in dirty loose trousers and slippers, and
without a coat.   He recognized his fellow-traveller, and,
in answer to his inquiry if Monsieur Jorrocks was at
home, grinned and answered, ' Oh oui, certainement,
Monsieur le *Colonel* Jorrockes est ici,' and motioned him
to come in.   The Yorkshireman entered the little ante-
room—a sort of scullery, full of mops, pans, dirty shoes,
dusters, candlesticks—and the first thing that caught
his eye was Jorrocks's sword, which Agamemnon had
been burnishing up with sand-paper and leather, lying
on a table before the window.   This was not very en-
couraging, but Agamemnon gave no time for reflection,
and, opening half a light salmon-coloured folding door
directly opposite the one by which he entered, the
Yorkshireman passed through unannounced, and unperceived by Mr. Jorrocks or the Countess, who were
completely absorbed in a game of dominoes, sitting on
opposite sides of a common deal table, whose rose-
coloured silk cover was laid over the back of a chair.
Jorrocks was sitting on a stool with his back to the door,
and the Countess being very intent on the game, Mr.
Stubbs had time for a hasty survey of the company

and apartment before she looked up. It was about one o'clock, and of course she was still *en déshabille*, with her nightcap on, a loose robe de chambre of flannel, and a flaming broad-striped red-and-black Scotch shawl thrown over her shoulders, and swan's-down lined slippers on her feet. Mr. Jorrocks had his leather pantaloons on, with a rich blue and yellow brocade dressing-gown, and blue morocco slippers to match. His jack-boots, to which he had added a pair of regimental heel-spurs, were airing before a stove, which contained the dying embers of a small log. The room was low, and contained the usual allowance of red figured velvet-cushioned chairs, with brass nails ; the window curtains were red-and-white on rings and gilded rods ; a secretaire stood against one of the walls, and there was a large mirror above the marble mantelpiece, which supported a clock surmounted by a flying Cupid, and two vases of artificial flowers covered with glass, on one of which was placed an elegant bonnet of the newest and most approved fashion. The floor, of highly-polished oak, was strewed about with play-bills, slippers, curl-papers, boxes, cards, dice, ribbons, dirty handkerchiefs, etc. ; and on one side of the deal table was a plate containing five well-picked mutton-chop bones, and hard by lay Mr. Jorrocks's mustachios and a dirty small-tooth comb.

Just as the Yorkshireman had got thus far in his survey, the Countess gave the finishing stroke to the game, and Mr. Jorrocks, jumping up in a rage, gave his leathers such a slap as sent a cloud of pipeclay flying into his face. ' Vous avez the *devil's* own luck ! ' exclaimed he, repeating the blow, when, to avoid the cloud, he turned short round, and encountered the Yorkshireman.

' How now ? ' roared he at the top of his voice, ' who sent for you ? Have you come here to insult me in my *own* house ? I'll lay my soul to an 'oss-shoe, I'll be too many for ye ! Where's my sword ? '

' Now, my good Mr. Jorrocks,' replied the Yorkshireman, very mildly, ' pray don't put yourself into a passion—consider the lady, and don't let us have any unpleasantness in Madame la Duchesse Benvolio's house,' making her a very low bow as he spoke, and laying his hand on his heart.

'D—n your displeasancies!' roared Jorrocks, 'and that's *swearing*—a thing I've never done since my brother Joe fobbed me of my bottom piece of muffin. Out with you, I say! Out with ye! you're a nasty dirty blackguard, I'm done with you for ever. I detest the sight of you, and hate ye afresh every time I see you!'

'Doucement, mon cher Colonel,' interposed the Countess, ' ve sall play anoder game, and you sall had von better chance,' clapping him on the back as she spoke. ' I *von't*!' bellowed Jorrocks ; 'turn this chap out first, I'll do it myself. H'Agamemnon! H'Agamemnon! happortez my sword! bring my sword! *tout suite*, directly!'

'Police! Police! Police!' screamed the Countess out of the window ; ' Police! Police! Police!' bellowed Agamemnon from the next one; ' Police! Police! Police!' re-echoed the grisly porter down below ; and before they had time to reflect on what had passed, a sergeant's file of the National Guard had entered the hotel, mounted the stairs, and taken possession of the apartment. The sight of the soldiers with their bright bayonets, all fixed and gleaming as they were, cooled Mr. Jorrocks's courage in an instant, and, after standing a few seconds in petrified astonishment, he made a dart at his jack-boots and bolted out of the room. The Countess Benvolio then unlocked her secretaire, in which was a plated liqueur-stand with bottles and glasses, out of which she poured the sergeant three, and the privates two glasses each of pure eau-de-vie, after which Agamemnon showed them the top of the stairs.

In less than ten minutes all was quiet again, and the Yorkshireman was occupying Mr. Jorrocks's stool. The Countess then began putting things a little in order, adorned the deal table with the rose-coloured cover— before doing which she swept off Mr. Jorrocks's mustachios, and thrust a dirty white handkerchief and the small-tooth comb under the cushion of a chair,—

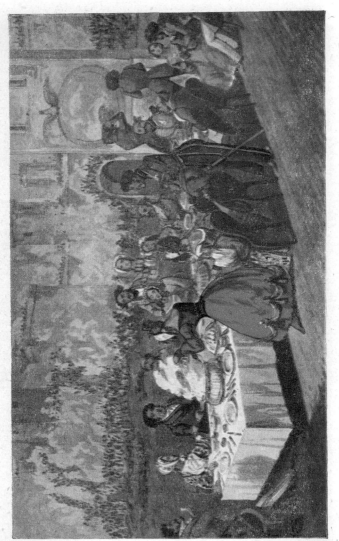

"WATER I DO DECLARE— WITH WORMS IN IT".

MR. JORROCKS RENOUNCES THE ACQUAINTANCE OF THE YORKSHIREMAN

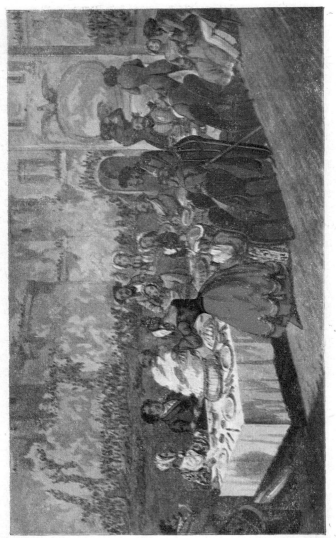

"WATER I DO DECLARE—WITH WORMS IN IT"

MR. JORROCKS RENOUNCES THE ACQUAINTANCE OF THE YORKSHIREMAN

while Agamemnon carried away the plate with the bones. ' Ah, le pauvre Colonel,' said the Countess, eyeing the bones as they passed, ' he sall be von grand homme to eat—him eat toujours—all day long. Oh, him mange beaucoup—beaucoup—beaucoup. He is von varé amiable man, but he sall not be moch patience. I guess he sall be varé rich—n'est-ce pas ? have many guinea ?—He say he keep beaucoup des chiens—many dogs for the hont—he sall be vot dey call rom customer (rum customer) in Angleterre, I think.'

Thus she went rattling on, telling the Yorkshireman all sorts of stories about the pauvre Colonel, whom she seemed ready to change for a younger piece of goods with a more moderate appetite ; and finding Mr. Stubbs more complaisant than he had been in the diligence, she concluded by proposing that he should accompany the Colonel and herself to a soirée-dansante that evening at a friend of hers, another Countess, in the ' Rue des Bon-Enfants.'

Being disengaged as usual, he at once assented, on condition that the Countess would effect a reconciliation between Mr. Jorrocks and himself, for which purpose she at once repaired to his room, and presently re-appeared arm and arm with our late outrageously indignant hero. The Colonel had been occupying his time at the toilette, and was en grand costume—finely cleaned leathers, jack boots and brass spurs, with a spic and span new blue military frock-coat, hooking and eyeing up to the chin, all covered with braid, frogs, tags, and buttons.

' Dere be von beau garçon ! ' exclaimed the Countess, turning him round after having led him into the middle of the room—' dat habit does fit you like vax.' ' Yes,' replied Mr. Jorrocks, raising his arm as though he were going to take flight, ' but it is rather tight—partiklarly round the waist—shouldn't like to dine in it. What do you think of it ? '—turning round and addressing the Yorkshireman as if nothing had happened—' suppose you get one like it ? ' ' Do,' rejoined the Countess, ' and some of the other things—vot you call them, Colonel ? ' ' What—breeches ? ' ' Yes, breeches—but

6

the oder name—vot you call dem ? ' ' Oh, leathers ? '
replied Mr. Jorrocks. ' No, no, another name still.'
' I know no other. Pantaloons, perhaps you mean ? '
' No, no, not pantaloons.' ' Not pantaloons ?—then I
know of nothing else. You don't mean those sacks of
things, called trousers ? ' taking hold of the Yorkshireman's. ' No, no, not trousers.' ' Then, really, my lady,
I don't know any other name.' ' Oh yes, Colonel, you
know the things I intend. Vot is it you call Davil in
Angleterre ? ' ' Oh, we have lots of names for him—
Old Nick, for instance.' ' Old Nick breeches,' said the
Countess thoughtfully ; ' no, dat sall not be it—vot
else ? ' ' Old Harry ? ' replied Mr. Jorrocks. ' Old
Harry breeches,' repeated the Countess in the hopes of
catching the name by the ear—' no, nor dat either,
encore anoder name, Colonel.' ' Old Scratch, then ? '
' Old Scratch breeches,' re-echoed the Countess—' no
dat shall not do.' ' Beelzebub ? ' rejoined Mr. Jorrocks.
' Beelzebub breeches,' repeated the Countess—' nor dat.'
' Satan, then,' said Mr. Jorrocks. ' Oui, oui ! ' responded
the Countess with delight, ' sat*an* ! black sat*an* breeches
—you shall von pair of black sat*an* breeches, like the
Colonel.'

' And the Colonel will pay for them, I presume ? '
said the Yorkshireman, looking at Mr. Jorrocks.

' I carn't,' said Mr. Jorrocks in an undertone ; ' I'm
nearly cleaned out, and shall be in *Short's gardens*
before I know where I am, unless I hold better cards
this evening than I've done yet. Somehow or other,
these French are rather too sharp for me, and I've been
down upon my luck ever since I came. Lose every
night, in fact, and then they are so werry anxious for
me to have my rewenge, as they call it, that they make
parties expressly for me every evening ; but, instead of
getting my rewenge, I only lose more and more money.
They seem to me *always* to turn up the king, whenever
they want him. To-night we are going to a Countess's
of werry great consequence, and, as you know écarté
well, I'll back your play, and, perhaps, we may do
something between us.'

This being all arranged, Mr. Stubbs took his departure,

and Mr. Jorrocks having girded on his sword, and the Countess having made her morning toilette, they proceeded to their daily promenade in the Tuileries gardens.

A little before nine that evening, the Yorkshireman again found himself toiling up the dirty staircase, and, on reaching the third landing, was received by Agamemnon in a roomy uniform of a chasseur—dark green and tarnished gold, with a cocked hat and black feather, and a couteau de chasse, slung by a shining patent-leather belt over his shoulder. The opening of the inner door displayed the worthy Colonel sitting at his ease, with his toes on each side of the stove (for the evenings had begun to get cool), munching the last bit of crust of the fifth perigord pie that the Countess had got him to buy. He was extremely smart : thin black gauze-silk stockings, black satin breeches ; well-washed, well-starched white waistcoat with a rolling collar, showing an amplitude of frill ; a blue coat with yellow buttons and a velvet collar, while his pumps shone as bright as polished steel.

The Countess presently sidled into the room, all smirks and smiles as dressy ladies generally are when well ' got up.' Rouge and the milliner had effectually reduced her age from five-and-forty down to five-and-twenty. She wore a dress of the palest pink satin, with lilies of the valley in her hair, and an exquisitely wrought gold armlet, with a most Liliputian watch in the centre.

Mr. Jorrocks having finished his pie-crust, and stuck on his mustachios, the Countess blew out her ' bougies,' and the trio, preceded by Agamemnon with a lanthorn in his hand, descended the stairs, whose greasy, muddy steps contrasted strangely with the rich delicacy of the Countess's beautifully slippered feet. Having handed them into the voiture, Agamemnon mounted up behind, and in less than ten minutes they rumbled into the spacious courtyard of the Countess de Jackson, in the Rue des Bons-Enfants, and drew up beneath a lofty arch at the foot of a long flight of dirty black-and-white marble stairs, about the centre of which was stationed a ' lacquey de place ' to show the company

up to the ball. The Countess de Jackson (the wife of
an English horse-dealer) lived in an *entre-sol au troisième*,
but the hotel being of considerable dimensions, her
apartment was much more spacious than the Countess
Benvolio's. Indeed, the Countess de Jackson, being a
" marchande des modes," had occasion for greater
accommodation and she had five low rooms, whereof
the centre one was circular, from which four others,
consisting of an ante-room, a kitchen, a bedroom, and
a ' salle à manger,' radiated.

Agamemnon having opened the door of the fiacre,
the Countess Benvolio took the Yorkshireman's arm,
and at once proceeded to make the ascent, leaving the
Colonel to settle the fare, observing, as they mounted
the stairs, that he was ' von exceeding excellent man,
but varé slow.'

' Madame la Comtesse Benvolio and Monsieur *Stoops!* '
cried the ' lacquey de place,' as they reached the door
of the low ante-room, where the Countess Benvolio
deposited her shawl, and took a final look at herself
in the glass. She again took the Yorkshireman's arm
and entered the round ballroom, which, though low
and out of all proportion, had an exceedingly gay
appearance, from the judicious arrangement of the
numerous lights, reflected in costly mirrors, and the
simple elegance of the crimson drapery, festooned with
flowers and evergreens against the gilded walls. Indeed,
the hotel had been the residence of an ambassador before
the first revolution, and this entresol had formed the
private apartment of his Excellency. The door immediately opposite the one by which they entered, led
into the Countess de Jackson's bedroom, which was
also lighted up, with the best furniture exposed, and her
toilette-table set out with numberless scent bottles,
vases, trinkets, and knick-knacks, while the ' salle à
manger ' was converted into a card-room. Having been
presented in due form to the hostess, the Yorkshireman
and his new friend stood surveying the gay crowd of
beautiful and well-dressed women, large-frilled and well-
whiskered men, all chatting, and bowing, and dancing,
when a half-suppressed titter that ran through the room

attracted their attention, and turning round, Mr. Jorrocks was seen poking his way through the crowd with a number of straws sticking to his feet, giving him the appearance of a feathered Mercury. The fact was, that Agamemnon had cleaned his shoes with the liquid varnish (French polish), and forgetting to dry it properly, the carrying away half the straw from the bottom of the fiacre was the consequence, and Mr. Jorrocks having paid the Jehu rather short, the latter had not cared to tell him about it.

The straws were, however, soon removed without interruption to the gaiety of the evening. Mr. Stubbs, of course, took an early opportunity of waltzing with the Countess Benvolio, who, as all French women are, was an admirable dancer, and Jorrocks stood by fingering and curling his mustachios, admiring her movements, but apparently rather jealous of the Yorkshireman. ' I wish,' said he, after the dance was over, ' that you would sit down at écarté, and let us try to win some of these mouncheers' tin, for I'm nearly cleaned out. Let us go into the card-room, but first let us see if we can find anything in the way of nourishment, for I begin to be hungry. Gar*soon*,' said he, catching a servant with a tray full of eau sucré glasses, ' avez-vous kickshaws to eat ? ' putting his finger in his mouth—' ge wouderay some refreshment.' ' Oh oui,' replied the garçon, taking him to an open window overlooking the courtyard, and extending his hand in the air, ' voilà, monsieur, de très bon rafraîchissement.'

The ball proceeded with the utmost decorum, for though composed of shopkeepers and such like, there was nothing in their dress or manner to indicate anything but the best possible breeding. Jorrocks, indeed, fancied himself in the very élite of French society, and but for a little incident would have remained of that opinion. In an unlucky moment he took it into his head he could waltz, and surprised the Countess Benvolio by claiming her hand for the next dance. ' It seems werry easy,' said he to himself, as he eyed the couples gliding round the room ;—' at all ewents there's nothing like trying, '' for he who never makes an effort never risks a

failure." ' The couples were soon formed and ranged for
a fresh dance. Jorrocks took a conspicuous position
in the centre of the room, buttoned his coat, and as the
music struck up put his arm round the waist of his
partner. The Countess, it seems, had some misgivings
as to his prowess in the dancing line, and used all her
strength to get him well off, but the majority of the
dancers started before him. At length, however, he
began to move, and went rolling away in something
between a gallop and a waltz, effecting two turns, like
a great cart-wheel, which brought him bang across the
room, right into the track of another couple, who were
swinging down at full speed, making a cannon with his
head against both theirs, and ending by all four coming
down upon the hard boards with a tremendous crash—
the Countess Benvolio undermost, then the partner of
the other Countess, then Jorrocks, and then the other
Countess herself. Great was the commotion, and the
music stopped ; Jorrocks lost his wig, and split his
Beelzebub breeches across the knees, while the other
gentleman cracked his behind—and the Countess Benvolio and the other Countess were considerably damaged ;
particularly the *other* Countess, who lost four false teeth
and broke an ear-ring. This, however, was not the
worst, for as soon as they were all scraped together and
set up right again, the *other* Countess's partner attacked
Jorrocks most furiously, calling him a sacré-nom-de-
Dieu'd bête of an Englishman, a mauvais sujet, a cochon,
etc. etc., then spitting on the floor—the greatest insult
a Frenchman can offer—he vapoured about being one
of the ' grand nation,' ' that he was brave—the world
knew it,' and concluded by thrusting his card—' Monsieur
Charles Adolphe Eugène, Confiturier, No. 15 bis, Rue
Poupée '—into Jorrocks's face.

It was now Jorrocks's turn to speak, so doubling his
fists, and getting close to him, he held one to his nose,
exclaiming, ' D—n ye, sir, je suis—JORROCKS—Je suis
an Englishman ! je vous lick within an inch of your
life !—Je vous kick !—Je vous mill !—je vous flabber-
gaster ! ' and concluded by giving him his card, ' Monsieur
le Colonel Jorrocks, No. 3, Rue des Mauvais-Garçons.'

A friend of the confectioner's interposed and got him
away, and Mr. Stubbs persuaded Mr. Jorrocks to
retire into the card-room, where they were speedily
waited upon by the friend of the former, who announced
that the Colonel must make an apology or fight, for he
said, although Jorrocks was a 'Colonel Anglais,' still
Monsieur Eugène was of the Legion of Honour, and
consequently, very brave and not to be insulted with
impunity. All this the Yorkshireman interpreted to
Mr. Jorrocks, who was most anxious to fight, and wished
it was light that they might go to work immediately.
Mr. Stubbs therefore told the confectioner's friend (who
was also his foreman), that the Colonel would fight him
with pistols at six o'clock in the Bois de Boulogne, but
no sooner was the word 'pistols' mentioned than the
friend exclaimed, with a grimace and shrug of his
shoulders, 'Oh, horror, no! Monsieur Adolphe is
brave, but he will not touch pistols—they are not the
weapons of his country.' Jorrocks then proposed to
fight him with broadswords, but this the confectioner's
foreman declined on behalf of his principal, and at last
the Colonel suggested that they could not do better
than fight it out with fists. Now, the confectioner was
ten years younger than Jorrocks, tall, long-armed, and
not over-burdened with flesh, and had moreover taken
lessons of Harry Hammer when that worthy had his
school in Paris, so he thought the offer was a good one,
and immediately closed with it. Jorrocks, too, had been
a patron of the prize-ring, having studied under Bill
Richmond, the man of colour, and was reported to have
exhibited in early life (incog.) with a pugilist of some
pretensions at the Fives Court; so, all things considered, fists seemed a very proper mode of settling the
matter, and that being agreed upon, each party quitted
the Countess de Jackson's—the confectioner putting
forth all manner of high-flown ejaculations and prayers
for success, as he groped about the ante-room for his
hat, and descended the stairs. 'O God of war!' said
he, throwing up his hands, 'who guided the victorious
army of this grand nation in Egypt, when, from the
pyramids, forty centuries beheld our actions—O brilliant

sun, who shone upon our armies at Jaffa, at Naples,
Montebello, Marengo, Austerlitz, Jena, and Algiers,
who blessed our endeavours, who knowest that we are
brave—brave as a hundred lions—look down on Charles
Adolphe Eugène, and enable him to massacre and
immolate on the altar of his wrath, this sacré-nom-de-
Dieu'd beastly hog of an Englishman '—and thereupon
he spit upon the flags with all the venom of a viper.

Jorrocks, too, indulged in a few figures of speech, as
he poked his way home, though of a different description. ' Now blister my kidneys,' said he, slapping
his thigh, ' but I'll sarve him out ! I'll baste him as
Randall did ugly Borrock. I'll knock him about as
Belcher did the Big Ikey Pigg. I'll damage his mug as
Turner did Scroggins'. I'll *fib* him till he's as black
as Agamemnon—for I *do* feel as though I could fight
a few.'

The massive folding doors of the Porte-Cocher at
the Hôtel d'Hollande had not received their morning
opening, when a tremendous loud, long-protracted rat-
tat-tat-tat-tan sounded like thunder throughout the
extensive square, and brought numerous night-capped
heads to the windows, to see whether the hotel was on
fire, or another revolution had broken out. The maître
d'hotel screamed, the porter ran, the chef de cuisine
looked out of his pigeon-hole window, and the garçons
and *male* femme des chambres rushed into the yard, with
fear and astonishment depicted on their countenances,
when, on peeping through the grating of the little door,
Mr. Jorrocks was descried, knocker in hand, about to
sound a second edition. Now, nothing is more offensive
to the nerves of a Frenchman than a riotous knock, and
the impertinence was not at all mitigated by its proceeding from a stranger who appeared to have arrived
through the undignified medium of a co-cou.[1] Having
scanned his dimensions and satisfied himself that, notwithstanding all the noise, Jorrocks was mere mortal
man, the porter unbolted the door, and commenced a

[1] Co-cous are nondescript vehicles that ply in the environs of
Paris. They are a sort of cross between a cab and a young
diligence.

loud and energetic tirade of abuse against ' Monsieur
Anglais,' for his audacious thumping, which he swore was
enough to make every man of the National Guard rush
' to arms.'

In the midst of the torrent, very little of which Mr.
Jorrocks understood, the Yorkshireman appeared, whom
he hurried into the ' co-cou,' bundled in after him, cried
' *alley !* ' to the driver, and off they jolted at a miserable
slow trot.   A little before seven they reached the village
of Passy, where it was arranged they should meet and
proceed from thence to the Bois de Boulogne, to select
a convenient place for the fight ; but neither the confectioner nor his second, nor any one on his behalf, was
visible, and they walked the length and breadth of the
village, making every possible inquiry without seeing
or hearing anything of them.   At length, having waited
a couple of hours, Mr. Jorrocks's appetite overpowered
his desire for revenge, and caused him to retire to the
Chapeau-Rouge to indulge in a ' fork breakfast.'

Nature being satisfied, he called for pen and ink, and
with the aid of Mr. Stubbs drew up the following proclamation, which to this day remains posted in the salle à
manger, a copy whereof was transmitted by post to the
confectioner at Paris :—

' PROCLAMATION !

' I, John Jorrocks, of Great Coram Street, in the County
of Middlesex, Member of the Surrey Hunt, in England,
and Colonel of the army when I'm in France, having
been grossly insulted by Charles Adolphe Eugène of
No. 15 bis, Rue Poupée, Confectioner, this day repaired
to Passy, with the intention of sarving him out with
my fists ; but, neither he not anyone for him having
come to the scratch, I, John Jorrocks, do hereby proclaim the said Charles Adolphe Eugène to be a shabby
fellow and no soldier, and totally unworthy the notice of
a fox-hunter and a gentleman sportsman.

' (Signed)   JOHN JORROCKS.

' (Countersigned)   STUBBS.'

6*

This being completed, and the bill paid, they returned leisurely on foot to Paris, looking first at one object, then at another, so that the Countess Benvolio's dinner-hour was passed ere they reached the Tuileries gardens, where after resting themselves until it began to get dusk, and their appetites returned, they repaired to the Café de Paris to destroy them again. The lofty well-gilded salon was just lighted up, and the numberless lamps reflected in costly mirrors in almost every partition of the wall, aided by the graceful figures and elegant dresses of the ladies, interspersed among the sombre-coated gentry with here and there the gay uniforms of the military, imparted a fairy air to the scene, which was not a little heightened by the contrast produced by Mr. Jorrocks's substantial figure stumping through the centre with his hat on his head, his hands behind his back, and the dust of the day hanging about his Hessians.

'Gar*soon*,' said he, hanging up his hat, and taking his place at a vacant table laid for two, 'ge wouderai some wittles,' and, accordingly, the spruce-jacketed, white-aproned garçon brought him the usual red-backed book with gilt edges, cut and lettered at the side, like the index to a ledger, and, as Mr. Jorrocks said, 'containing reading enough for a month.' 'Quel potage voulez-vous, monsieur?' inquired the garçon at last, tired of waiting while he studied the carte and looked the words out in the dictionary. 'Avez-vous any potted lobster?' 'Non,' said the garçon, 'potage au vermi-celle, au riz, à la Julienne, consommé, et potage aux choux.' 'Old shoe! who the devil do you think eats old shoes here? Have you any mock-turtle or gravy soup?' 'Non, monsieur,' said the garçon, with a shrug of the shoulders. 'Then avez-vous any roast beef?' 'Non, monsieur; nous avons bœuf au naturel—bœuf à la sauce piquante—bœuf aux cornichons—bœuf à la mode—bœuf aux choux—bœuf à la sauce tomate—bifteck aux pommes des terres.' 'Hold hard,' said Jorrocks; 'I've often heard that you can dress an egg a thousand ways, and I want to hear no more about it; bring me a beef-steak and pomme de terres for three.' 'Stop!' cried Mr. Stubbs, with dismay—'I see you don't understand ordering a dinner in France—let me teach you. Where's the carte ? ' 'Here,' said Mr. Jorrocks, ' is the " bill of lading," ' handing over the book. ' Garçon, apportez une douzaine des huitres, un citron, et du beurre frais,' said the Yorkshireman, and, while they were discussing the propriety of eating them before or after the soup, a beautiful dish of little green oysters made their appearance, which were *encored* before the first supply was finished. ' Now, Colonel,' said the Yorkshireman, ' take a bumper of Chablis,' lifting a pint bottle out of the cooler. ' It has had one plunge in the ice-pail and no more—see what a delicate rind it leaves on the glass ! '—eyeing it as he spoke. ' Aye, but I'd rayther it should leave something in the mouth than on the side of the glass,' replied Mr. Jorrocks ; ' I loves a good strong, generous wine—*military* port, in fact—but here comes fish and soup—wot are they ? ' ' Filet de sole au gratin, et potage au macaroni avec fromage de Parmesan. I'll take fish first, because the soup will keep hot longest.' ' So will I,' said Mr. Jorrocks, ' for I think you understand the thing—but they seem to give werry small penn'orths—it really looks like trifling with one's appetite—I likes the old joint—the cut-and-come-again system, such as we used to have at Sugden's, in Cornhill —joint, wegitables, and cheese, all for two shillings.' ' Don't talk of your joints here,' rejoined the Yorkshire-man—' I told you before, you don't understand the art of eating—the dexterity of the thing consists in titivating the appetite with delicate morsels so as to prolong the pleasure. A well-regulated French dinner lasts two hours, whereas you go off at score, and take the shine out of yourself before you turn the Tattenham Corner of your appetite. But come, take another glass of Chablis, for your voice is husky as though your throat was full of dust. Will you eat some of this boulli-vert ? ' ' No, not no boulevard for me, thank ye.' ' Well, then, we will have the " entré de bœuf "—beef with sauce tomate—and there is a cotelette de veau en papilotte ; which will you take ? ' ' I'll trouble the beef, I think ; I don't like that ere pantaloon cutlet much, the skin is so tough.' ' Oh, but you don't eat the paper, man ;

that is only put on to keep this nice layer of fat ham from melting ; take some, if it is only that you may enjoy a glass of champagne after it. There is no meat like veal for paving the way for a glass of champagne.' 'Well, I don't care if I do, now you have explained how to eat it, for I've really been troubled with indigestion all day from eating one wholesale yesterday ; but don't you stand potatoes—pommes des *terres*, as we say in France ! ' ' Oh, yes, fried, and à la maître d'hôtel ; here they come, smoking hot. Now, J., for a glass of champagne—take it out of the pail—nay, man ! not with both hands round the middle, unless you like it warm—by the neck, so,' showing him how to do it, and pouring him out a glass of still champagne. ' This won't do,' said Jorrocks, holding it up to the candle ; ' *garsoon ! garsoon !*—no good—no bon—no fizzay, no fizzay,' giving the bottom of the bottle a slap to rouse it. ' Oh, but this is still champagne,' explained the Yorkshireman, ' and far the best.' ' I don't think so,' retorted Mr. Jorrocks, emptying the glass into his water-stand. ' Well, then, have a bottle of the other,' rejoined the Yorkshireman, ordering one. ' And who's to pay for it ? ' inquired Mr. Jorrocks. ' Oh, never mind that— care killed the cat—give a loose to pleasure for once, for it's a poor heart that never rejoices. Here it comes, and " may you never know what it is to want," as the beggar boys say. Now, let's see you treat it like a philosopher—the wire is off, so you've nothing to do but cut the string, and press the cork on one side with your thumb—Nay ! you've cut both sides ! ' fizz—pop— bang, and away went the cork close past the ear of an old deaf general, and bounded against the wall. ' Come, there's no mischief done, so pour out the wine. Your good health, old boy, may you live for a thousand years, and I be there to count them ! Now, that's what I call good,' observed the Yorkshireman, holding up his glass, ' see how it dulls the glass, even to the rim— champagne isn't worth a copper unless it's iced—is it, Colonel ? ' ' Vy, I don't know—I carn't say I like it so werry cold ; it makes my teeth chatter, and cools my courage as it gets below—champagne certainly gives one werry gentlemanly ideas, but for a continuance, I don't know but I should prefer mild h'ale.' 'You're right, old boy, it does give one very gentlemanly ideas, so take another glass, and you'll fancy yourself an emperor. Your good health again.' 'The same to you, sir. And now what do you call this chap?' 'That is a quail the other a snipe—which will you take?' 'Vy, a bit of both, I think; and do you eat these chaps with them?' 'Yes, nothing nicer—artichokes à la sauce blanche; you get the real eating part, you see, by having them sent up this way, instead of like haystacks, as they come in England, diving and burning your fingers amid an infinity of leaves.' 'They are werry pretty eating, I must confess; and this upper Binjimin of ham the birds are cooked in is delicious. I'll trouble you for another plateful.' 'That's right, Colonel, you are yourself again; I always thought you would come back into the right course. And now you are good for a glass of claret of light Hermitage. Come, buck up, and give a loose to pleasure for once.' 'For *once*, aye, that's what you always say; but your *once* comes so werry often.' 'Say no more. Garçon! Une demi-bouteille de St. Julien; and here, J., is a dish upon which I will stake my credit as an experienced caterer—a Charlotte de pommes—upon my reputation it is a fine one, the crust is browned to a turn, and the rich apricot sweetmeat lies ensconced in the middle, like a sleeping babe in its cradle. If ever man deserved a peerage and a pension, it is this cook.' 'It's werry delicious—order another.' 'Oh, your eyes are bigger than your stomach, Mr. J. According to all mathematical calculation this will more than suffice. Aye, I thought so—you are regularly at a stand-still. Take a glass of whatever you like. Good—I'll drink Chablis to your champagne. And now, that there may be no mistake as to our country, we will have some cheese—fromage de Roquefort, Gruyère, Neufchatel, or whatever you like, and a beaker of Burgundy after, and then remove the cloth, for I hate dabbling in dowlas after dinner is done.'

SPORTING IN FRANCE

'RUM beggars, these French,' said Mr. Jorrocks to himself, laying down the newspaper and taking a sip of Churchman's chocolate, as on the Sunday morning he sat with the Countess Benvolio, discussing rolls and butter, with *Galignani's Messenger*, for breakfast.

' Rum beggars, indeed,' said he, resuming the paper, and reading the programme of the amusements for the day, commencing with the hour of Protestant service at the Ambassador's chapel, followed on by Palace and Gallery of Pictures of the Palais Royal—Review with Military Music in the Place du Carousel—Horse-races in the Champs de Mars—Fête in the Park of St. Cloud —Combat d'Animaux, that is to say, dog-fighting and bull-baiting, at the Barrière du Combat, Tivoli, etc. etc. ' It's not werry right, but I suppose at Rome we must do as Romans do,' with which comfortable reflection Mr. Jorrocks proposed that the Countess and he should go to the races. Madame was not partial to animals of any description, but having got a new hat and feathers, she consented to show them, on condition that they adjourned to the fête at St. Cloud in the evening.

Accordingly, about noon, the ostler's man of a neighbouring English livery stable, drew up a dark-coloured job cab, with a red-and-white striped calico lining, drawn by a venerable long-backed white horse, at the Countess's gateway in the Rue des Mauvais-Garçons, into which Mr. Jorrocks having handed her ladyship, and Agamemnon, who was attired in his chasseur uniform, having climbed up behind, the old horse, after two or three flourishes of his dirty white tail, as a sort of acknowledgment of the whip on his sides, got himself into motion, and proceeded on his way to the races. The Countess, being resolved to cut a dash, had persuaded our hero to add a smart second-hand cocked hat, with a flowing red-and-white feather, to the rest of his military attire ; and the end of a scarlet handkerchief, peeping out at the breast of his embroidered frock-coat, gave him the appearance of wearing a decoration, and procured him the usual salute from the soldiers and veterans of the Hospital of Invalids, who were lounging about the ramparts and walks of the edifice. The Countess's costume was simple and elegant ; a sky-blue satin pelisse with boots to match, and a white satin bonnet with white feathers tipped with blue, and delicate primrose-coloured gloves. Of course the head of the cab was well thrown back to exhibit the elegant inmates to the world.

Great respect is paid to the military in France, as Mr. Jorrocks found by all the hack cab and fiacre drivers pulling up and making way for him to pass, as the old crocodile-backed white horse slowly dragged its long length to the gateway of the Champ de Mars. Here the guard, both horse and foot, saluted him, which he politely acknowledged, under direction of the Countess, by raising his chapeau bras, and a subaltern was despatched by the officer in command to conduct him to the place appointed for the carriages to stand. But for this piece of attention Mr. Jorrocks would certainly have drawn up at the splendid building of the Ecole Militaire, standing as it does like a grand stand in the centre of the gravelly dusty plain of Champ de Mars. The officer, having speared his way through the crowd with the usual courtesy of a Frenchman, at length drew up the cab in a long line of anonymous vehicles under the rows of stunted elms by the stone-lined ditch, on the southern side of the plain, when, turning his charger round, he saluted Mr. Jorrocks, and bumped off at a trot. Mr. Jorrocks then stuck the pig-driving whip into the socket, and, throwing forward the apron, handed out the Countess, and installed Agamemnon in the cab.

A fine day and a crowd make the French people thoroughly happy, and on this afternoon the sun shone brightly and warmly on the land ;—still there was no apparently settled purpose for the assembling of the multitude, who formed themselves in groups upon the plain, or lined the grass-burnt mounds at the side, in most independent parties. The Champ de Mars forms a regular parallelogram of 2700 feet by 1320, and the course, which is of an oblong form, comprises a circuit of the whole, and is marked out with strong posts and ropes. Within the course, equestrians—or more properly speaking, ' men on horseback '—are admitted under the surveillance of a regiment of cavalry, while infantry and cavalry are placed in all directions with drawn swords and fixed bayonets to preserve order. Being a gravelly, sandy soil, in almost daily requisition for the exercise and training of troops, no symptoms of vegetation can be expected, and the course is as hard as the ride in Rotten Row or up to Kensington Gardens.

About the centre of the south side, near where the carriages were drawn up, a few temporary stands were erected for the royal family and visitors, the stand for the former being in the centre, and hung with scarlet and gold cloth, while the others were tastefully arranged with tri-coloured drapery. These are entered by tickets only, but there are always plenty of platforms formed by tables and ' chaises à louer ' (chairs to let) for those who don't mind risking their necks for a sight. Some few itinerants tramped about the plain, offering alternately tooth-picks, play-bills, and race-lists for sale. Mr. Jorrocks of course purchased one of the latter, which was decorated at the top with a woodcut representing three jockeys riding two horses, one with a whip as big as a broadsword. On pages 172 and 173 we subjoin the list as a specimen of ' Sporting in France.'

Foreigners accuse the English of claiming every good-looking horse, and every well-built carriage met on the continent, as their own, but we think that few would be ambitious of laying claim to the honour of supplying France with jockeys or race-horses. Mr. Jorrocks, indeed, indifferent as he is to the affairs of the turf, could not suppress his ' conviction ' of the difference between the flibberty-gibberty appearance of the Frenchmen, and the quiet, easy, close-sitting jockeys of Newmarket. The former all legs and elbows, spurting and pushing to the front at starting, in tawdry, faded jackets and nankeen shorts, just like the frowsy door-keepers of an Epsom gambling-booth ; the latter in clean, neat-fitting leathers, well-cleaned boots, spick and span new jackets, feeling their horses' mouths, quietly in the rear, with their whip hands resting on their thighs. Then such riding ! A hulking Norman with his knees up to his chin, and a long, lean, half-starved-looking Frenchman set astride like a pair of tongs, with a wet sponge applied to his knees before starting, followed by a runaway English stable lad, in white cords and drab gaiters, and half a dozen others equally singular, spurring and tearing round and round, throwing the gravel and sand into each other's faces, until the field was so separated as to render it difficult to say which was leading and which was tailing, for it is one of the rules of their races that each heat must be run in a certain time, consequently, though all the horses may be distanced, the winner keeps working away. Then what an absence of interest and enthusiasm on the part of the spectators ! Three-fourths of them did not know where the horses started, scarcely a man knew their names, and the few tenpenny bets that were made, were sported upon the colour of the jackets. A Frenchman has no notion of racing, and it is on record that after a heat in which the winning horse, after making a waiting race, ran in at the finish, a Parisian observed, that ' although ' Annette ' had won at the finish, he thought the greater honour was due to ' Hercule, he having kept the lead the greater part of the distance.' On some one explaining to him that the jockey on ' Annette ' had purposely made a waiting race, he was totally incredulous, asserting that he was sure the jockeys had too much *amour propre* to remain in the rear at any part of the race, when they might be in front.[1]

' Moderate sport,' said Mr. Jorrocks to himself, curling his mustachios, and jingling a handful of five-franc pieces in the pocket of his leathers,—' moderate sport indeed,' and therefore he turned his back to the course and walked the Countess off towards the cab.

From beneath a low, tenth-rate-looking booth, called ' The Cottage of Content,' supported by poles placed on the stunted trees of the avenue, and exhibiting on a

[1] *New Sporting Magazine*, vol. vii., p. 139.

PROGRAMME DES COURSES DE CHEVAUX

QUI AURONT LIEU AU CHAMP DE MARS LE DIMANCHE A UNE HEURE,

EN PRESENCE DE LL. MM. LE ROI ET LA REINE, ET DES PRINCES DE LA FAMILLE ROYALE,

DEUX PRIX ROYAUX.

PRIX ROYAL DE 5000 FR. pour les chevaux et jumens de deuxième espèce.—En partie liée.

Noms De Chevaux.	Signalemens Et Ages.	Noms Des Propriétaires.	Poids que les chevaux doivent porter.	Noms Des Jockeys.	Costumes Des Jockeys.	Notes sur les Chevaux.
Moina	Bai-clair, 4 ans.	Haras de Meudon	102l.	Tom Hall	Veste rouge, toque tricolore	Issu de Candid et de Miltonia.
Corisandre	Bai-brun, 5 ans.	M. Bonvié fils.	115	Tom Wilson.	Veste orange, manches et toque noires	Issu d'Holbein et de Lisbeth.
Flore	Bai-cerise, 4 ans.	M. de Laroque	102	Tony Montel.	Veste noire, manches blanches, toque noire	Issue de Tigris et de Biche.
Eléanor	Alezan-brûlé, 5 ans.	M. de Royère.	112	Bernou	Veste verte, toque noire	Issue de Moulay et de Cadette.
Diomède	Bai, 4 ans.	M. le baron de la Bastide	105	Baptiste	Veste bleue, manches jaunes, toque bleue et jaune	Issu de Prémium et de Gabrielle.
Cirus	Bai-brun, 5 ans.	Lord Seymour	115	North	Veste orange, toque noire	Issu de Toley et de Miss.
Aline	Bai-clair, 4 ans.	M. Noel.	102	Tom	Veste ponceau, manches blanches, toque bleue	Issue de Snail et d'une jument Normande.
Léonie	Alezan-doré, 5 ans.	M. Belhomme	112	Pichon.	Veste jaune, toque verte	Issue de Massoud et d'une fille de D-y-o.

PRIX ROYAL DE 6000 FR. pour les chevaux de jumens de deuxième espèce.—En partie liée.

Young-Milton ·	Bai, 4 ans.	M. Fasquel ·	105l.	Tom Webb ·	Veste et toque noires ·	Issu de Milton et de Betzi.
Mouna ·	Bai-clair, 4 ans.	M. de Laroque	102	Tony Montel	Veste noire, manches blanches, toque noire.	Issu de Rainbow et de Mouna.
Paméla ·	Bai, 4 ans.	Haras de Meudon	102	Tom Hall ·	Veste rouge, toque tricolore.	Issue de Candid et de Géane.
Eglé ·	Gris-sanguin, 5 ans.	Lord Seymour	112	Mous ·	Veste orange, toque noire ·	Issu de Rainbow et de Young-Urganda.
Cédéric ·	Bai, 5 ans.	M. le baron de la Bastide	115	Baptiste	Veste bleue, manches jaunes, toque bleue et jaune	Issue de Candid et de Prestesse.
Young-Tandem	Bai-cerise, 4 ans.	M. Schickler	105	Webb ·	Veste rouge, toque noire ·	Issu de Multum-in-Parvo et d'Oïda.
Oubiou ·	Alezan, 6 ans.	MM. Salvador et Tassinari	121	Tom Johns	Veste bleue, manches blanches, toque rouge	Issu d'Oubiou et d'une fille de Stradlam-lad.
Coradin ·	Bai, 5 ans.	M. Moreil ·	115	René ·	Veste bleue, manches jaunes, toque bleue et jaune	Issu de Candid et de Prestesse.

NOTA.—Les chevaux de première espèce sont ceux nés en France de pères et mères étrangers ; ceux de la deuxième espèce sont ceux nés de pères et mères Français ou seulement de l'un des deux.—Chaque épreuve comprenda les deux tours du Champs de Mars.—Les courses commenceront par la première épreuve des chevaux de deuxième espèce.—La seconde course se fera pour la première épreuve des chevaux de première espèce ; suivie de la deuxième épreuve des chevaux de deuxième espèce : et elles seront terminées par la deuxième épreuve des chevaux de première espèce.

blue board, ' John Jones, dealer in British beer,' in gilt
letters, there issued the sound of voices clamouring
about odds and weights and scales ; and on looking in,
a score of ragamuffin-looking grooms, imitation jockeys,
and the usual hangers-on of race-horses and livery-
stables, were seen drinking beer, smoking, playing at
cards, dice, and chuck-farthing.   Before the well-
patched canvas curtain that flapped before the entrance,
a crowd had collected round one of the horses which
was in the care of five or six fellows, one to hold him,
another to whistle to him, a third to whisk the flies
away with a horse's tail, a fourth to scrape him, a fifth
to rinse his mouth out,—while the stud-groom, a tall,
gaunt, hairy-looking fellow, in his shirt sleeves, with
ear-rings, a blue apron and trousers (more like a
gardener than a groom), walked round and round with
mystified dignity, sacréing and muttering, ' Ne parlez
pas, ne parlez pas,' as anyone approached who seemed
likely to ask questions.   Mr. Jorrocks, having well
ascertained the importance of his hat and feather,
pushed his way with the greatest coolness into the ring,
just to cast his eye over the horse and see whether he
was fit to go with the Surrey, and the stud-groom
immediately took off his lavender-coloured foraging cap,
and made two profound salaams, one to the Colonel,
the other to the Countess.   Mr. Jorrocks, all politeness,
took off his chapeau, and no sooner was it in the air,
than with a wild exclamation of surprise and delight,
the groom screamed, ' O, Monsieur Shorrock, mon ami
comment vous portez-vous ? ' threw his arms round the
Colonel's neck, and kissed him on each cheek.

' Hold ! ' roared the Colonel, half smothered in the
embrace, and, disengaging himself, he drew back a few
paces, putting his hand on the hilt of his sword, when
in the training groom of Paris he recognized his friend
the Baron of Newmarket.   The abruptness of the
incident disarmed Mr. Jorrocks of reflection, and being
a man of impulse and warm affections, he at once forgave
the novelty of the embrace, and most cordially joined
hands with those of his friend.   They then struck up a
mixture of broken English, and equally broken French,

in mutual inquiries after each other's healths and movements, and presuming that Mr. Jorrocks was following
up the sporting trade in Paris, the Baron most considerately gave him his best recommendations which
horse to back, kindly betting with him himself, but,
unfortunately, at each time assigning Mr. Jorrocks the
losing horse. At length, being completely cleaned out,
he declined any further transactions, and having got
the Countess into the cab, was in the act of climbing in
himself, when some one took him by the sword as he
was hoisting himself up by the wooden apron, and drew
him back to the ground. ' Holloa, Stubbs, my boy ! '
cried he, ' I'm werry 'appy to see ye,' holding out his
hand, and thereupon Mr. Stubbs took off his hat to the
Countess. ' Well, now, the deuce be in these French,'
observed Mr. Jorrocks confidentially, in an undertone,
as, resigning the reins to Agamemnon, he put his arm
through the Yorkshireman's and drew out of hearing
of the Countess behind the cab—' the *deuce* be in them,
I say. There's that beggarly Baron as we met at Newmarket, has just diddled me out of four naps and a half,
by getting me to back 'osses that he said were *certain*
to win, and I really don't know how we are to make
" tongue and buckle " meet, as the coachmen say.
Somehow or other they are *far* too sharp for me. Cards,
dominoes, dice, backgammon, and racing, all one—they
inwariably beat me, and I declare I haven't as much
pewter as will coach me to Calais.' The Yorkshireman,
as may be supposed, was not in a condition to offer any
great pecuniary assistance ; but after a turn or two
along the mound, he felt it would be a reproach on his
country if he suffered his friend to be done by a Frenchman, and on consideration he thought of a trick that
Monsieur would not be up to. Accordingly desiring Mr.
Jorrocks to take him to the Baron, and behave with
great cordiality, and agree to the proposal he should
make, they set off in search of that worthy, who, after
some trouble, they discovered in the ' Cottage of
Content,' entertaining John Jones and his comrades
with an account of the manner in which he had fleeced
Monsieur Shorrock. The Yorkshireman met him with

the greatest delight, shook hands with him over and over again, and then began talking about racing, pigeon-shooting, and Newmarket, pretended to be full of money and very anxious for the Baron's advice in laying it out. On hearing this, the Baron beckoned him to retire, and joining him in the avenue, walked him up and down, while he recommended his backing a horse that was notoriously amiss. The Yorkshireman consented, lost a nap with great good humour, and banteringly told the Baron he thought he could beat the horse on foot. This led them to talk of foot-racing, and at last the Yorkshireman offered to bet that Mr. Jorrocks would run fifty yards with him on his back before the Baron would run a hundred. Upon this the Baron scratched his head and looked very knowing, pretended to make a calculation, when the Yorkshireman affected fear, and professed his readiness to withdraw the offer. The Baron then plucked up his courage, and after some haggling, the match was made for six naps, the York-shireman reckoning the Baron might have ten francs in addition to what he had won of Mr. Jorrocks and himself. The money was then deposited in the hands of the Countess Benvolio, and away went the trio to the 'Cottage of Content,' to get men and ropes to measure and keep the ground. The English jockeys and lads, though ready enough to pigeon a countryman them-selves, have no notion of assisting a foreigner to do so, unless they share in the spoil, and the Baron being a notorious screw, they all seemed heartily glad to find him in a trap. Out then they all sallied, amid cheers and shouts, while John Jones, with a yard-wand in his hand, proceeded to measure a hundred yards along the low side of the mound. This species of amusement being far more in accordance with the taste of the French than anything in which horses are concerned, an immense mob flocked to the scene, and the Baron having ex-plained how it was, and being considered a safe man to follow, numerous offers were made to bet against the performance of the match. The Yorkshireman, being a youth of discretion and accustomed to bet among strangers, got on five naps more with different parties,

who, to ' prevent accidents,' submitted to deposit the
money with the Countess, and all things being adjusted,
and the course cleared by a picket of infantry, Mr.
Jorrocks ungirded his sword and depositing it with his
frock-coat in the cab, walked up to the fifty yards he
was to have for start. ' Now, Colonel,' said the Yorkshireman, backing him to the mound, so that he might
leap on without shaking him, ' put your best leg first,
and it's a hollow thing; if you don't fall, you *must*
win,'—and thereupon taking Mr. Jorrocks's cocked hat
and feather from his head, he put it sideways on his
own, so that he might not be recognized, and mounted
his man. Mr. Jorrocks then took his place as directed
by John Jones, and at a signal from him—the dropping
of a blue cotton handkerchief—away they started amid
the shouts, the clapping of hands, and applause of the
spectators, who covered the mound and lined the course
on either side. Mr. Jorrocks's action was not very
capital, his jack-boots and leathers rather impeding his
limbs, while the Baron had as little on him as decency
would allow. The Yorkshireman feeling his man rather
roll at the start, again cautioned him to take it easy, and
after a dozen yards he got into a capital run, and though
the lanky Baron came tearing along like an ill-fed greyhound, Mr. Jorrocks had full two yards to spare, and
ran past the soldier, who stood with his cap on his
bayonet as a winning-post, amid the applause of his
backers, the yells of his opponents, and the general
acclamation of the spectators.

The Countess, anticipating the victory of her hero,
had despatched Agamemnon early in the day for a
chaplet of red and yellow *immortelles*, and having
switched the old cab horse up to the winning-post, she
gracefully descended, without showing more of her foot
and ankle than was strictly correct, and decorated his
brow with the wreath, as the Yorkshireman dismounted.
Enthusiasm being always the order of the day in France,
this act was greeted with the loudest acclamations, and,
without giving him time to recover his wind, the popu-
lace bundled Mr. Jorrocks neck and shoulders into the
cab, and, seizing the old horse by the head, paraded

him down the entire length of the Champ de Mars, Mr.
Jorrocks bowing and kissing his hands to the assembled
multitude, in return for the *vivas* ! the clapping of
hands, and the waving of ribbons and handkerchiefs
that greeted him as he went.

Popularity is but a fickle goddess, and in no country
more fickle than in France. Ere the procession reached
the end of the dusty plain, the mob had tailed off very
considerably, and as the leader of the old white horse
pulled him round to return, a fresh commotion in the
distance, caused by the apprehension of a couple of pick-
pockets, drew away the few followers that remained,
and the recently-applauded and belauded Mr. Jorrocks
was left alone in his glory. He then pulled up, and
taking the chaplet of *immortelles* from his brow, thrust
it under the driving cushion of the cab, and proceeded
to reinstate himself in his tight military frock, regird
himself with his sword, and resume the cocked hat and
feather.

Nothing was too good for Mr. Stubbs at that moment,
and, had a pen and ink been ready, Mr. Jorrocks would
have endorsed him a bill for any amount. Having
completed his toilette, he gave the Yorkshireman the
vacant seat in the cab, flopped the old horse well about
the ears with the pig-driving whip, and trotted briskly
up the line he had recently passed in triumphal procession, and wormed his way among the crowd in search
of the Countess. There was nothing, however, to be
seen of her, and after driving about, and poking his way
on foot into all the crowds he could find, bolting up to
every lady in blue, he looked at his great double-cased
gold repeater, and finding it was near three o'clock and
recollecting the fête of St. Cloud, concluded her ladyship
must have gone on, and Agamemnon, being anxious to
see it, of course was of the same opinion, so again
flopping the old horse about the ears, he cut away down
the Champ de Mars, and, by the direction of Agamemnon,
crossed the Seine by the Pont des Invalides, and gained
the route to Versailles.

Here the genius of the people was apparent, for the
road swarmed with voitures of every description, dili-

gences, gondoles, co-cous, cabs, fiacres, omnibuses, dame-
blanches, all rolling and rumbling along, occasionally
interrupted by the lilting and tilting of a light English
cab or tilbury, drawn by a thorough-bred, and driven
by a dandy. The spirit of the old white horse even
seemed roused, as he got among the carriages, and heard
the tramping of hoofs and the jingling of bells round
the necks of other horses, and he applied himself to the
shafts with a vigour his enfeebled-looking frame appeared incapable of supplying. So they trotted on,
and after a mile travelling at a foot's pace after they
got into close line, they reached the *porte Maillot*, and,
resigning the cab to the discretion of Agamemnon, Mr.
Jorrocks got himself brushed over by one of the gentry
who ply in that profession at all public places, and tuck-
ing his sword under one arm, he thrust the other through
Mr. Stubbs's, and, John-Bull-like, strutted up the long
broad grass avenue, through the low part of the wood
of St. Cloud, as if all he saw belonged to himself. The
scene was splendid, and nature, art, and the weather
appeared confederated for effect. On the lofty heights
arose the stately palace, looking down with placid
grandeur on the full foliage of the venerable trees, over
the beautiful gardens, the spouting fountains, the rushing
cascades, and the gay and countless myriads that
swarmed the avenues, while the circling river flowed
calmly on, without a ripple on its surface, as if in
ridicule of the sound of trumpets, the clang of cymbals,
and the beat of drums that rent the air around.

Along the broad avenue were ranged shows of every
description—wild beasts, giants, jugglers, tumblers,
mountebanks, and monsters, while in spots sheltered
from the sun by lofty trees were dancing places, swings,
round-abouts, archery-butts, pistol-ranges, ball-kicking,
and head-thumping places, montagnes-Suisses, all the
concomitants of fairs and fêtes—beating ' Bartlemy-
fair,' as Mr. Jorrocks candidly confessed, all to nothing.

The chance of meeting the Countess Benvolio in such
a multitude was very remote indeed, but, to tell the
truth, Mr. Jorrocks never once thought of her, until
having eat a couple of cold fowls and drunk a bottle of

porter at an English booth, he felt in his pocket for his purse, and remembered it was in her keeping. Mr. Stubbs, however, settled the account, and in high glee Mr. Jorrocks resumed his peregrinations, visiting first one show, then another, shooting with pea-guns, then dancing a quadrille, until he was brought up short before a splendid green and gold round-about, whose magic circle contained two lions, two swans, two black horses, a tiger, and a giraffe. ' Let's have a ride,' said he, jumping on to one of the black horses, and adjusting the stirrups to his length. The party was soon made up, and as the last comer crossed his tiger, the engine was propelled by the boys in the centre, and away they went at Derby pace. In six rounds Mr. Jorrocks lost his head, turned completely giddy, and bellowed out to them to stop. They took no heed—all the rest were used to it—and, after divers yells and ineffectual efforts to dismount, he fell to the ground like a sack. The machine was in full work at the time, and swept round three or four times before they could stop it. At last Mr. Stubbs got to him, and a pitiful plight he was in. He had fallen on his head, broken his feather, crushed his ' chapeau bras,' lost his mustachios, was as pale as death, and very sick. Fortunately the accident happened near the gate leading to the town of St. Cloud, and thither, with the aid of two gendarmes, Mr. Stubbs conveyed the fallen hero, and having put him to bed at the Hôtel d'Angleterre, he sent for a ' médecin,' who of course shook his head, looked very wise, ordered him to drink warm water—a never-failing specific in France —and keep quiet. Finding he had an Englishman for a patient, the ' médecin ' dropped in every two hours, always concluding with the order ' encore l'eau chaud.' A good sleep did more for Mr. Jorrocks than the doctor, and when the ' médecin ' called in the morning and repeated the injunction ' encore l'eau chaud,' he bellowed out, ' Cuss your l'eau chaud, my stomach arn't a reservoir ! give me some wittles ! ' The return of his appetite being a most favourable symptom, Mr. Stubbs discharged the doctor, and forthwith ordered a ' déjeuner à la fourchette,' to which Mr. Jorrocks did pretty fair justice, though trifling in comparison with his usual performances. They then got into a Versailles diligence that stopped at the door, and, rattling along at a merry pace, very soon reached Paris and the Rue des Mauvais-Garçons.

'Come up and see the Countess,' said Mr. Jorrocks, as they arrived at the bottom of the dirty flight of stairs, and, with his hands behind his back and his sword dragging at his heels, he poked upstairs, and, opening the outer door, entered the apartment. He passed through the small ante-room, without observing his portmanteau and carpet-bag on the table, and there being no symptoms of the Countess in the next one, he walked forward into the bedroom beyond.

Before an English fireplace that Mr. Jorrocks himself had been at the expense of providing, snugly ensconced in the luxurious depths of a well-cushioned easy-chair sat a monstrous man with a green patch on his right eye, in slippers, loose hose, a dirty grey woollen dressing-gown and black silk nightcap, puffing away at a long meerschaum pipe, with a figure of Bacchus on the bowl. At a sight so unexpected, Mr. Jorrocks started back, but the smoker seemed quite unconcerned, and, casting an unmeaning grey eye at the intruder, puffed a long-drawn respiration from his mouth.

'How now!' roared Mr. Jorrocks, boiling into a rage, which caused the monster to start upon his legs as though he were galvanized, 'Vot brings *you* here?'

'Sprechen sie Deutsch?' responded the smoker, opening his eye a little wider, and taking the pipe from his mouth. 'Speak English, you fool!' bawled Mr. Jorrocks. 'Sie sind sehr unverschämt' (you are very impudent), replied the Dutchman, with a thump on the table. 'I'll run you through the gizzard!' rejoined Mr. Jorrocks, half drawing his sword,—'skin you alive, in fact!' when in rushed the Countess and threw herself between them.

Now, Mynheer Van Rosembom, a burgomaster of Flushing, was an old friend of the Countess's, and an exceedingly good paying one, and having cast up that morning quite unexpectedly by the early diligence from

Dunkirk, and the Countess being enraged at Mr. Jorrocks
for not sharing the honours of his procession in the cab
on the previous day, and believing, moreover, that his
treasury was pretty well exhausted, thought she could
not do better than instal Rosembom in his place, and
retain the stakes she held for the Colonel's board and
lodging.

This arrangement she kept to herself, simply giving
Rosembom, who was a not much better Frenchman than
Col. Jorrocks, to understand that the room would be
ready for him shortly, and Agamemnon was ordered to
bundle Mr. Jorrocks's clothes into his portmanteau and
bag, and place them in readiness in the ante-room.
Rosembom, fatigued with his journey, then retired to
enjoy his pipe at his ease, while the Countess went to the
Marché St. Honoré to buy some sour crout, roast beef,
and prunes for his dinner.

'Turn this great slush bucket out of my room!'
cried Mr. Jorrocks, as the Countess rushed into his
apartment. 'Vot's he doing here?'

'Doucement, mon cher Colonel,' said she, clapping
him on the back, 'he sall be my brodder.'

'Never such a thing!' roared Mr. Jorrocks, eyeing
him as he spoke. 'Never such a thing! no more than
myself—out with him, I say, or I'll cut my stick—toute
suite—directly!'

'Avec tout mon cœur!' replied the Countess, her
choler rising as she spoke. 'You're another,' rejoined
Mr. Jorrocks, judging by her manner that she called
him something offensive—'Vous êtes one mauvaise
woman!' 'Monsieur,' said the Countess, her eyes
flashing as she spoke, 'vous êtes un polisson!—von
rascal!—von dem villain!—un charlatan!—von nasty—
bastely—ross bif!—dem dog,' and thereupon she curled
her fingers and set her teeth on edge as though she would
tear his very eyes out. Rosembom, though he didn't
exactly see the merits of the matter, exchanged his pipe
for the poker,—so what with this, the sword, and the
nails, things wore a very belligerent aspect.

Mr. Stubbs, as usual, interposed, and the Countess,
still keeping up the semblance of her rage, ordered them

to quit her apartment directly, or she would have recourse to her old friends the police. Mr. Stubbs was quite agreeable to go, but hinted that she might as well hand over the stakes that had been entrusted to her keeping on the previous day ; upon which she again indulged in a torrent of abuse, swore they were a couple of thieves, and that Mr. Jorrocks owed her far more than the amount for board and lodging. This made the Colonel stare, for on the supposition that he was a visitor, he had been firing away his money in all directions, playing at everything she proposed, buying her bonnets, perigord pies, hiring remises, and committing every species of extravagance, and now to be charged for what he thought was pure friendship, disgusted him beyond expression.

The Countess speedily summoned the porter, the man of letters of the establishment, and with his aid drew Mr. Jorrocks out a bill, which he described as ' reaching down each side of his body and round his waist,' commencing with 2 francs for savon, and then proceeding in the daily routine of café, 1 franc ; déjeuner à la fourchette, 5 francs ; dîner avec vin, 10 francs ; tea, 1 franc ; souper, 3 francs ; bougies, 2 francs ; apartement, 3 francs ; running him up a bill of 700 francs ; and when Mr. Stubbs remonstrated on the exorbitance of the charges, she replied, ' It sall be, sare, as small monnae as sall be consistent avec my dignified respectability, you to charge.'

There seemed no help for the matter, so Mr. Stubbs paid the balance, while Mr. Jorrocks, shocked at the duplicity of the Countess, the impudence of Rosembom, and the emptiness of his own pockets, bolted away without saying a word.

That very night the Malle-Poste bore them from the capital, with two cold fowls, three-quarters of a yard of bread, and a bottle of porter, for Mr. Jorrocks on the journey ; and ere another sun went down, the sandy suburbs of Calais saw them toiling towards her ramparts, and rumbling over the drawbridges and under the portcullis that guard the entrance to her gloomy town. Calais ! cold, cheerless, lifeless Calais ! Whose soul has ever warmed as it approached thy town ? but how many hearts have turned with sickening sorrow from the mirthless tinkling of thy bells ! [1]

'We'll not stay here long, I guess,' said Mr. Jorrocks, as the diligence pulled up at the post-office, and the conducteur requested the passengers to descend. 'That's optional,' said a bystander, who was waiting for his letters, looking at Mr. Jorrocks with an air as much as to say, 'What a rum-looking fellow you are !' and not without reason, for the Colonel was attired in a blue sailor's jacket, white leathers, and jack-boots, with the cocked hat and feather. The speaker was a middle-aged, middle-statured man, with a quick, intelligent eye, dressed in a single-breasted, green riding-coat, striped toilenette waistcoat, and drab trousers, with a whip in his hand. 'Thank you for nothing !' replied Mr. Jorrocks, eyeing him in return, upon which the speaker turned to the clerk, and asked him if there were any letters for Monsieur Apperley or Nimrod. 'NIMROD !' exclaimed Mr. Jorrocks, dropping on his knees as though he were shot, 'Oh, my vig ! what have I done ? Oh dear ! oh dear ! what a dumbfounderer—flummoxed, I declare.'

'*Hold up !* old un,' said Nimrod in astonishment. 'Why, what's the matter now ? you don't *owe* me anything, I dare say !'

'*Owe* you anything ! yes, I does,' said Mr. Jorrocks, rising from the ground, 'I owes you a debt of gratitude that I can never wipe off—you'll be in the day book and ledger of my memory for ever and a year.'

'Who are you ?' inquired Nimrod, becoming more and more puzzled, as he contrasted his dialect with his dress.

'Who am I ?—Why, I'm Mr. Jorrocks.'

'Jorrocks, by Jove ! Who'd have thought it ? I declare I took you for a horse-marine. Give us your hand, old boy. I'm proud to make your acquaintance.'

'Ditto to you, sir, twice repeated. I considers you

[1] At the Hôtel de Ville is a clock that chimes the quarters and keeps up a most monotonous tinkle by day and by night.

the werry first man of the age ! '—and thereupon they shook hands with uncommon warmth.

' You've been at Paris, I suppose,' resumed Nimrod, after their respective digits were released ; ' were you much gratified with what you saw ? What pleased you most—the Tuileries, Louvre, Garden of Plants, Père la Chaise, Notre Dame, or what ? '

' Why now, to tell you the truth, singular as it may seem, I saw nothing but the Tuileries and Naughty Dame,—I may say a werry naughty dame, for she fleeced me uncommonly, scarcely leaving me a dump to carry me home.'

' What, you've been among the ladies, have you ? that's gay for a man at your time of life.'

' Yes, I certain*lie* have been among the ladies,— Countesses I may say—but, dash my vig, they are a rum set, and made me pay for their acquaintance. The Countess Benwolio certain*lie* is a bad 'un.'

' Oh, the deuce !—did that old devil catch you ? ' inquired Nimrod.

' Vot, do you know her ? '

' Know her ! ay—everybody here knows her with her black boy. She's always on the road, and lives now by the flats she catches between Paris and the coast. She was an agent for Morrison's Pills,—but having a fractious Scotch lodger that she couldn't get out, she physicked him so dreadfully that he nearly died, and the police took her licence away. But you are hungry, Mr. Jorrocks, come to my house and spend the evening, and tell me all about your travels.'

Mr. Stubbs objected to this proposition, having just learned that the London packet sailed in an hour, so the trio adjourned to Mr. Roberts' Royal Hotel, where over some strong eau-de-vie they cemented their acquaintance, and Mr. Jorrocks, finding that Nimrod was to be in England the following week, insisted upon his naming a day for dining in Great Coram Street.

' Permits ' to embark having been considerately granted ' *gratis* '[1] by the government for a franc apiece,

---

[1] Though ' gratis ' is stamped conspicuously on the document, they always charge something for them.

at the hour of ten our travellers stepped on board; and Mr. Jorrocks, having wrapped himself up in his martial cloak, lay down in the cabin, and, like Ulysses in Ithaca, as Nimrod would say, ' arrived in London asleep.'

MR. JORROCKS'S DINNER PARTY

THE general postman had given the final flourish to his bell, and the muffin-girl had just begun to tinkle hers, when a capacious yellow hackney-coach, with a faded scarlet hammer-cloth, was seen jolting down Great Coram Street, and pulling up at Mr. Jorrocks's door.

Before Jarvey had time to apply his hand to the area bell, after giving the usual three knocks and a half to the brass lion's head on the door, it was opened by the boy Benjamin in new drab coat, with a blue collar, and white sugar-loaf buttons, drab waistcoat, and black velveteen breeches, with well-darned white cotton stockings.

The knock drew Mr. Jorrocks from his dining-room, where he had been acting the part of butler, for which purpose he had put off his coat and appeared in his shirt sleeves, dressed in nankeen shorts, white gauze silk stockings, white neckcloth, and white waistcoat, with a frill as large as a hand-saw. Handing the bottle and cork-screw to Betsy, he shuffled himself into a smart new blue saxony coat with velvet collar and metal buttons, and advanced into the passage to greet the arrivers.

' O gentlemen, gentlemen,' exclaimed he, ' I'm so 'appy to see you—so werry 'appy you carn't think,' holding out both hands to the foremost, who happened to be Nimrod ; ' this is werry kind of you, for I declare it's six to a minute. 'Ow are you, Mr. Nimrod ? Most proud to see you at my humble crib. Well, Stubbs, my boy, 'ow do you do ? Never knew you late in life,' giving him a hearty slap on the back. ' Mr. Spiers, I'm werry

MR. JORROCKS MAKES A FAUX PAS

MR. JORROCKS BEATS THE BARON FOR SPEED

MR. JORROCKS MAKES A FAUX PAS

MR. JORROCKS BEATS THE BARON FOR SPEED

'appy to see you. You are just what a sporting publisher ought to be—punctuality itself. Now, gentlemen, dispose of your tiles, and come upstairs to Mrs. J., and let's get you introduced.'

'I fear we are late, Mr. Jorrocks,' observed Nimrod, advancing past the staircase end to hang up his hat on a line of pegs against the wall.

'Not a bit of it,' replied Mr. Jorrocks—'not a bit of it—quite the contrary—you are the first, in fact ! '

'Indeed ! ' replied Nimrod, eyeing a table full of hats by where he stood—'why, here are as many hats as would set up a shop. I really thought I'd got into *Beaver* (Belvoir) Castle by mistake ! '

'Haw ! haw ! haw ! werry good, Mr. H'Apperley, werry good indeed.—I owes you one.'

'*I* thought it was a *Castor*-Oil Mill,' rejoined Mr. Spiers.

'Haw ! haw ! haw ! werry good, Mr. Spiers, werry good indeed,—owes you one also,—but I see what you're driving at. You think these 'ats have a cocoanut apiece belonging to them upstairs. No such thing, I assure you ; no such thing. The fact is, they are what I've won at warious times of the members of our 'unt ; and as I've got you great sporting coves dining with me, I'm going to set them out on my sideboard, just as racing gents exhibit their gold and silver cups, you know. Binjimin ! I say, Binjimin, you blackguard,' holloaing down the kitchen stairs, ' Why don't you set out the castors as I told you ? and see you brush them well ! '

' Coming, sir, coming, sir,' replied Benjamin from below, who at that moment was busily engaged, taking advantage of Betsy's absence, in scooping marmalade out of a pot with his thumb. ' There's a good lot of them,' said Mr. Jorrocks, resuming the conversation, ' four, six, eight, ten, twelve, thirteen,—all trophies of sporting prowess. Real good hats. None o' your nasty gossamers, or dog-hair ones. There's a tile ! ' said he, balancing a nice new white one with green rims on the top of his finger. ' I won that in a most *mi*raculous manner.— A most wonderful way, in fact. I was driving to Croydon one morning in my four-wheeled one-'oss chay, and just

7

as I got to Lilley-white, the blacksmith's, below Brixton
Hill, they had thrown up a drain—a *gulph* I may call it
—across the road for the purpose of repairing the gas-
pipe. I was *ray*ther late as it was, for our 'ounds are
werry punctual, and there was nothing for me but either
to go a mile and a half about, or drive slap over the gulph.
Well, I looked at it, and the more I looked at it the less
I liked it ; but just as I was thinking I had seen enough
of it, and was going to turn away, up tools Timothy
Trueman in his buggy, and he, too, began to crane and
look into the abyss—and a terrible place it was, I assure
you—*quite frightful*, and he liked it no better than
myself. Seeing this, I takes courage, and said, " Why,
Tim, your 'oss will do it ! " " Thank'e, Mr. J.," said
he, " I'll *follow* you." " Then," said I, " if you'll change
wehicles "—for, mind ye, I had no notion of damaging
my own—" I'll bet you a hat I gets over." " Done,"
said he, and out he got, so I takes his 'oss by the head,
looses the bearing-rein, and, leading him quietly up to
the place and letting him have a look at it, gave him a
whack over the back, and over he went, gig and all, as
clever as could be ! '

Stubbs. Well done, Mr. J., you are really a most
wonderful man ! You have the most extraordinary
adventures of any man breathing—but what did you
do with your own machine ?

Jorrocks. Oh ! you see, I just turned round to
Binjimin, who was with me, and said, ' You may go
home,' and, getting into Timothy's buggy, I had my
ride for nothing, and the hat into the bargain. A nice
hat it is too—regular beaver—a guinea's worth at least.
All true what I've told you, isn't it, Binjimin ?

' Quite ! ' replied Benjamin, putting his thumb to
his nose, and spreading his fingers like a fan as he slunk
behind his master.

' But come, gentlemen,' resumed Mr. Jorrocks, ' let's
be after getting upstairs. Binjimin, announce the
gentlemen as your missis taught you. Open the door
with your left hand, and stretch the right towards her,
to let the company see the point to make up to.'

The party ascended the stairs one at a time, for the

flight is narrow and rather abrupt, and Benjamin, obeying his worthy master's injunctions, threw open the front drawing-room door, and discovers Mrs. Jorrocks sitting in state at a round table, with annuals and albums spread at orthodox distances around. The possession of this room had long been a bone of contention between Mr. Jorrocks and his spouse, but at length they had accommodated matters, by Mr. Jorrocks gaining un-divided possession of the back drawing-room (communi-cating by folding-doors), with the run of the front one equally with Mrs. Jorrocks on non-company days. A glance, however, showed which was the master's and which was the mistress's room. The front one was papered with weeping willows, bending under the weight of ripe cherries on a white ground, and the chair cushions were covered with pea-green cotton velvet with yellow worsted bindings.

The round table was made of rosewood, and there was a ' what-not ' on the right of the fireplace of similar material, containing a handsomely-bound collection of Sir Walter Scott's works, in wood. The carpet-pattern consisted of most dashing bouquets of many-coloured flowers, in winding French horns on a very light drab ground, so light, indeed, that Mr. Jorrocks was never allowed to tread upon it except in pumps or slippers. The bell-pulls were made of foxes' brushes. and in the frame of the looking-glass, above the white marble mantelpiece, were stuck visiting-cards, cards of invitation, thanks for ' obliging inquiries,' etc. etc. The hearth-rug exhibited a bright yellow tiger, with pink eyes, on a blue ground, with a flossy green border ; and the fender and fire-irons were of shining brass. On the wall, immediately opposite the fireplace, was a portrait of Mrs. Jorrocks before she was married, so unlike her present self that no one would have taken it for her. The back drawing-room, which looked out upon the gravel walk and house-backs beyond, was papered with broad scarlet and green stripes in honour of the Surrey-Hunt uniform, and was set out with s green-covered library table in the centre, with a red morocco hunting chair between it and the window, and several good strong hair-bottomed mahogany chairs around the walls. The table had a very literary air, being strewed with Sporting Magazines, odd numbers of *Bell's Life,* pamphlets, and papers of various descriptions, while on a sheet of foolscap on the portfolio were ten lines of an elegy on a giblet pie which had been broken in coming from the baker's, at which Mr. Jorrocks had been hammering for some time. On the side opposite the fireplace, on a hanging range of mahogany shelves, were ten volumes of *Bell's Life in London,* the *New Sporting Magazine,* bound, gilt, and lettered, the *Memoirs of Harriette Wilson, Boxiana,* Taplin's *Farriery,* Nimrod's *Life of Mytton,* and a backgammon board that Mr. Jorrocks had bought by mistake for a History of England.

Mrs. Jorrocks, as we said before, was sitting in state at the far side of the round table, on a worsted-worked ottoman, exhibiting a cock pheasant on a white ground, and was fanning herself with a red-and-white paper fan, and turning over the leaves of an annual. How Mr. Jorrocks happened to marry her, no one could ever divine, for she never was pretty, had very little money, and not even a decent figure to recommend her. It was generally supposed at the time, that his brother Joe and he having had a deadly feud about a bottom piece of muffin, the lady's friends had talked him into the match, in the hopes of his having a family to leave his money to, instead of bequeathing it to Joe or his children. Certain it is they never were meant for each other ; Mr. Jorrocks, as our readers have seen, being all nature and impulse, while Mrs. Jorrocks was all vanity and affectation. To describe her accurately is more than we can pretend to, for she looked so different in different dresses, that Mr. Jorrocks himself sometimes did not recognize her. Her face was round, with a good strong brick-dust sort of complexion, a turn-up nose, eyes that were grey in one light and green in another, and a middling-sized mouth with a double chin below. Mr. Jorrocks used to say that she was ' warranted ' to him as twelve years younger than himself, but many people supposed the difference of age between them was not so great. Her stature was of the middle height, and she was of one breadth from the shoulders to the heels. She was dressed in a flaming scarlet satin gown, with swan's down round the top, as also at the arms, and two flounces of the same material round the bottom. Her turban was of green velvet, with a gold fringe, terminating in a bunch over the left side, while a bird of Paradise inclined towards the right. Across her forehead she wore a gold band, with a many-coloured glass butterfly (a present from James Green), and her neck, arms, waist (at least what ought to have been her waist), were hung round and studded with mosaic—gold chains, brooches, rings, buttons, bracelets, etc., looking for all the world like a portable pawn-broker's shop or the lump of beef that Sinbad the Sailor threw into the Valley of Diamonds. In the right of a gold band round her middle, was an immense gold watch, with a bunch of mosaic seals appended to a massive chain of the same material ; and a large minia-ture of Mr. Jorrocks when he was a young man, with his hair stiffly curled, occupied a place on her left side. On her right arm dangled a green velvet bag, with a gold cord, out of which one of Mr. Jorrocks's silk handker-chiefs protruded, while a crumpled, yellowish-white cambric one, with a lace fringe, lay at her side.

On an hour-glass stool, a little behind Mrs. Jorrocks, sat her niece Belinda (Joe Jorrocks's eldest daughter), a nice laughing pretty girl of sixteen, with languishing blue eyes, brown hair, a nose of the 'turn-up' order, beautiful mouth and teeth, a very fair complexion, and a gracefully-moulded figure. She had just left one of the finishing and polishing seminaries in the neigh-bourhood of Bromley, where, for two hundred a year and upwards, all the teasing accomplishments of life are taught, and Mrs. Jorrocks, in her own mind, had already appropriated her to James Green, while Mr. Jorrocks, on the other hand, had assigned her to Stubbs. Belinda's dress was simplicity itself ; her silken hair hung in shining tresses down her smiling face, confined by a plain tortoise-shell comb behind, and a narrow pink velvet band before. Round her swan-like neck was a plain white cornelian necklace ; and her well-washed

white muslin frock, confined by a pink sash, flowing
behind in a bow, met in simple folds across her swelling
bosom. Black sandal shoes confined her fairy feet, and
with French cotton stockings completed her toilette.
Belinda, though young, was a celebrated eastern beauty,
and there was not a butcher's boy in Whitechapel, from
Michael Scales downwards, but what eyed her with
delight as she passed along from Shoreditch on her
daily walk.

The presentations having been effected, and the
heat of the day, the excellence of the house, the cleanli-
ness of Great Coram Street—the usual topics, in short,
when people know nothing of each other—having been
discussed, our party scattered themselves about the
room to await the pleasing announcement of dinner.
Mr. Jorrocks, of course, was in attendance upon Nimrod,
while Mr. Stubbs made love to Belinda behind Mrs.
Jorrocks.

Presently a loud, long-protracted '*rat-rat-tat-tat-tan,
rat-tat-tat-tat-tan*,' at the street door sounded through
the house, and Jorrocks, with a slap on his thigh,
exclaimed, ' By Jingo ! there's Green. No man knocks
with such wiggorous wiolence as he does. All Great
Coram Street and parts adjacent know when he comes.
Julius Cæsar himself couldn't kick up a greater row.'
' What Green is it, Green of Rollestone ? ' inquired
Nimrod, thinking of his Leicestershire friend. ' No,'
said Mr. Jorrocks, ' Green of Tooley Street. You'll
have heard of the Greens in the Borough, 'emp, 'op,
and 'ide (hemp, hop, and hide) merchants—numerous
family, numerous as the 'airs in my vig. This is James
Green, jun., whose father, old James Green, jun., *verd
antique* as I calls him, is the son of James Green, sen.,
who is in the 'emp line, and James is own cousin to
young old James Green, sen., whose father is in the 'ide
line.' The remainder of the pedigree was lost by
Benjamin throwing open the door and announcing Mr.
Green ; and Jemmy, who had been exchanging his
cloth boots for patent-leather pumps, came bounding
upstairs like a racket-ball. ' My dear Mrs. Jorrocks ! '
cried he, swinging through the company to her, ' I'm

delighted to see you looking so well. I declare you are fifty per cent. younger than you were. Belinda, my love, 'ow are you? Jorrocks! my friend, how do ye do?'

'Thank ye, James,' said Jorrocks, shaking hands with him most cordially, 'I'm werry well indeed, and delighted to see you. Now let me present you to Nimrod.'

'Aye, Nimrod!' said Green, in his usual flippant style, with a nod of his head, ''ow are ye, Nimrod? I've heard of you, I think,—Nimrod, Brothers and Co., bottle merchants, Crutched Friars, ain't it?'

'No,' said Jorrocks, in an undertone with a frown, '—Mr. H'Apperley Nimrod, the great sporting h'author.'

'True,' replied Green, not at all disconcerted, 'I've heard of him—Nimrod—the mighty 'unter before the Lord. Glad to see ye, Nimrod. Stubbs, 'ow are ye?' nodding to the Yorkshireman, as he jerked himself on to a chair on the other side of Belinda.

As usual, Green was as gay as a peacock. His curly flaxen wig projected over his forehead like the roof of a Swiss cottage, and his pointed gills were supported by a stiff black mohair stock, with a broad front and black frill confined with jet studs down the centre. His coat was light green, with archery buttons, made very wide at the hips, with which he sported a white waistcoat, bright yellow ochre leather trousers, pink silk stockings and patent-leather pumps. In his hand he carried a white silk handkerchief, which smelt most powerfully of musk; and a pair of dirty wristbands drew the eye to sundry dashing rings upon his fingers.

Jonathan Crane, a little long-nosed old city wine merchant, a member of the Surrey Hunt, being announced and presented, Mrs. Jorrocks declared herself faint from the heat of the room, and begged to be excused for a few minutes. Nimrod, all politeness, was about to offer her his arm, but Mr. Jorrocks pulled him back, whispering, '*Let her go, let her go.*' 'The fact is,' said he, in an undertone after she was out of hearing, 'it's a *way* Mrs. J. has when she wants to see that dinner's all right. You see she's a terrible high-bred woman, being a cross between a gentleman-usher and a lady's maid, and doesn't like to be supposed to look after these things, so when she goes, she always pretends to faint. You'll see her back presently,' and, just as he spoke, in she came with a half-pint smelling bottle at her nose. Benjamin followed immediately after, and, throwing open the door, proclaimed, in a half-fledged voice, that 'dinner was sarved,' upon which the party all started on their legs.

'Now, Mr. H'Apperley Nimrod,' cried Jorrocks, 'you'll trot Mrs. J. down—according to the book of etiquette, you know, giving her the wall side.[1] Sorry, gentlemen, I haven't ladies apiece for you, but my sally-manger, as we say in France, is *ray*ther small, besides which I never like to dine more than eight. Stubbs, my boy, Green and you must toss up for Belinda —here's a halfpenny, and let it be " Newmarket "[2] if you please. Wot say you ? a voman ! Stubbs wins ! cried Mr. Jorrocks, as the halfpenny fell head downwards. 'Now, Spiers, couple up with Crane, and James and I will whip into you. But stop, gentlemen ! ' cried Mr. Jorrocks, as he reached the top of the stairs, 'let me make one request—that you von't eat the windmill you'll see on the centre of the table. Mrs. Jorrocks has hired it for the evening, of Mr. Farrell, the confectioner, in Lamb's Conduit Street, and it's engaged to two or three evening parties after it leaves this.' 'Lauk, John ! how wulgar you are. What matter can it make to your friends where the windmill comes from ! ' exclaimed Mrs. Jorrocks in an audible voice from below ; Nimrod, with admirable skill, having piloted her down the straits and turns of the staircase. Having squeezed herself between the backs of the chairs and the wall, Mrs. Jorrocks at length reached the head of the table, and with a bump of her body and wave of her hand motioned Nimrod to take the seat on her right. Green then pushed past Belinda and Stubbs, and took the place on Mrs. Jorrocks's left, so Stubbs, with a

[1] 'In your passage from one room to another, offer the lady the wall in going downstairs,' etc.—*Spirit of Etiquette.*

[2] 'We have repeatedly decided that Newmarket is *one* toss.'— *Bell's Life.*

dexterous manœuvre, placed himself in the centre of
the table, with Belinda between himself and her uncle.
Crane and Spiers then filled the vacant places on Nimrod's
side, Mr. Spiers facing Mr. Stubbs.

The dining-room was the breadth of the passage
narrower than the front drawing-room, and, as Mr.
Jorrocks truly said, was *ray*ther small, but the table
being excessively broad, made the room appear less
than it was. It was lighted up with spermaceti candles,
in silver holders, one at each corner of the table, and
there was a lamp in the wall between the red-curtained
windows, immediately below a brass nail on which
Mr. Jorrocks's great hunting-whip and a bunch of
boot-garters were hung. Two more candles in the
hands of bronzed Dianas on the marble mantelpiece
lighted up a coloured copy of Barraud's picture of John
Warde, on Blue Ruin ; while Mr. Ralph Lambton, on
his horse Undertaker, with his hounds and men, occupied
a frame on the opposite wall. The old-fashioned
cellaret sideboard, against the wall at the end, supported a large bright burning brass lamp, with raised
foxes round the rim, whose effulgent rays shed a brilliant
halo over eight black hats and two white ones, whereof
the four middle ones were decorated with evergreens
and foxes' brushes. The dinner table was crowded,
not covered. There was scarcely a square inch of cloth
to be seen on any part. In the centre stood a magnificent finely-spun barley sugar windmill, two feet and a
half high, with a spacious sugar foundation, with a cart
and horses and two or three millers at the door, and
a she-miller working a ball dress flounce at a lower
window.

The whole dinner, first, second, third, fourth course
—everything, in fact, except dessert—was on the table,
as we sometimes see it at ordinaries and public dinners.
Before both Mr. and Mrs. Jorrocks were two great
tureens of mock turtle soup, each capable of holding a
gallon, and both full up to the brim. Then there were
two sorts of fish ; turbot and lobster sauce, and a great
salmon. A round of boiled beef and an immense piece
of roast occupied the rear of these, ready to march on

7*

the disappearance of the fish and soup—and behind the
walls formed by the beef of old England, came two
dishes of grouse, each dish holding three brace.   The
side dishes consisted of a calf's head hashed, a leg of
mutton, chickens, ducks, and mountains of vegetables ;
and round the windmill were plum puddings, tarts,
jellies, pies, and puffs.

Behind Mrs. Jorrocks's chair stood Batsay with a
fine brass-headed comb in her hair, and stiff ringlets
down her ruddy cheeks.   She was dressed in a green
silk gown, with a coral necklace, and one of Mr. Jorrocks's
lavender and white coloured silk pocket-handkerchiefs
made into an apron.   Binjimin stood with the door
in his hand, as the saying is, with a towel twisted round
his thumb, as though he had cut it.

' Now, gentlemen,' said Mr. Jorrocks, casting his
eye up the table, as soon as they had all got squeezed
and wedged round it, and the dishes were uncovered,
' *you see your dinner*, eat whatever you like except the
windmill—hope you'll be able to satisfy nature with
what's on—would have had more, but Mrs. J. is so
werry fine, she won't stand two joints of the same sort
on the table.'

Mrs. J.   Lauk, John, how can you be so wulgar !
Who ever saw two rounds of beef, as you wanted to
have ?   Besides, I'm sure the gentlemen will excuse
any little defishency, considering the short notice we have
had, and that this is not an elaborate dinner.

Mr. Spiers.   I'm sure, ma'am, there's no de*fish*ency
at all.   Indeed I think there's as much fish as would
serve double the number—and I'm sure you look as if
you had your soup ' on sale or return,' as we say in the
magazine line.

Mr. J.   Haw ! haw ! haw ! werry good, Mr. Spiers.
I owe you one.   Not bad soup though—had it from
Birch's.   Let me send you some ; and pray lay into
it, or I shall think you don't like it.   Mr. H'Apperley,
let me send you some—and, gentlemen, let me observe,
once for all, that there's every species of malt liquor
under the side-table.   Prime stout, from the Marquess
Cornwallis, hard by.   Also ale, table, and what my

friend calls lamen*table*,—*he says* because it's so werry small—but, in truth, because I don't buy it of him. There's all sorts of drench, in fact, except water—a thing I never touch—rots one's shoes, don't know what it would do with one's stomach if it was to get there. Mr. Crane, you're eating nothing. I am quite shocked to see you ; you don't surely live upon h'air ? *Do* help yourself, or you'll faint from werry famine. Belinda, my love, does the Yorkshireman take care of you ? Who's for some salmon ?—bought at Luckey's, and there's both Tally-ho and Tantivy *sarce* to eat with it. Somehow or other I always fancies I rides harder after eating their sarces with fish. Mr. H'Apperley Nimrod, you are the greatest man at table, consequently I axes you to drink wine first, according to the book of etiquette —help yourself, sir. Some of Crane's particklar hot and strong, real stuff, none of your wan de bones (vin de beaume) or rot-gut French stuff—hope you like it—if you don't, pray speak your mind freely, now that we have Crane among us. Binjimin, get me some of that duck before Mr. Spiers ; a leg and a wing, if you please, sir, and a bit of the breast.

Mr. Spiers. Certainly, sir, certainly. Do you prefer a right or a left wing, sir ?

Mr. Jorrocks. Oh, either. I suppose it's all the same.

Mr. Spiers. Why, no, sir, it's not exactly all the same ; for it happens there is only one remaining, therefore it must be the *left* one.

Mr. J. (chuckling). Haw ! haw ! haw ! Mr. S., werry good that—werry good, indeed. I owes you *two*.

' I'll trouble you for a little, Mr. Spiers, if you please,' says Crane, handing his plate round the windmill.

' I'm sorry, sir, it is all gone,' replies Mr. Spiers, who had just filled Mr. Jorrocks's plate ; ' there's nothing left but the neck,' holding it up on the fork.

' Well, send it,' rejoins Mr. Crane, ' neck or *nothing*, you know, Mr. Jorrocks, as we say with the Surrey.'

' Haw ! haw ! haw ! ' grunts Mr. Jorrocks, who is

busy sucking a bone ; ' haw ! haw ! haw ! werry good,
Crane, werry good—owes you one. Now, gentlemen,'
added he, casting his eye up the table as he spoke, ' let
me adwise ye, before you attack the grouse, to take
the hedge (edge) off your appetites, or else there won't
be enough ; and, you know, it does not do to eat the
farmer after the gentleman. Let's see, now—three and
three are six, six brace among eight—oh dear, that's
nothing like enough. I wish, Mrs. J., you had followed
my adwice, and roasted them all. And now, Binjimin,
you're going to break the windmill with your clumsi-
ness, you little dirty rascal ! Why von't you let *Bat-*
say arrange the table ? Thank you, Mr. Crane, for
your assistance,—your politeness, sir, exceeds your
beauty.' [A barrel organ strikes up before the window,
and Jorrocks throws down his knife and fork in an
agony.] ' Oh dear, oh dear, there's that cursed h'organ
again. It's a regular annihilator. Binjimin, run and
kick the fellow's werry soul out of him. There's no
man suffers so much from music as I do. I wish I had
a pocketful of sudden deaths, that I might throw one
at every thief of a musicianer that comes up the street.
I declare the scoundrel has set all my teeth on edge.
Mr. Nimrod, pray take another glass of wine after your
roast beef.—Well, with Mrs. J. if you *choose*, but I'll
join you—always says that you are the werry cleverest
man of the day—read all your writings—anny-tommy
(anatomy) of gaming, and all. Am a h'author myself,
you know—once set to, to write a werry long and elaborate
h'article on scent, but after cudgelling my brains, and
turning the thing over and over again in my mind, all
that I could brew on the subject was that scent was a
werry rum thing ; nothing rummer than scent, except a
woman.'

' Pray,' cried Mrs. Jorrocks, her eyes starting as
she spoke, ' don't let us have any of your low-lifed
stable conversation here—you think to show off before
the ladies,' added she, ' and flatter yourself you talk
about what we don't understand. Now, I'll be bound
to say, with all your fine sporting h'information, you
carn't tell me whether a mule brays or neighs ! '

'Vether a mule brays or neighs?' repeated Mr.
Jorrocks, considering, 'I'll lay I can!'

'Which, then?' inquired Mrs. Jorrocks.

'Vy, I should say it brayed.'

'*Mule bray!*' cried Mrs. Jorrocks, clapping her
hands with delight, 'there's a cockney blockhead for
you! It *brays*, does it?'

Mr. Jorrocks. I meant to say *neighed.*

'Ho! ho! ho!' grinned Mrs. J., '*neighs*, does it?
you are a nice man for a fox-'unter—a mule neighs—
thought I'd catch you some of these odd days with
your wain conceit.'

'Vy, what does it do, then?' inquired Mr. Jorrocks,
his choler rising as he spoke. 'I hopes at all ewents
he don't make the 'orrible noise you do.'

'Why, it *screams*, you great h'ass!' rejoined his
loving spouse.

A single but very resolute knock at the street door,
sounding quite through the house, stopped all further
ebullition, and Benjamin, slipping out, held a short
conversation with some one in the street, and
returned.

'What's happened now, Binjimin?' inquired Mr.
Jorrocks, with anxiety on his countenance, as the
boy re-entered the room; 'the 'osses arn't amiss, I
'ope?'

'Please, sir, Mr. Farrell's young man has come for
the windmill—he says you've had it two hours,' replied
Benjamin.

'The deuce be with Mr. Farrell's young man! he
does not suppose we can part with the mill before the
cloth's drawn—tell him to mizzle, or I'll mill him.
"Now's the day and now's the hour"; who's for some
grouse? Gentlemen, make your game, in fact. But
first of all, let's have a round robin. Pass the wine,
gentlemen. What wine do you take, Stubbs?'

'Why, champagne is good enough for me.'

Mr. Jorrocks. I *dare say*; but if you wait till you
get any here, you will have a long time to stop. Shampain, indeed! had enough of that nonsense abroad—
declare you young chaps drink shampain like h'ale.

There's red and wite, port and sherry, in fact ; and them as carn't drink, they must go without.

> X. was expensive, and soon became poor ;
> Y. was the wise man, and kept want from the door.

'Now for the grouse ! ' added he, as the two beefs disappeared, and they took their stations at the top and bottom of the table. 'Fine birds, to be sure ! hope you haven't burked your appetites, gentlemen, so as not to be able to do justice to them—smell high— werry good—gamey, in fact—Binjimin, take an 'ot plate to Mr. Nimrod—sarve us all round with them.

The grouse being excellent, and cooked to a turn, little execution was done upon the pastry, and the jellies had all melted long before it came to their turn to be eaten. At length, every one, Mr. Jorrocks and all, appeared satisfied, and the noise of knives and forks was succeeded by the din of tongues and the ringing of glasses, as the eaters refreshed themselves with wine or malt liquors. Cheese and biscuit being handed about on plates, according to the *Spirit of Etiquette*, Binjimin and Batsay at length cleared the table, lifted off the windmill, and removed the cloth. Mr. Jorrocks then delivered himself of a most emphatic grace.

The wine and dessert being placed on the table, the ceremony of drinking healths all round was performed. 'Your good health, Mrs. J., Belinda, my loove, your good health—wish you a good 'usband.—Nimrod, your good health.—James Green, your good health. Old *verd antique's* good health.—Your uncle's good health.—All the Green family.—Stubbs, your good health.—Spiers, Crane, etc. etc.' The bottles then pass round three times, on each of which occasions Mrs. Jorrocks makes them pay toll. The fourth time she let them pass ; and Jorrocks began to grunt, hem, and haw, and kick the leg of the table, by way of giving her a hint to depart. This caused a dead silence, which at length was broken by the Yorkshireman's exclaiming, 'Horrid pause ! '

'Horrid paws ! ' vociferated Mrs. J., in a towering rage, ' so would yours, let me tell you, sir, if you had helped to cook all that dinner : ' and gathering herself up and repeating the word, ' horrid paws, indeed, I like your imperence,' she sailed out of the room like an exasperated turkey-cock ; her face, from heat, anger, and the quantity she had drunk, being as red as her gown. Indeed, she looked for all the world as if she had been put into a furnace and blown red-hot. Jorrocks having got rid of his ' worser half,' as he calls her, let out a reef or two of his acre of white waistcoat, and each man made himself comfortable according to his acceptation of the term. ' Gentlemen,' says Jorrocks, ' I'll trouble you to charge your glasses, 'eel-taps off—a bumper toast—no sky-lights, if you please. Crane, pass the wine—you are a regular old stop-bottle—a turnpike gate, in fact. *I think you take back hands*—gentlemen, are you all charged ?—then I'll give you THE NOBLE SPORT OF FOX-'UNTING ! gentlemen, with three times three, and Crane will give the 'ips,—all ready— now, 'ip, 'ip, 'ip, 'uzza, 'uzza, 'uzza,—'ip, 'ip, 'ip, 'uzza, 'uzza, 'uzza,— 'ip, 'ip, 'ip, 'uzza, 'uzza, 'uzza—one cheer more, 'uzza ! ' After this followed ' The Merry Harriers,' then came ' The Staggers,' after that ' The Trigger, and bad luck to Cheetum,' all bumpers ; when Jorrocks, having screwed his courage up to the sticking place, called for another, which being complied with, he rose and delivered himself as follows :—

' Gentlemen, in rising to propose the toast which I am now about to propose—I feel—I feel—(Yorkshireman —" Very queer ? ") *J.* No, not werry queer, and I'll trouble you to hold your jaw. (Laughter.) Gentlemen, I say, in rising to propose the toast which I am about to give, I feel—I feel—(Crane—" Werry nervous ? ") *J.* No, not werry nervous, so none of your nonsense ; *let me alone, I say.* I say, in rising to propose the toast which I am about to give, I feel—(Mr. Spiers—" Very foolish ? " Nimrod—" Very funny ? " Crane—" Werry rum ? ") *J.* No, *werry proud* of the distinguished honour that has been conferred upon me—conferred upon me —conferred upon me—distinguished honour that has been conferred upon me by the presence, this day, of one of the most distinguished men—distinguished men —by the presence, this day, of one of the most dis-

tinguished men and sportsmen—of modern times.
(Cheers.) Gentlemen—this is the proudest moment of
my life ! the eyes of England are upon us ! I give you
the health of Mr. H'Apperley Nimrod." (Drunk with
three times three.)

When the cheering and dancing of the glasses had
somewhat subsided, Nimrod rose and spoke as follows :—

' Mr. Jorrocks, and Gentlemen,—

' The handsome manner in which my health has been
proposed by our worthy and estimable host, and the
flattering reception it has met with from you, merit my
warmest acknowledgments. I should, indeed, be unworthy of the land which gave me birth, were I insensible
of the honour which has just been done me by so enlightened and distinguished an assembly as the present.
My friend, Mr. Jorrocks, has been pleased to designate
me as one of the most distinguished sportsmen of the
day, a title, however, to which I feel I have little claim ;
but this I may say that I have portrayed our great
national sports in their brightest and most glowing
colours, and that on sporting subjects my pen shall yield
to none. (Cheers.) I have ever been the decided advo-
cate of manly sports and exercises, not only on account
of the health and vigour they inspire, but because I
feel that they are the best safeguards of a nation's
energies, and the best protection against luxury, idleness,
debauchery, and effeminacy. (Cheers.) The authority
of all history informs us, that the energies of countries
flourished whilst manly sports have flourished, and de-
cayed as they died away. (Cheers.) What says Juvenal,
when speaking of the entry of luxury into Rome ?—

> " Sævior armis
> Luxuria incubuit, victumque ulciscitur orbem."

And we need only refer to ancient history, and to the
writings of Xenophon, Cicero, Horace, or Virgil, for
evidence of the value they have all attached to the
encouragement of manly, active, and hardy pursuits,
and the evils produced by a degenerate and effeminate
life on the manners and characters of a people. (Cheers.)
Many of the most eminent literary characters of this

and of other countries have been ardently attached to
field sports ; and who that has experienced their bene-
ficial results can doubt that they are the best promoters
of the *mens sana in corpore sano*—the body sound and
the understanding clear. (Cheers.) Gentlemen, it is
with feelings of no ordinary gratification that I find
myself at the social and truly hospitable board of one
of the most distinguished ornaments of one of the most
celebrated Hunts in this great country, one whose name
and fame have reached the four corners of the globe—
to find myself after so long an absence from my native
land—an estrangement from all that has ever been
nearest and dearest to my heart, once again surrounded
by those cheerful countenances which so well express
the honest, healthful pursuits of their owners. Let us,
then,' added Nimrod, seizing a decanter and pouring
himself out a bumper, ' drink in true Kentish fire, the
health and prosperity of that brightest sample of civic
sportsmen, the great and renowned JOHN JORROCKS ! '

Immense applause followed the conclusion of this
speech, during which time the decanters buzzed round
the table, and, the glasses being emptied, the company
rose, and a full charge of Kentish fire followed ; Mr.
Jorrocks sitting all the while, looking as uncomfortable
as men in his situation generally do.

The cheering having subsided, and the parties having
resumed their seats, it was his turn to rise ; so, getting
on his legs, he essayed to speak, but finding, as many
men do, that his ideas deserted him the moment the ' eyes
of England ' were turned upon him, after two or three
hitches of his nankeens, and as many hems and haws,
he very coolly resumed his seat, and spoke as follows :—

' Gentlemen, unaccustomed as I am to public speaking,
I am quite taken aback by this werry unexpected compliment—(cheers) ;—never since I filled the h'ancient
and h'onerable h'office of churchwarden in the populous
parish of St. Botolph Without, have I experienced a
gratification equal to the present. I thank you from
the werry bottom of my breeches-pocket. (Applause.)
Gentlemen, I'm no h'orator, but I'm a h'onest man.
(Cheers.) I should indeed be undeserving the name of

a sportsman—undeserving of being a member of that
great and justly celebrated 'unt, of which Mr. H'Apperley
Nimrod has spun so handsome and flattering a yarn, if
I did not feel deeply proud of the compliment you have
paid it. It is impossible for me to follow that great
sporting scholar fairly over the ridge and furrow of his
werry intricate and elegant h'oration, for there are many
of those fine gentlemen's names—French, I presume—
that he mentioned, that I never heard of before, and
cannot recollect ; but if you will allow me to run 'eel a
little, I would make a few h'observations on a few of his
h'observations. Mr. H'Apperley Nimrod, gentlemen,
was pleased to pay a compliment to what he was pleased
to call my something 'ospitality. I am extremely obliged
to him for it. To be surrounded by one's friends is
in my mind the " *A1* " of 'uman 'appiness. (Cheers.)
Gentlemen, I am most proud of the honour of seeing
you all here to-day, and I hope the grub has been to
your likin'—(cheers),—if not, I'll discharge my butcher.
On the score of quantity there might be a little deficiency,
but I hope the quality was prime. Another time this
shall be all remedied. (Cheers.) Gentlemen, I understand those cheers, and I'm flattered by them—*I likes*
'ospitality ! I'm not the man to keep my butter in a
'pike-ticket, or my coals in a quart pot. (Immense
cheering.) Gentlemen, these are my sentiments, I leaves
the flowers of speech to them as is better acquainted
with botany. (Laughter.) I likes plain English, both in
eating and talking, and I'm happy to see Mr. H'Apperley
Nimrod has not forgot his, and can put up with our
homely fare, and do without pantaloon cutlets,[1] blankets
of woe,[2] and such like miseries. I hates their 'orse
douvers (hors-d'œuvres), their rots, and their poisons
(poissons) ; 'ord rot 'em, they near killed me, and right
glad am I to get a glass of old British black strap. And
talking of black strap, gentlemen, I call on old Crane,
the man what supplies it, to tip us a song. So now I'm
finished, and you, Crane, lap up your liquor and begin.'
(Applause.)

Crane was shy—unused to sing in company—never-

---

[1] ' Côtelette en papillote.'   [2] ' Blanquette de veau.'

theless, if it was the wish of the party, and it would oblige his good customer, Mr. Jorrocks, he would try his hand at a stave or two *made* by himself [1] in honour of the immortal Surrey. Having emptied his glass and cleared his windpipe, Crane commenced :—

> ' Here's a health to them that can ride !
> Here's a health to them that can ride !
> And those that don't wish good luck to the *cause*
> May they roast by their own fireside !
> It's good to drown care in the chase,
> It's good to drown care in the bowl,
> It's good to support Daniel Haigh and his hounds,
> Here's his health from the depth of my soul.

> ### CHORUS.
>
> Hurrah for the loud tally-ho !
> Hurrah for the loud tally-ho !
> It's good to support Daniel Haigh and his hounds,
> And echo the shrill tally-ho !

> ' Here's a health to them that can ride !
> Here's a health to them that ride bold !
> May the leaps and the dangers that each has defied,
> In columns of sporting be told !
> Here's freedom to him that would walk !
> Here's freedom to him that would ride !
> There's none ever feared that the horn should be heard
> Who the joys of the chase ever tried.

> Hurrah for the loud tally-ho !
> Hurrah for the loud tally-ho !
> It's good to support Daniel Haigh and his hounds,
> And halloo the loud tally-ho ! '

' Beautiful ! beautiful ! ' exclaimed Jorrocks, clapping his hands and stamping as Crane had ceased.

> ' A werry good song, and it's werry well sung,
> Jolly companions every one !

' Gentlemen, pray charge your glasses—there's one toast we must drink in a bumper if we ne'er take a bumper again. Mr. Spiers, pray charge your glass—

[1] Crane deceived himself when he said he wrote this song. It was published in the *Sporting Magazine* before he was a member of the Hunt. It is in honour of the popular sportsman who for a long series of years has hunted Surrey with a patience and keenness worthy of a better country.

Mr. Stubbs, vy don't you fill up ?   Mr. Nimrod, off with
your 'eel taps, pray—I'll give ye the " Surrey 'Unt,"
with all my 'art and soul. Crane, my boy, here's your
werry good health, and thanks for your song ! ' (All
drink the Surrey Hunt and Crane's good health, with
applause, which brings him on his legs with the following
speech.)

   ' Gentlemen, unaccustomed as I am to public speaking
—(laughter)—I beg leave, on behalf of myself and the
absent members of the Surrey 'Unt, to return you our
own most 'artfelt thanks for the flattering compliment
you have just paid us, and to assure you that the esteem
and approbation of our fellow-sportsmen is to us the
magnum bonum of all earthly 'appiness. (Cheers and
laughter.) Gentlemen, I will not trespass longer upon
your valuable time, but as you seem to enjoy this wine
of my friend Mr. Jorrocks's, I may just say that I have
got some more of the same quality left, at from forty-
two to forty-eight shillings a dozen, also some good
stout draught port, at ten-and-sixpence a gallon—some
ditto werry superior at fifteen ; also foreign and British
spirits, and Dutch liqueurs, rich and rare.'

   The conclusion of the vintner's address was drowned
in shouts of laughter. Mr. Jorrocks then called upon
the company in succession for a toast, a song, or a senti-
ment.   Nimrod gave, ' The Queen [1] and her Stag-
hounds ' ; Crane gave, ' Champagne to our real friends,
and real pain to our sham friends ' ; Green sang, ' I'd
be a Butterfly ' ; Mr. Stubbs gave, ' Honest Men and
Bonnie Lasses ' ; and Mr. Spiers, like a patriotic printer,
gave ' The Liberty of the Press,' which he said was like
fox-hunting—' if we have it not, we die '—all of which
Mr. Jorrocks applauded as if he had never heard them
before, and drank in bumpers. It was evident that
unless tea was speedily announced, he would soon
become—

            ' O'er the ills of life victorious,'

for he had pocketed his wig, and had been clipping the

---

[1] To save any pains-taking critic the trouble of remarking
that we laid the earlier part of these scenes in the late King's
time, we beg to say that ' *we know it.*'

MR JORROCKS TAKES A RIDE AT ST. CLOUD

"LIFT ME UP!—TIE ME IN MY CHAIR!—FILL MY GLASS"

Queen's English for some time. After a pause, during which his cheeks twice changed colour, from red to green and back to red, he again called for a bumper toast, which he prefaced with the following speech, or parts of a speech :—

" Gentlemen,—in rising—propose toast about to give—feel werry—feel werry—(Yorkshireman, " Werry muzzy ? ") *J*.—feel werry—(Mr. Spiers, " Werry sick?") *J*.—werry—(Crane, " Werry thirsty ? ") *J*.—feel werry —(Nimrod, " Werry wise ? ") *J*.—no ; but werry *sensible*—great compliment—eyes of England upon us— give you the health—Mr. H'Apperley Nimrod—three times three ! '

He then attempted to rise for the purpose of marking the time, but his legs deserted his body, and, after two or three lurches, down he went with a tremendous thump under the table. He called first for ' Batsay,' then for ' Binjimin,' and, game to the last, blurted out, ' Lift me up !—tie me in my chair !—fill my glass ! '

PRINTED BY
MORRISON AND GIBB LTD
LONDON AND EDINBURGH

Date Due